For Nomes. Without you, Portugal would only be a country.

# LUCY COURTENAY

HODDER CHILDREN'S BOOKS

First published in Great Britain in 2018 by Hodder and Stoughton

1 3 5 7 9 10 8 6 4 2

Text copyright © Lucy Courtenay, 2018

The moral rights of the author have been asserted.

A CIP catalogue record for this book
is available from the British Library.

ISBN 978 1 444 93075 7

Typeset in Berkeley Oldstyle by Hewer Text UK Ltd, Edinburgh
Printed and bound in Great Britain by Clays Ltd, Elcograf S.p.A.

The paper and board used in this book
are made from wood from responsible sources.

Hodder Children's Books
An imprint of
Hachette Children's Group
Part of Hodder and Stoughton
Carmelite House
50 Victoria Embankment
London EC4Y 0DZ

An Hachette UK Company
www.hachette.co.uk

Life hurls us like a stone, and we sail through the air saying, 'Look at me move.'

Fernando Pessoa
*The Book of Disquiet*

# PROLOGUE

# NATHAN

## AUGUST

The package is tightly wrapped in brown paper, and bound with enough tape to ruin a game of pass the parcel. It's not very big. Easy enough to tuck under my arm.

'What is it?' I ask.

'Something to give Ricky a headache.'

'Is it drugs?'

Dad's eyes narrow, the way they always do when I ask questions. 'Board the boat, put the parcel down, get off the boat again. Simple.'

I moisten my lips and eye the package. We both know I'll do it, so why am I stalling? Maybe because this is it. The line that you're not supposed to cross. The other stuff feels like nothing.

'Simple,' Dad repeats.

Nothing about my dad is simple.

It must be drugs. I think with horrible fascination about the people my father must deal with, people who can get

1

hold of enough drugs to fill a parcel. I consider peeling off some of the tape and helping myself before putting it where Dad wants me to.

What if it isn't drugs, though?

What then?

# PRECIOUS

## JUNE

For a short man, Dad cast a long shadow. My parents used to look like freaks dancing together, back in the days when they had parties in the London house. I would watch through the banisters as Mum, in low heels, held Dad's hairy hand and spun around like a surgically enhanced ballerina in a cramped music box.

Dad loved flashing his money, his possessions and his family, in that order. If you're born poor in the back end of Europe, sticking it to the man counts for a lot. Naturally enough, I hated his loud insistence on the best of everything. But then he built me a ship around the gnarled tree in the back garden. It was hard to hate him after that. For a while, at least.

The tree ship had three masts including the tree trunk, rigging, angled sails, a deck, a brig and a crow's nest with actual crows in it. In the summer, the rustling leaves sounded like the sea. In my tree ship, I was Vasco da Gama with a chestnut beard that whipped about in the wind. I was Pedro Álvares Cabral, whose name sounded like 'goat' in Portuguese and whose head I had always pictured with a little set of horns. I didn't like the brig with its oak bars, but I spent as much time in the crow's nest as I could (crows permitting), hiding from the piano teachers and the karate sensei and the Mandarin instructors that Mum kept on a permanent loop through the house in her bid to improve me. I often wanted to leap from the crow's nest and fly with the crows myself, but something always stopped me. Confidence in my own ability to fly, most likely.

'Find the end of the world,' Dad would instruct, laughing in the grassy ocean below with his cigar in his hand as I sailed waves as high as mountains and discovered lands hot with coconuts and brightly coloured birds. 'And when you have found it, sail around it. *É só mar e dragões.*' It is only sea and dragons.

Sea and dragons were in Dad's blood. He had a temper, and he broke things, and he drank, and he disappeared sometimes for weeks on end. There were other things I didn't understand: whispers in the playground, men with long-lens cameras hanging around outside the house. Tea round a friend's house could be tricky when your minder had to come too. Lotta was the only one who invited me round on minder days. That's why we were still friends at the start of last summer. Sharing pesto spaghetti in the shadow of a big, silent man with a shaved head and a gun cements something, I think.

Mum had the ship demolished last year, along with the tree, so she could level the garden and build a home cinema and a gym. Dad was too busy building empires and sailing yachts and playing golf to notice. Then the photos of him with three women in a hotel bedroom in Spain showed up in the papers. More men with long lenses showed up that day than for the rest of his career put together.

If I've learned anything over the past few months, it's that the sea is big; but the dragons are bigger.

# HARRY

'Sometimes,' my father told me as we walked together to the shops at the end of the road on the last day I saw him, 'you just have to jump off the cliff. Bungee off the bridge.'

I was assessing the road for traffic at the time, squinting at the big white van at the end of the road in case there were armed robbers in it waiting for their chance to knock off the corner shop. It had been knocked off three times in the previous four months, so it was due another overhaul.

'Kiss the scariest girl in the seediest bar. Pet the mad dog on the side of the road. It's where you'll find life.'

On a normal day, Dad was a Bunsen burner turned up to full eyebrow-burn. That day, with the final Atlantic adventure looming, he was Dad squared, which made him exhausting and me irritated. If life could only be found in seedy bars and on the end of frayed elastic ropes, then what exactly was I experiencing? Maybe I was a hologram, someone you could put your fist through, something with no shadow. But there were definitely two people moving along the pavement in the bright sunlight that day, even though one of them was larger in every way than the other.

'Embrace it. Chew it. Taste it.'

I kept nodding, hoping that this father–son talk would dry up and allow us to focus on fetching our Saturday croissants before the shop ran out.

'Now is all we have. Next is never guaranteed.'

He was full of stuff like that. Motivational mottos, he called them.

'You only live once, Harry boy.'

*And ideally for as long as possible*, I thought.

Dad was leaving that afternoon for the airport, bound for the Bahamas. He was going to sail home via the Azores, the last piece in the 3D jigsaw entitled 'Sailing Round the World Before I'm Fifty', which he'd been assembling for most of his life. I used to wonder where he'd take himself once he finished with the world. Space seemed likely.

As I checked the white van at the end of the road again (it appeared to be full of builders, but vigilance was everything), he laid his hand on my shoulder. I was aware of the meatiness of it, the manliness of him.

'Grasp the nettle, Harry. Bite the hornet. That's all I'm saying.'

When we got the news that his boat had gone down with no survivors off the west coast of Ireland three weeks later, Mum went mad for a while. She worked eighteen-hour days in the bank, and dyed her hair jet-black, and took up kick-boxing, and rescued five dogs of indeterminate colour and breed, and made a collage of Dad photos that turned the living-room wall into a creepy shrine, and cried inside the wardrobe every night with her face buried in his old suits.

I didn't see the point of a breakdown. I didn't drop out of school, my grades were fine, I found girlfriends and still hadn't got drunk by the time I was fifteen. My bereavement counsellor was impressed by my maturity and discharged me after a few months. When Mum took me on holiday to Mallorca to celebrate my GCSE results, I threw up when I saw the sea. So far, so normal.

The main thing I remember about that whole time is this question.

What kind of idiot bites a hornet?

# NATHAN

Dad leaves the house early on the day of the party, shortly before reminding me to make a hair appointment. My hand goes protectively to my head.

'Exams aren't over yet,' I say, not meeting his eye. 'Last one's on Monday. I said I'd take the dreads off after that.'

He checks his TAG Heuer. 'Art is a hobby, not an exam.'

'Art is my future,' I say, feeling brave. I'm eighteen years old. I can say what I like.

'A future I'm not going to pay for.'

I feel the usual flare of impotence deep in my guts. I have to go to Art School, I *have* to. The rats of self-doubt hurl themselves around inside my head.

'I hope I don't need to remind you not to smash up the house tonight,' Dad says.

'I'm sure Nathan's friends will be respectful,' says Mum with a worried glance in my direction.

Dad shoots his cuffs. 'If they aren't, I'll know who to blame.'

I think of the box of vodka in my bedroom, the pills Dirk's bringing later. Dad pecks Mum on the cheek with his beaky little mouth. As he walks out of the kitchen, it's clear his mind is already on profit margins.

'Your father,' Mum begins as the front door gives its heavy, oiled click.

'Is a dear, dear man?' I offer.

Her eyes get teary. They do that a lot. I wonder sometimes if her eyes will dissolve one day. 'The business is going through a tough patch. He has to find solutions or they'll fire him and then what will happen to us? To our house?'

I don't want this argument tonight.

'Be kind, Nathan,' Mum implores. 'The pressure is taking it out of him.'

'And he's taking it out on me,' I say. 'On my sodding birthday.'

'Don't swear—'

'Right, because sodding swearing is so very sodding awful,' I return sourly. My father hasn't even wished me Happy Birthday.

'Nathan, your father works hard to provide for us. You need to respect him for that.'

It's an old speech, no more convincing now than it was when Mum first parroted it at me. It continues in the usual vein for a bit. Still so young . . . understand the value of a worthwhile career . . . grateful for all your father does for us . . .

10

'Are you leaving soon?' I interrupt.

She stops, sniffs and nods. She's not got any make-up on today. It makes her look old.

'Make it sooner,' I say.

I intend the box of vodka to be down at least half a bottle before the guests arrive. If this party really does mark the end of one thing and the start of something else, then it better be a good one.


Johnny Depp knows what he's doing with this eyeliner stuff. The chicks are all over me.

'You're crazy,' Lotta says with a scream of laughter.

I lift her hair from her sweaty neck, all the better to inhale her. The kitchen is a mass of bodies, writhing around us like tadpoles. 'And you're hot.'

I love the way she giggles, all eyelashes and flicking hair. It makes me feel all-powerful. I start wrapping her hair around my fist and pulling her towards me. Kissing her is like sinking my teeth into a warm apple pie.

The first telephone complaint of the night shrills through the house, competing with the bass, and losing. There's a scream from outside, and a splash. Someone's in the pool, and not before time. On cue, the crowd heads through the French windows. The splashes and shrieks intensify. On the decks, Dirk looks pissed off about his deserted dance floor, but makes do with popping something small and blue that puts the smile back on his face and turns the sound up louder.

11

'Let's go swimming,' I suggest against Lotta's mouth. 'Naked.'

She almost chokes. 'In front of all these people? You have to be kidding.'

The hallway is lit only by the candles and LED balloons that Mum ordered in. The place is dark, and smoky with weed as I push Lotta against the wall at the bottom of the stairs. Someone's broken off a banister about three steps up, and bottles litter the treads. We'll make our way up, I decide, one step at a time.

'Don't mind me,' says someone around the halfway point.

Lotta detaches herself with a shriek and I almost lose my balance in the dark. Precious Silva unfolds herself limb by limb and stands up. The girl who never joins in, but can't quite go away. The music shakes the stairs under our feet.

'You look like a deckchair, Precious Metal,' I cackle, tweaking the striped fabric of her dress. 'Can I sit on you?'

'He's drunk,' says Lotta, visibly swaying where she stands.

I'm bored and already losing the vibe. Even though we're on the same step, I stare up into Precious Silva's bulgy brown eyes and she stares down into mine. Exactly how tall *is* she?

'This is a party,' I inform her. 'You are advised to get drunk or get lost.'

'I was thinking of going,' says Precious, ducking her head. Her thick black hair swings around her face. 'It's pretty late.'

'Fine,' I say with a hiccup. 'Bye bye.'

I'm suddenly aware of some whirling blue lights outside that aren't coming from Dirk's decks. The blue gets brighter and whirlier, and I realise that someone has opened the door. Two police officers are silhouetted in the doorway. One of them sniffs the air like the sodding Child Catcher.

In an extreme version of Musical Statues, the tunes stop and people freeze. The first one to move is Dirk, who shoots out of the house with his head down in a streak of energy that speaks volumes for what's in his pockets. Outside, I glimpse wet bodies sidling round the house and squelching at speed down the drive. Guided by a strong sense of self-preservation, the rest of the guests pour out of the building on the squelchers' heels in a thundering river, parting around the police officers and rejoining on the other side to vanish without trace into the shrubbery. Somewhere in the kitchen, a glass bottle drops off a table and smashes.

'Are you responsible for this party, sir?' says the Sniffer after the long and dramatic moment of silence that follows the breaking bottle.

Precious Metal and Lotta have gone, swept away in the departing tide, and I'm alone on the stairs. My best painting is hanging at an angle by the front door, the one I had framed after GCSE. It's covered in scrawled Post-it messages for Dad to pick up whenever he comes in through the door after one of his trips to the refinery offices in Spain. I have an urgent desire to straighten it and sweep off the yellow cluster of fluttering notes. But, not quite trusting my legs, I

13

sit down on the stairs instead and gesture vaguely at the empty, shattered space around me. The ice of tomorrow is already creeping through my veins.

'What party?' I say, in one final show of defiance. 'I don't see a party.'

# PRECIOUS

'Still here, Mum.'

In the process of pulling away from the kerb, one painted fingernail hovering over her phone, my mother cranes round and looks at me in surprise. The craning makes her neck look wrinklier than she would like. I don't point it out.

'What are you still doing in the car?'

'You didn't stop,' I say. 'Not properly.'

'Oh, baby, I'm so sorry! My head is everywhere today.' She jams on the brakes in the middle of Mr Hegarty's smooth-running drop-off zone, making the large silver Lexus behind us stop and honk. I smile gamely as she detonates an explosion of snaps of her and me, taken from her favourite angle.

'I love you, have fun,' she says, blowing kisses that don't wreck her lipstick.

I'm not sure how much fun a final GCSE is, in the grand scheme of things. She swings away again the moment I have shut the car door. Fortunately I don't trap my kilt in the hinges like Yetunde Abiola with her father's Porsche Cayenne last term.

'You had one job,' I say out loud.

Mum has a thousand jobs. Committee meetings, charity boards, fitness schemes, social media platforms for her latest fashion designs, divorcing my father, household accounts, counselling the permanently miserable Ilynka as she vacuums the hallway. A thousand jobs plus me, and none of us ever done.

'Oh, and thanks for the pep talk,' I add as her tail lights disappear down Queen's Gate. 'Appreciated. Really. I don't know how I'd get through this last exam without your faith and encouragement.'

'Talking to yourself, Presh?'

Lotta is grinning by the polished wooden doors. Lotta Cooper, curvy and gorgeous with the most expensive teeth in the school. I think she's waiting for me, but you can never be totally sure with Lotta.

'First sign of madness?' I offer weakly.

'I went mad weeks ago,' Lotta says with the breezy certainty that she's the sanest person in London. 'Are you coming in?'

We head inside – sort of side by side and sort of not – through the high, cool corridor with its shiny tiles and glossy scholarship boards.

'Legendary night, wasn't it?' says Lotta as we walk. 'I can't believe we were invited to an eighteenth.'

The thing I mainly remember about the party, apart from the impressive level of damage, was Lotta and Nathan Payne. That and the step on Nathan's stairs where I sat with a disgusting drink and tried to look like I was enjoying my own company while the music and fun and snogging all went on somewhere else.

'Instagram went mental over that picture of Nathan Payne's lips on your neck,' I say. 'I hear he broke his nose after the police showed up. Is that true?'

'Apparently,' says Lotta. 'You know, that picture got over five hundred likes?'

I can't imagine *knowing* five hundred people, let alone making them like me.

'So aren't you going to ask?' she says.

A number of unprintable questions rush through my head. 'Ask what?'

'If I'm going to see him again.'

'Are you?'

Lotta gives the kind of shrug that only golden people get to do. Shall I accept this life achievement award? Perhaps. Shall I kiss the wild-haired, chisel-cheeked god of the departing sixth form? Maybe. 'I don't think Nathan is dating material,' she says airily. 'But it was fun while it lasted.'

I'll bet it was. My stomach twists. No one has ever kissed me like Nathan Payne was kissing Lotta at the weekend.

'You are coming for definite this summer?' Lotta asks as we pass the old schoolroom with its wooden desks ordered in a shiny brown army parade.

The holiday with Lotta is the brightest beacon on my horizon. I have packed at least six times, and bought five new bikinis online. I have agonised over whether four suitcases is too much, and how many Lotta will take. I've packed four pairs of sunglasses curated from an extensive selection of panic buys, and seven pairs of shoes, all flats. When you nudge six foot, heels make you look like a drag queen.

Mum took surprisingly little persuasion when I raised this holiday with her. Since Dad's latest hostile takeover of a golf hotel sent all the business papers into a feeding frenzy last month, she's decided that being anywhere near him could be dangerous. Hostile golf takeovers make me think of Dad bludgeoning some poor suit with one of those golf clubs that look like conkers on steroids. But when I told her about the Swintons' place in Vilamoura, she caved within a couple of days. Seemed genuinely excited, actually.

'On condition that I can come too,' she said. 'To keep an eye on you.'

She and Mrs Swinton are yoga buddies, so it was easy enough to fix up. It might be quite nice having her there, I suppose. A bit of mother–daughter time.

'Yes,' I say now with absolute focus. 'I'm definitely coming this summer.'

'Only I was wondering because Olivia was thinking she might come,' says Lotta now.

I feel a rush of anxiety. Olivia Trott-Parke is as dark and gorgeous as Lotta is bright and blond. If Olivia comes we'll be a threesome for a fortnight, and mother–daughter time will take on a fresh and sinister significance as my only social option.

'Do you want Olivia to come?' I ask cautiously.

'I was just wondering,' Lotta says again.

We're early. Lotta takes out her phone while we loiter. I study my own phone in a puddle of self-loathing. Unlike my mother and her angled expertise, my selfies are universally crap. Shot from above, my bony proportions look even stranger. Shot from below, my chin looks like a mountain ledge that should have Bear Grylls dangling off it. Side shots and I'm all nose; straight on and I look like a skeletal murderer. I sidle up to Lotta and snap us both from above. At least with Lotta in the picture, more people will comment.

'Hun!'

'Babes!'

Lotta and Olivia embrace like sisters as the corridor clock creeps ever closer to nine. I lower my phone and shuffle backwards with my nose in my pencil case, in order to blend better with the panelling on the corridor walls as they fountain away about life and parties and the joys of being them.

'You know the best bit about today?' says Lotta, detaching herself from Olivia as Ms Matthews comes along the line to collect our phones. 'We can take off this uniform for ever and burn it.'

Lotta and Olivia will pass everything with top grades and never look back from the glorious successes of their future lives. I slide my thumbs under my waistband and lean back against the wall and close my eyes. Two hours of my life, that's all. Just two hours and then the summer will begin.

I'll worry about the rest of it when it comes.

# HARRY

## JULY

My palms have broken into a sweat, and I'm not even looking at the sea. It's so enormous, and blue, and loud, like a party guest you're doing your best to ignore. I didn't think the Med had noisy waves. No tides and all that. But it does. Slosh, slosh, slosh. Then there's the herring gulls, and the boats, and the endlessly clinking sails. It's hard to concentrate through the drilling sound in my head.

Sasha is opposite me, lining up sugar sachets on our café table. We met on the train to Paris, and we've got to know each other pretty well over the past couple of weeks. She's from Minnesota, and she has pink hair, and a collection of gold nose studs featuring the different signs of the zodiac which she matches to the lunar calendar. She talks about emotions a lot and plans to study psychology in London next year. We've mentioned my dad a couple of times. Lightly. In passing. The sea thing hasn't come up till now.

21

'So we'll be in Barcelona by Tuesday at the latest, but I've booked hostel rooms for Monday as well just in case we make the last train out of Nice,' I say. 'The best route looks like it'll be via Toulouse. We can stay overnight and get the train over the Pyrenees to Barcelona.'

'It's quite a long way round,' Sasha says as she selects the middle sachet and rips it open, sprinkling it in her cup. The sugar stays on the surface of the coffee for a minute as though surprised by its sudden release, then sinks before it has a chance to think it through.

'It just means a night in Toulouse,' I say.

'There's nothing in Toulouse.' She tidies away the sachets again, tucking them back into the little pot in the middle of the table. A huge herring gull stares at us with eyes like pale death.

'The people of Toulouse might disagree with you on that,' I say, in an attempt at joviality.

'I thought we were going along the coast,' she says.

I feel the old prickling on the back of my neck. What is it about the sea that everyone finds so wonderful? It's just lots of deep, dark water, full of sunken boats and the ghosts of the drowned. I'm not going along the coast, even if Sasha plucks my eyeballs out and feeds them to the herring gull.

'Going that way involves a complicated change at the border and then a really long wait on the platform and the train gets in quite late too,' I say out loud. 'The Toulouse way is better. It would be really bad if we arrived in Barcelona at night and didn't have anywhere to stay.'

Sasha stirs her coffee round and round and looks over my shoulder at the beach. It's too easy to imagine all the bodies down there, bloated scraps of flesh and bone, and I pull my chair round a little to cut out the view, and pull up a selection of Toulouse factoids on my phone.

'Toulouse is "one of the most vibrant cities in France". It says so here. The beauty of interrailing is that we can make these random diversions any time we want.'

'Harry,' she says. 'I don't care about complicated border crossings or long waits on platforms. I want to stick to the coast.'

I moisten my lips. The herring gull is still watching me. The clattering sails over my shoulder won't shut *up*.

'I just don't see the fuss about the sea,' I say.

Sasha's nostrils flare, making Leo (as of yesterday) move and flash in the sunlight. 'Maybe if you actually *looked* at it,' she says, 'you'd understand.'

'The sea is a geographical fact,' I point out. 'Not a philosophical statement.'

'It's like you're avoiding it.'

'That's stupid,' I say. 'You can't avoid the sea. It's the sea.'

Something in my face must trigger a page she read recently in *Psychiatry Today* because she narrows her gaze.

'You are,' she says. 'You're avoiding it.'

I don't know where to direct my efforts: at not looking at the sea, or at arguing the toss.

'I'm not,' I say weakly.

She leans in. 'First you don't want to go on that walk by the shore. Then there was the beach party those hostel guys invited us to that you didn't want to do. And now there's this Toulouse thing.'

I tuck a loose strand of pink hair behind her ear, focusing on the soft feel of her cheek on my hand. I have to give her something.

'I don't like thinking of all the refugees who've drowned out there,' I say. 'All that stuff on the news has changed the way I look at it. It's not a pretty blue paradise. It's an oily soup full of bodies.'

She whitens. 'That's gross.'

I realise I may have gone too far. The trouble is, I believe it one hundred per cent. And of course, it's not just the refugees that I think about, swirling about in the unknowable darkness.

Sasha sees the thought whisking past my eyes.

'Is this about your dad?' she says suddenly. 'He drowned so you don't like the sea?'

She looks like I just plugged her in. I am her fantasy scenario. The boy who needs fixing. The guy who will provide her with ample resource material for a groundbreaking study into bereavement and teenage boys. Dr Sasha Olson, PhD. The herring gull edges closer. I like birds, watching them as they fly and nest and make the air their own, but I'm fantasising about stabbing this one with my coffee spoon.

'Maybe,' I say, as though I haven't thought about it.

She reaches for my hand like she's already wearing the

24

white coat. 'Have you ever talked to anyone about this? You know, properly? With a professional?'

'Of course I have,' I say shortly.

'You don't talk about your dad much,' she says, tipping her head to one side as she assesses her prize specimen. 'Oh, Harry, you must still be so sad.'

The taste of defeat mingles with the coffee. 'I just don't like the sea,' I repeat.

'But that's not normal.'

'Having a dead parent isn't entirely normal either.' I can't help my voice rising.

'It's natural to be angry,' she says with excitement. 'But if you can't even look at the sea because it reminds you of your father – that's not right. It's unhealthy.'

She's got the language down. Hearing her use it sends me right back to that hellish room with the counsellor nodding away.

'I'm not angry,' I say.

'There are bereavement specialists, people who've devoted their lives to helping guys like you—'

This is it, isn't it? She's going to chew and chew and she's not going to let go until she breaks me. She's going to ruin this holiday, and ruin everything.

'For God's sake,' I say. 'I don't need help. I just want to go to Toulouse.'

She blinks. 'I was only—'

'What's so great about professionals anyway?' I demand. 'They can't change anything, they can't stop Dad getting on that fricking boat. All they do is yap, the same as you're doing now. The only difference is, they yap at me in rooms full of beige furniture with views of a car park and Van Gogh prints on the walls. You're yapping at me in a café with fricking sea views on my fricking *holiday*.'

At some point in my speech, I have stood up. Half the people in the café have edged away. So has the herring gull. Sasha stares at me in astonishment.

'I'm sorry,' I say, trying to calm myself. 'It's just . . . there are trigger points and I think . . . I don't want to mess up this holiday. It will be cool in Toulouse, I promise. And we can get the Barcelona train over the Pyrenees, see some snow.'

The sun has turned Sasha's hair to rose-gold and her skin to chestnut velvet. I lean across the table to kiss her. She turns her head away.

# NATHAN

Dad's fingers are pressed together as he swivels back and forth on his big leather chair. As a kid, I used to push the tips of my fingers together like that and move them up and down, imagining that they were separated by a pane of glass. I'd like a pane of glass between me and my father right now, but I'm making do with a desk and a computer. The view outside the window is of the sea, hard and glittering. I'm still not used to the feeling of air conditioning on my neck.

'This is an opportunity for you, finally, to prove useful.' Dad gets up from his desk and walks to the window. Palm trees stud the view as the gardens slope down to the shore, their rough pineapple trunks within touching distance if anyone bothered to open a window around here. He's wearing a cream-coloured suit, a nod to the fact that it's thirty-five degrees outside. Tucked somewhere inland, away from this pretty part of the Spanish coast, the refinery churns endlessly through its stinking raw contents. When

Dad took me up there last week, it was like I had arrived in hell.

'A chance to make up for some of your crap,' Dad says. 'And there's been a lot of crap lately, so there's a lot of making up to do.'

I rub at the bridge of my nose silently. Ever since the party, I've lost the will to fight back, if I ever had the will to begin with.

'I don't expect you to say anything.' He comes to stand behind me, and I recoil slightly at the feel of his hands on my shoulders. 'I simply expect you to listen and make notes. Can you do that?'

'Yes,' I say.

Dad squeezes. 'Watch his expression, read his emotions. Write it down. Don't blink, don't turn away. I will do all the talking, and you will do all the watching. Then you will tell me what you have observed.'

The buzzer goes on Dad's desk.

'Mr Silva is here, sir.'

Dad lets go of me and leans into the intercom. 'Five more minutes, Maria. Then send him in.'

I wonder sometimes if Dad's sleeping with Maria. He's secretive like that, out in the evenings without much explanation. He does it in London too. I don't ask. What's the point?

Approximately four and a half minutes sooner than expected, the door clatters back on its hinges and Precious Silva's dad comes into the room. I glimpse Maria's apologetic face for an instant before the door swings shut again.

For such a short man, Ricky Silva manages to fill the space he occupies. Dad looks a little startled as he shakes the hairy hand being thrust at him. 'Good to see you, Ricky!' he says, attempting to sound hearty. 'Been a while, been a while. This is my son, Nathan. He's working with me this summer, showing him the ropes, you know the drill.'

My hand is crushed to dust.

'Forgive me. I have very little time today.'

Ricky Silva sounds like someone rolled his larynx in sand. The shark of the Algarve sits himself down on the long white leather sofa by the window and spreads his arms out along the top. I get the fleeting sense that he's trying to fill the space even further, more pufferfish than shark. The pen is in my hand as my fingers reach for the pad of paper on which I am meant to be making notes.

'So tell me,' says Dad after a cloud of small talk as Maria brings in coffee. 'Are the rumours true?'

Ricky grimaces. 'The run-off from the cement works has caused a terrible mess. It will cost a lot of money to clear up before development can begin.'

'Tell me what I can do to help,' Dad says earnestly. 'The oil industry doesn't have a great record in environmental responsibility, but we know people who can clean up a mess like this. I can put in a call.'

Ricky Silva rubs his head. 'I appreciate the gesture, but the problems run deeper than cement.'

There's an expectant pause.

'I have very little time,' Ricky Silva repeats, his brow creasing.

Dad clears his throat. 'I appreciate that you're a busy man,' he says. 'We all are. But I believe I have the solution to your problems, Ricky. And the elegance of it is that we can both benefit.'

I lean forward slightly. This is the part where I'm supposed to concentrate. Make notes.

'What is this solution?' Ricky enquires.

'I want to buy some of your land,' says Dad.

Ricky looks startled. 'You are not a hotel man.'

Dad leans back in his chair. 'I'm not interested in hotels. I'm interested in oil,' he says. 'There is oil in the Algarve, as you know. Both onshore and off. This company wants to drill in Portugal and bring the crude oil to our refineries in Spain. But we need sites. I am responsible for finding those sites.'

Ricky tips his head. 'I'm listening.'

'One of your sites has come up in a recent survey,' Dad continues. 'It will be costly to extract the oil, but I could pitch it to the board as a long-term investment.'

'Where is this site?' says Ricky.

Dad writes something down, passes it across the table. Ricky takes it. His eyes widen at what's written there. I crane my neck to see what's on the paper, but can't.

'We keep the surveys to ourselves as a rule,' Dad is saying. 'Drilling sites are not popular. *Potential* drilling sites, even less so. Environmentalists, expatriate communities, local estate agents, holiday companies – you name it, they are all on our backs. But oil is there, yes.'

Several emotions chase each other across the leathery plains of Ricky Silva's face, which I find myself itching to draw. Caution is one. Reluctance another. I can't identify the rest.

'I have plans for this site,' Ricky says. 'Plans I have been working towards for most of my career. I don't want to sell it.'

'Consider it, at least,' says Dad.

'Perhaps,' Ricky says stiffly, standing up again with a swift pull on the knees of his pale grey suit.

'It's a difficult site,' warns Dad, shaking Ricky's hand. 'You'll need to invest a huge amount to develop it. With the way things are going for you . . .'

'I am well aware of how things are going,' says Ricky.

'Yes,' says Dad soothingly. 'Of course you are.'

Ricky looks again at the piece of paper in his hairy paw. He seems smaller now than he was when he came into the room. The pufferfish deflated.

'Let's meet again next month,' Dad suggests, steering Ricky to the door with his thin-fingered hand. 'Things may be clearer by then.'

'Things will be *better* by then,' Ricky says, almost to himself.

'Perhaps,' Dad says. He tips his head. 'Perhaps not.'

Almost as soon as Ricky Silva has left, Dad lifts the pad from my hand. He stares at the deflated shark on the top sheet. I'm almost as surprised to see it there as he is.

# PRECIOUS

'God, it's hot,' sighs Lotta. 'I'm sweating like anything.'

Lotta doesn't have a drop of sweat on her long brown body. Not even on that bit under your hair where your neck creases up. Her blondness, after two weeks in the sun, is blinding, glimmering, like molten gold, or butter. Lotta's mum doesn't believe in butter. She doesn't seem to believe in food either, I noted glumly at the start of this holiday. There's never anything in the state-of-the-art fridge apart from champagne and organic face packs. There's not much point in keeping food here when we eat at the club every day, but sometimes it would be nice to have something to graze on.

Olivia adjusts her Ray-Bans, flicks a ladybird off one perfect thigh and snaps a flurry of pictures. Her phone starts purring as appreciation pours in. Five hundred likes right there, without even trying. I shift on my lounger and pick up my phone, wondering if I should do the same. On the screen, sweat sits lightly on the dark facial hair fringing my top lip. There isn't a filter for that so I take a few random shots of the pool instead. One of the maids is sweeping something on the wrap-around terrace, the sound of her bristles swishing rhythmically along with the sound of the crickety things in the grass. The air always smells nice here: piney and fresh. I like to think it stirs my Portuguese DNA on some level, my ancestral genes blinking and breathing alongside me.

'I'm completely *dying* of heat,' says Olivia, putting her phone down.

'We could go inside,' I suggest, as I feel somehow that it's my turn to expand on this hotness conversation.

'Not on our last day.' Lotta lies back down on her lounger and fluffs out her hair. 'Who knows when we'll see the sun again?'

'Not until Tuscany in September,' says Olivia. '*If* we're lucky.'

Olivia's hair is developing gorgeous light-brown highlights, like perfectly toasted Homepride. The thought brings me back to butter again, and my stomach plays an embarrassing little tune in a perfect rumble of gas and liquid. Lotta and Olivia both giggle. I sit up, hot with more than just the sun. My bikini didn't exactly deliver on the curve-boosting promises. I feel like a plank that someone left outside a builder's yard. A plank decorated with a couple of super-expensive bandanas.

'I'm going for a swim,' I say.

I cheer up as I sink beneath the blue. Water is my favourite element. I have been swimming since I was four months old, when Ilynka first took me to baby snorkelling. We have photos somewhere of me underwater in my swim nappy with my eyes wide open, as chilled as a fish. I could spin and turn in its cool blueness for ever. Maybe it's all those hours I spent on my imaginary back-garden ocean, but getting back on solid ground is always a disappointment.

'You're like Ariel in *The Little Mermaid*,' says Lotta from the lounger as I dip down and swim the length of the pool.

'Only without the boobs,' I say as I push my wet, dark hair out of my eyes.

'You ought to get them done if they bother you,' says Lotta. She adjusts her own perfect baps. 'It's only a few thou.'

When Mum gets a procedure, she sits around bandaged like Tutankhamun, furious with everyone and weeping with agony. I've never seen the appeal. I duck down again and swim an entire length of the curving pool, far below the water so I'm skimming the tiled floor. I feel more like a crocodile than a mermaid, if I'm honest. Dark. Scaly. Maybe even a bit dangerous, like something inside me is waiting to burst out.

'Do you think you'll see your dad before we leave?' asks Lotta when I surface, gasping for breath.

I have been trying not to think about my father this holiday. It's not been easy. Whenever I picture him, with his inky-black hair and skin as dark as the dried beef strips Mum once went through a phase of eating, he is always silhouetted against the masts of the marina, on the boardwalks, in all the good restaurants in this town.

'No,' I say.

'I always thought he was nice. Fun, you know?'

'Mum thought so too,' I say. 'Once.'

I hope I have picked the right tone of voice: jokey, sarcastic. Olivia and Lotta make sympathetic faces at me, and I feel warmed by their friendship again. They've both been through this. Lotta's done it twice.

'I'm going to be a divorce lawyer when I leave uni,' says Lotta as she oils her arms. 'I will be excellent at empathising with the victims and I'll make loads of money.'

'They aren't victims, Lots,' says Olivia. 'They're clients.'

'That makes it sound like I'm going to be a prostitute.'

'Mum says divorce lawyers are worse than prostitutes,' I say.

'Because you never even get to sleep with them?' offers Olivia. Lotta snorts with laughter.

'Our divorce lawyer wears fat rings on every finger,' I tell them. 'She buys a ring every time she wins a case worth more than ten million pounds.'

'What happens when she runs out of fingers?'

'"Upgrades, Mrs Silva," she says.' I rest my head back on the pillow of cool water. '"That's what this business is all about."'

36

Lotta squeals with shocked delight. Olivia joins in. As Lotta makes us all pose for a pic, I allow myself to enjoy the feeling that I have made them laugh on purpose.

# HARRY

I hate the sea. And yet somehow here I am, standing in it, the skin on my feet wrinkled and blue. If I stay here long enough, they'll probably dissolve into the brine like a tooth in a glass of cola, and float away to join all the other body parts sloshing around the seabed.

*Come and get me, you bastard*, I think, *in all your big bastard blueness. Come and bloody get me.*

'I'm here, Dad,' I tell the waves hopelessly. 'Again. But I can't stay long.'

I consider the definition of 'long'. Is three days long? It's felt long. But I don't seem able to leave. Believe me, I've tried.

'You all right, mate?'

A guy with a large brown gut hanging over the top of a small pair of blue Speedos is looking at me. On a brightly coloured towel behind him sits someone I'm guessing is his wife.

'You been standing there for ages,' he says. 'You know you still got your guitar on your back?'

I fiddle with the strap across my chest. I'm never going to play the thing. I should probably sell it, if I can find a taker. I bought it in Barcelona off a guy in the street, even though Sasha was gone by then.

*'You ought to buy a guitar,' Sasha says as we laugh at the buskers along the Seine. 'You can't be much worse than half of these guys. I'll sing, you play. We'll be millionaires before we reach Nice.'*

*I roll my eyes at her. 'Why do you keep going on about Nice?'*

'What you gonna do, son?' says Speedo Man. 'Serenade the fishes?'

I move towards him suddenly, making him stumble backwards. The look in his eyes reminds me of the herring gull in Nice all those millions of years ago. With three weeks of beard growth I probably look like a very thin, scary Jesus.

'I'm biting the hornet,' I inform him. 'It tastes like shit.'

'I think he's drunk, Brian,' says the wife, clambering off her towel. 'Let's head back, there's Aqua Zumba on in twenty minutes.'

'Do you want a guitar?' I say, suddenly keen to make amends. They were only trying to be friendly and I've frightened them. 'Thirty euros and it's yours.'

But they're hurrying away from me without looking back.

There are some little black and white wading birds nearby, black-winged stilts I think, with long red legs bent like pipe cleaners under them and heads moving like feathered pistons. I'm swaying where I stand. I'm not drunk, just hungry. I ought to take eating more seriously but I've lost interest. I swivel the strap round and contemplate my guitar. It's scratched and brown and the number of strings still matches the number of pegs. I strum it experimentally. It sounds terrible. My phone is dead, or I would Google how to tune it.

I rub my face like a kid, and try to ignore the sting of salt and sand in my eyes. I'm lost and sad and alone, with a guitar I can't play and a face that scares fat Englishmen. But hey. I'm looking at the sea. I'm standing in the sea.

That's what you wanted, isn't it, Dad?

I pull my feet from the water, and head up the beach to buy a bread roll from the guy in the corrugated tin van parked on the little road running into the middle of town. It tastes of dust and sand, like everything in this place.

'I don't have to be here,' I say out loud. 'I can leave any time I want.'

I feel bolstered by the sound of my own voice. There's nothing to stop me heading for the station and finding a nice comfy train to take me back to sanity. I breathe deeply. Once again, I summon a picture of myself sitting down on an orange vinyl seat, the smell of diesel and hot rubber in the air, smiling at a train attendant who looks like Sasha but isn't angry with me.

The image propels me down the dusty street to the station. Within minutes I am sweating like a racehorse, the guitar slick against my back. I wave my pass at the guy behind the glass. Five minutes until the next train, and I can leave. I sit down on the platform, pull the guitar round on to my lap and stare at the strings. Several fellow travellers watch me hopefully. Like most people in my life, they are in for disappointment.

Only now do I let myself consider exactly where this train is going to take me. I can't check my phone because it's dead. I didn't ask the guy in the station, and I don't want to go back in because then I will look stupid as well as thin and crazy. Besides, there's the risk that I might keep walking, back to drown my feet in the salt and sand, where I will stand until I am dead too, growing thinner and madder with every sunset. I've done three sunsets in this place already, I can't do any more. I focus on the storks' nest on the house across the platform, the large structure threatening to tip sideways every time the storks shift about, and attempt to calm myself down.

There's an old payphone tucked inside the cool of the station house. I should probably call Mum to let her know I'm still alive. We haven't spoken since Nice. But I'm not up to explaining anything at the moment, not even to myself, and I'm definitely not up to figuring out how Spanish telephones work. I'll call when I reach the next town. It'll be a bigger place than this dusthole, a place where they sell solar battery packs for phones. That's about the height of my aspirations right now.

The storks opposite turn their long necks as a grubby tin train approaches, clacking with diesel and purpose. I clench and unclench my fists, and stand up, and shuffle along the platform with everyone else, and put my foot on the plate and heave myself into the carriage. I am trembling so hard that the guitar is almost playing itself, singing tunelessly on my back.

I'm leaving. I'm leaving now.

The train doors start to close. Beyond them, the sea gives a final glimmer. Dad waves desperately from the prow of the boat with the sun sinking behind him. He's only there for a moment and then he's gone, along with the view.

The metal floor of the carriage sucks at me, vacuum-packing me into something impossibly small. I'm struggling to breathe. My vision narrows, my lungs labouring at nothing. The only thing I know is that if I don't get out of this train, I'll die like a fish on a slab. There's a strange whimpering sound, like a deflating mouse. Oh. That'll be me.

'STOP THE TRAIN,' I shout. 'STOP THE TRAIN STOP THE—'

I'm grappling with the doors, yanking them apart. Someone shouts at me as I jump, and I crash to my knees on the platform as the carriage moves away, my belongings clattering down beside me. The guitar is miraculously unscathed, but the only thing I care about is that I can breathe again, and I gasp and roll around in the dust to prove it.

The storks flap their wings disapprovingly above me. Far below the platform edge, past the white flats and cars, past the corrugated bread-roll van and Speedo Man's hotel, I can still see the bastard sea.

# PRECIOUS

Mum laughed too, in a savage kind of way, when she told me that anecdote about the lawyer's rings. I didn't laugh back at the time. If Dad's planning to upgrade, what does that make Mum and me? Rejects. Last year's line. Worthless.

'There's going to be nothing worthless about *me* when I've finished with that man,' said Mum when I raised this with her.

I'm so lost in thought, mindlessly sculling up and down the pool, that it takes me several moments to realise that Lotta and Olivia have gone inside and I'm alone. I immediately feel panicky. I'm not good at being alone. Being alone gives me too much time to think, and thinking digs me the kind of holes that are almost impossible to climb out of. *What is the point of me?* being one of the biggies.

It's not *entirely* true that I'm alone. There's a dog observing me on the other side of the wall. He's brown, scruffy, low-slung and ugly, and his lower jaw sticks out too far, making him look as if he's furious with the world.

'Hey,' I say, climbing out of the pool and wrapping my towel around me.

The dog sticks out his funny jaw a bit more. *That bikini don't do you no favours.*

I can take this from a dog. Dogs have no side, no agenda. They just say things the way they see them. The first thing I'm going to do when I leave home is get a dog, and the uglier the better.

'I think I've got thinner this holiday,' I tell him. 'I've basically been eating loads of fish and salad. There's never any food, you see.'

*Tell me about it.*

Voices drift towards me from the house.

'You didn't say your daughter would be here . . .'

'Shoo!'

I spin around to see my mother stalking across the lawn in a bright orange kaftan-style dress, flapping her red-polished nails in a dangerous kind of way. I've clapped eyes on so little of her this holiday that I'm almost surprised to see her now. There's a sharp-nosed guy lurking behind her, his grey hair streaked with blond in an old-footballer style. The guy she's spent most of her time with, I'm guessing. He doesn't look happy about being here.

'Baby, don't talk to strange dogs,' Mum tells me, still waving fiercely. 'They could have rabies and AIDS and all kinds of vile things.'

The dog raises its shaggy eyebrows at me. *She always like this?*

'He's on the other side of the wall,' I tell my mother. 'He won't come any closer.'

'Nasty flea-bitten thing. Come over here, I want you to say hello to Aiden.'

I hold my towel tightly against myself, horribly aware of my make-up free face and bony knees and plastered hair. I'm so cocooned in the towel that it's quite hard to walk forward. There's no way I can hold out a hand to shake the slim, long-fingered one the streaky guy is reluctantly holding out towards me. And to top it all off, I can't remember what Mum said his name was. The only word that comes to mind is Bacon. It's the streaky thing. Could he be called Bacon?

'Pleased to meet you,' Bacon says, looking anything but. His voice has a sharp London tang about it.

'Pleased to meet me too,' I say. 'I mean, you too.'

'Oh, Precious, could you be any more gauche?' Mum says. 'Luckily Aiden has a teenager too. He knows all about how hopeless you can be in company.'

Oh, *Aiden*. I prefer Bacon. Bacon isn't Mum's first romance since Dad, and he probably won't be the last. I guess she deserves a bit of fun, though it would have been nice to have seen more of her this fortnight than I have.

'He's wonderful, isn't he?' she says when Bacon retreats to the wall to study the dog.

'He seems OK,' I say. 'Based on the four words he said.'

'He's a tonic,' Mum says with a sigh. 'And really wise. He knows exactly how I'm feeling right now.'

She angles the phone for maximum kaftan coverage, then keys in a hundred hashtags along the lines of #koolkaftans, #yummymummy and #coverthebulges. She's so much better at this stuff than me.

'Now, Precious, I need you to listen,' she says. 'I have something very important to tell you.'

I feel a drip from my wet hair rolling down my nose. I can't wipe it because if I wipe it that means I have to take my hands off my towel which means I will drop my towel in front of Bacon and that won't do at all.

'I'm leaving this afternoon, assuming the car ever gets here,' Mum says. 'I can't miss my flight. I have a very important meeting at Howarth Steele this evening.'

I blink. 'Aren't I flying home with you tomorrow?'

'There's been a change of plan.' Mum raises her hand to her head to adjust her sunglasses. 'Now don't be angry, but I saw your father today.'

Feelings stab through me. I can't quite identify them, but they are sharp. I keep my voice steady for Bacon's sake. 'I thought we were staying away from Dad this holiday.'

Mum picks at a bit of fluff on her dress. 'He hadn't had the guts to speak to me face-to-face since that business in Spain,' she says fretfully. 'As we were here, Aiden thought I should hear direct from him what he thinks we're worth. Why should I hear it through his lawyers?'

I think about the rings on Hazel Howarth's fat fingers. 'Did he ask about me?' I say before I can filter the question.

'Of course not, that man only thinks of himself. Instead,

47

he made the most ludicrous offer you've ever heard, claiming bankruptcy. Bankruptcy! That man owns half this coastline. Bankrupt he is NOT.'

Mum's always gone out with fists flailing, manicured to within an inch of their lives, a bit like she was just now with the dog. I want her to hug me and tell me everything is going to be fine, but she's not the hugging kind. We just stand there instead, eyeball to polarised-prescription-Tom-Ford-aviator-lens, and let the unspoken stuff flow between us. Bacon stands at a safe distance and studies his watch a bit too obviously. Over the wall, the dog cocks his leg on a bush covered in bright pink flowers.

'So you're going back for a meeting tonight?' I say at last. 'About the divorce?'

Mum whips out her compact and pats powder around her nose. 'The sooner I get to Howarth Steele, the better. You can fly back with Lotta and Olivia tomorrow like we planned, your ticket will still be fine. Get a taxi from the airport, Ilynka will let you in. Where is that car?'

Someone appears to have heard her, because the gates swing open and a dark car with tinted windows glides up the villa's cobbled driveway.

Mum blows me a kiss. 'Take care now, baby,' she says. 'And remember, I love you and everything is going to be fine.'

The 'everything's going to be fine' thing feels like it came too late. I stand there, clutching my towel as Mum's pile of cases is loaded into the boot. Bacon turns his back and opens the door for her and she slides into the back seat. Her phone is already out, sunlight glinting on the screen. The engine is almost silent as it purrs away, back down the drive towards the glittering sea, and I'm alone again. Even the dog has gone.

# HARRY

I don't have to go inland. If I keep going, I'll end up in Calais, as long as the sea stays on my left at all times. Seems logical. Or as logical as I can get in my current state of mind.

You've got me for as long as you need me, Dad.

I still can't play this bloody guitar.

# NATHAN

It's all right here. Rich, full of life. A few good-looking women. I study the boats in the marina as they clink and bob, shifting around on their anchors. The brown paper package squats at my feet. I haven't opened it. Better not to know.

I squint at the waitress over the top of my sunglasses as she sets down the tiny cup of black oil in front of me.

'Anything else?' she says.

I lean back in my chair. 'What else are you offering?'

She blushes and backs away into the recesses of the café. Her teeth are a let-down. Losing interest, I return my gaze to the marina. And there it is. Dad said it would be obvious when I saw it, and he was right. It's massive. If you drew it, it would spill off the edges of the page.

I have to get this right.

# PRECIOUS

'Oh my gosh, Lots, you look AMAZING,' squeals Olivia.

'Shut UP,' Lotta squeals back. 'YOU look amazing. That dress is INCREDIBLE.'

'I've been saving it for our last night.' Olivia gives a twirl. The peacock colours glitter and Lotta squeals again.

'If we're really lucky,' I say, smoothing down my long golden skirt and backing towards the waiting car, 'we might still catch the others at the club, although they usually stop serving around midnight.'

'Oh, we're not eating tonight,' says Olivia.

I get the unnerving sense that she and Lotta have planned this evening without me. Above our heads, a load of scabby moths attack the porch light.

'But Lotta's mum said she'd booked a table for all of—'

Lotta interrupts. 'There's no way we're spending our last night with the 'rents, Presh. We're going to this place down by the beach that everyone on my feed has been raving about. It's, like, super-deluxe and the vibe is awesome.'

'Lotta has already texted her mum about it,' says Olivia. 'I'm sure the club will do food. But if it doesn't, there'll be a burger van or something, there are always loads of them around places like that.'

Lotta makes a retching sound. 'Swear to me you won't eat anything from those vans, Presh. They use dog meat in their burgers.'

I think of the ugly dog from earlier, and feel a little anxious. I don't want to eat dog meat, but I'm seriously hungry and might have to take the risk. I actually considered eating Lotta's mum's face pack tonight. It was green and looked like guacamole, and it would probably have tasted all right on one of those zero-calorie rice cracker things in the cupboard.

'I swear,' I say, crossing my fingers behind my back.

The drive only takes ten minutes. Propping my elbow on the sill in the car as Lotta and Olivia burble away about their plans, I gaze out at the lights of Vilamoura. How many happy families are behind those windows? How many parents sitting with their kids around a table, eating proper food and laughing?

*'Tell me about the feast,' I beg one night when Mum is out and Dad, for once, is in. 'Before King Sebastian leaves Portugal with his army.'*

*I feel Dad's weight as he settles on the edge of my mattress, and watch as he picks up the painted figure that I keep on my bedside table. He turns the figure of the little king thoughtfully in his thick fingers.*

*'The feast lasted three days,' he says finally, as though reluctant to begin the story. 'With chickens, geese, goats, pheasants, rabbits, veal, venison, beef and enough wine to fill the river and float all of the king's ships.'*

*'There were a lot of ships,' I prompt.*

*'Eight hundred ships, waiting for the feast to end. Eight hundred ships, full of men about to die.'*

*I shiver.*

*'A comet blazed through the sky as the king dined on golden cod and meats roasted and shining in honey, warning of death with its long, fiery finger. The king did not see it. The smell of the cloves and the nutmeg in the pies floated across the harbour, among the ships of waiting men . . .'*

*Dad's Portuguese vowels wash over me like waves on a beach, shifting and pulling at the sand of me as I drift to sleep. Re-forming me over and over again.*

The car drives through the marina, past the restaurants and clubs we normally go to. I watch them sadly, checking off all the safe, familiar eating opportunities they represent. There's even a guy sitting at one of my favourite tables who looks familiar, but the car has gone past before I can work out where I know him from, or even if I know him at all.

'Isn't that your dad's boat, Precious?' says Lotta suddenly.

A large silver yacht is moored in one of the more obvious spots in the marina, bobbing lazily on its mooring. It is strung with twinkling fairy lights and rainbow-coloured LEDs. I freeze, staring as the car whips by, glimpsing the name *Amalia* stencilled on its shining nose. My father isn't famous for his good taste, as we have already established. I knew I'd see some evidence of him this week.

'I don't know,' I mutter, sinking down in my seat. 'I didn't get a proper look.'

Lotta pulls out her bag, checks her make-up and fires off a selfie without even glancing at the camera. She's perfected the art of catching herself unawares. Olivia twists round and gawps at *Amalia* as the car glides past the marina towards the beach. I concentrate on looking out of the window, wondering where the burger vans are.

The car drops us by the long stretch of beach east of the town centre. Ahead of us, perched on the sand, stands a white building with a sloping roof. Lights whirl around a tented dance floor like a psychedelic lighthouse, with a crowd of people in shorts and T-shirts queuing up and dancing as they wait. I feel nervous and tall and overdressed, like an anxious lamp post at Christmas.

Whooping and screaming, Olivia and Lotta kick off their shoes and race towards the action. I follow more slowly until the smell of hot dogs pulls me up short. As promised, there are food vans parked all the way along the road that borders the beach. There's a homeless guy sitting on the pavement beside the first van, giving my dress a sideways look. I try not to catch his eye as I sidle up.

'*Que queres?*' says a man with a lot of black hair that runs from the top of his head and down his face and on to his shoulders and chest without stopping.

I point at a steel dish full of frankfurters, and he passes me one in a soft white roll. It's completely delicious. I don't care if it's made of dog. I wolf it down so fast that I can barely breathe.

'*Quatro euros.*'

I nod and smile, catching my breath at the last of my quivery, pink, smoky sausage of divinity. I fumble for my purse, yank out my card and hold it out. The hairy man shakes his head. Someone laughs. I guess a place like this doesn't do contactless. I need cash. I grab the bunch of notes Mum got me in case of emergency and pull one out.

Mr Hairy takes the note and studies it. He glances at me, then back at the note, then stuffs it into the grubby money belt round his waist. I wipe my hands as best I can on a slippery serviette before I catch up the folds of my dress and hurry down to the beach to find Lotta and Olivia in the club queue. I can't see a VIP line, so I guess they're waiting with everyone else. I walk up and down chattering groups who all seem to know each other, feeling self-conscious and alone as usual. Twitchy too, which is stupid. My father wouldn't hang out here, but I still get the feeling I'm being watched.

In the end, I return to the end of the line, fumble for my phone and dial Lotta, sticking my finger in my ear as

I wait for her to pick up. I really don't want to be here by myself.

'Change.'

The homeless guy from the van is standing in front of me, holding out his hand.

# HARRY

She's an overdressed beanpole in a deflated gold helium balloon, long dark hair that doesn't suit her, all hunched in on herself like she's trying not to take up as much space as her body requires. Definitely out of her comfort zone. Why is she alone? What did she think she was doing, wandering off without change from a fifty-euro note? Who does that? I get the strangest sense that she can't actually see me, even though I'm standing right in front of her. I've been feeling pretty invisible lately, so it wouldn't be a huge surprise.

She says something fast and crunchy-sounding in Portuguese, then realises I don't understand. 'Who are you?' she says in English, extra loudly, the way you do with mad people and foreigners. 'What do you want?'

I'm not entirely sure why I'm doing this. I could have kept the cash after the van guy asked me to find this girl. After all, forty-six euros is forty-six euros.

'Your change,' I repeat.

Her eyes dart about like black-lashed humming birds. 'I don't have any change. Please go away.'

Christ. She thinks I'm begging. It would be funny if it wasn't so tragic. Am I really looking so rough?

'It's. For. You,' I say, carefully, jingling the money at her. 'From your hot dog. You didn't stick around long enough for the guy to get the change together. He doesn't see fifty-euro notes very often.'

Her long dress gleams in the yellowish lights overhead. 'I didn't want any change.'

London accent. Not posh. Just clearly and stupidly rich.

'It wasn't lobster à la carte.' I can't help sounding sarcastic about this.

Her ears change colour. The rest of her face has no chance of revealing its true nature beneath the trowels of make-up she's wearing. The sea swishes ceaselessly beside us. I hated it four weeks ago when Sasha left. I can't begin to tell you how much I hate it now.

'Are you taking the money or what?'

She starts backing away from me. 'Keep it. Get a hot meal or something.'

'It's forty-six euros,' I say, perplexed. 'I could get a hotel room for that.'

'Do that then,' she says, before she hauls up her dress and legs it down the beach towards the club in a long streak of melted gold.

I trudge back to the hot dog van, my hands heavy with coins, and buy two hot dogs because I might as well. As I sit back down on the edge of the pavement beside my guitar to eat them, I scroll through the encounter in my head. It reads pretty badly, however many ways I look at it. I have got to the point where a girl in a Bacofoil frock thinks I'm a homeless. Maybe I need to shave off the beard. She was OK-looking, in an alien sort of way. Big eyes. Androgynous, that's the word.

As I catalogue and file her into the section in my head entitled Never Go There Again, there is a sharp boom behind me, followed by the distant sound of breaking glass. An odd silence follows. I turn my head and squint back towards the town, where the sky is suddenly glowing with fire. The air around me thickens with something more than frankfurter steam. I stuff what's left of my second hot dog into my mouth and get up.

'*Bomba*,' pronounces the guy in the food van.

Shouting people descend on the scooters parked in jumbled piles along the seafront, piling aboard, grabbing their girlfriends, and occasionally a helmet, and buzzing away. Some of them are heading for the action. Others are leaving by the coast road, getting out of the way. The music from the club on the beach is so loud that they probably haven't heard a thing.

Shouldering my rucksack and guitar, I weave through the clot of traffic snarling up along the front and walk towards the town to see what's happened. The sirens have started screeching like fried cats now, and a load of car alarms alongside the jetties have joined in. By the time I make it to the centre, there are three police cars parked across the road, preventing anything with an engine from passing through.

In the marina itself the water is rocking violently, and broken things are burning on its oily surface. It looks as if a boat just blew up, one of the flashy ones that are always moored up this end.

Among many others, there was a theory at Dad's inquest that the gas stove blew a hole through the hull, sinking the boat in seconds. No one aboard would have stood a gnat's chance. No one aboard this one would have either.

My mouth is dry and my head hurts. I walk away from the fire and the sirens and the screaming, back towards the darkness and the sand and the sound of the ceaseless sea.

# PRECIOUS

It's clear from the way they are studying their phones that Lotta and Olivia are trying not to look as if they are listening to the conversation over by the long glass windows that overlook the airport runway. But it's sort of unmissable.

'. . . matter of time before something like this happened, of course. You can take the man out of the gutter but *you'll never take the gutter out of the man.*'

This last bit is very hushed, like Lotta's mum and stepdad have just realised that I might be within earshot. I shift in my seat and wish myself a thousand miles away.

'Presh?'

Lotta and Olivia are staring right at me, their phones slack by their sides.

'Are you relieved?' says Lotta. 'That he wasn't on the boat, I mean?'

I have thought about this a lot since the news broke. 'I don't know,' I say, because it's sort of true.

'Do they really think it was an attempt to kill him?' There's a look in Olivia's eyes that I want to call 'greedy', although that probably doesn't make sense. 'That's what my feed is saying.'

I think of Mum. I don't *think* she knows how to make a bomb. 'It was probably an accident,' I say.

Mrs Swinton tip-taps across the marble departure lounge floor. I get to my feet. She addresses us while looking slightly over the top of my head, which takes a bit of doing.

'Girls, we'll head for our departure gate in a minute. What a mess,' she adds, tip-tapping off again.

I'm not exactly sure why my father's boat exploding and making headline news means things are a mess for Mrs Swinton. The holiday is over, and we're flying home, and she won't have to see me again for a while. Maybe she thinks she will be hounded by press photographers and nagged for a quote about holidaying with Ricky Silva's ex-wife and kid. I think she'll be OK, personally. My father is the only interesting thing about me, and the press already knows we're related.

I can't stop thinking about all the what ifs. What if he *had* been on board? What if he'd been blown up while I was out with Lotta and Olivia? What if bits of his body had landed on the beach – his hairy hands or something?

'Final call for flight BA507 to departure gate 4. Flight BA507.'

Mrs Swinton's head rears up. 'Final call? When was the first call?'

My phone rings as our party sets off at an anxious jog for the departure gate.

'Well, if this isn't just *typical* of that man,' says Mum when I pick up.

'I don't think he blew up his own boat,' I say.

'Who knows what goes through his head? The press are all over me like midges. Whatever happened? What are they saying?'

I don't want to go into it. 'Not much,' I say.

'If I've warned you about that man once, I've warned you about that man a thousand times.'

'I know,' I mumble.

'Remember that I love you and only want the best for you.'

*And the best that man is NOT*, I think.

'And the best that man is NOT,' says Mum with relish.

She rings off. Moments later the phone rings again and I sigh and lift it back to my ear. Only this time, it's not her.

'Precious?'

My stomach squeezes into a small, lemony ball at the sound of my father's voice. I haven't spoken to him in three months. He doesn't even know I'm in the Algarve, or that I saw his boat when it was still in one piece.

'I wanted to tell you in person that I'm still alive,' he says.

Why is it that his voice makes me feel like I'm five years old again?

'Fortunately I got lucky at the casino last night and never made it back to the boat.'

I feel like retching. 'I don't need to know the details, thanks.'

'The story will blow over soon enough, I promise.'

'There's a story?' I say without thinking.

'With me, there's always a story.'

That much is true. Although the stories used to be a little different.

There is a loud BING BONG overhead, followed by a stream of Portuguese. I'm right underneath a tannoy. There's no way Dad will have missed it.

'Where are you?' he says in surprise.

The tannoy goes again. '*O voo BA507 para Londres Heathrow . . .*'

'Faro airport? You are at Faro?'

Lotta and Olivia are vanishing up ahead. I ought to hang up and chase after them but I can't seem to move. Mum didn't want Dad to know I was here and now I'm piggy in the middle.

'She never said you were with her,' Dad growls. 'Hand her the phone.'

My skin prickles.

'Precious, *hand your mother the phone.*'

'I'm not with her,' I blurt. 'She left yesterday.'

The stream of swear words that follow this can probably be heard by the entire departure lounge. I realise I'm sweating.

'Stay where you are,' Dad says at last. 'You are not safe by yourself.'

My skin pimples. I think of the *Amalia*, lying in pieces in Vilamoura marina.

*With me, there's always a story.*

'You need to come back with me. I'll send someone for you.'

I rouse myself. 'I'm going home—' I begin.

'You're going nowhere. Stay where you are.'

I clench my hand so hard around my phone, it's a wonder I don't crack the screen.

'Don't move. My men will find you, and bring you to me.'

I don't want to spend any part of the summer with my father. Mum is expecting me back. *I'm* expecting me back.

'I'm going home,' I repeat. 'My flight's about to leave.'

'This isn't a request. It's an order!'

Do this, do that. That man, that woman. 'I'm catching my flight,' I say, courage flooding me from somewhere. 'And you can't stop me.'

I angrily stuff my phone into my bag, shoving it down as far as it will go so I won't hear it when he rings back. Bloody, bloody, bloody hell.

Lotta has finally realised that I'm not tagging along behind her, and is waiting up ahead. 'We were supposed to board fifteen minutes ago,' she says, twirling her hair around one manicured finger. 'Mum's massively stressed. She's not used to economy flights.'

There is a lot of urgent action at the gate. Lotta's mum tuts, and flaps Lotta and Olivia through the gate like chickens, and checks her watch, and rushes ahead. I pull my ticket clumsily from my bag.

'How old are you?' asks the attendant on the gate.

'Sixteen,' I say, a little unsteadily. The conversation with Dad has knocked the breath out of me.

'Travelling alone?'

'I'm travelling with them,' I say, pointing at where Mrs Swinton's heel is whisking around the corner.

'Your surname is Silva?'

'Yes,' I say cautiously. She's not going to ask about my dad, is she?

'We can't allow you to board the flight alone, Miss Silva.'

'I'm not alone,' I tell her. 'I'm with the party that just went through.'

The smile is bland. 'We need confirmation from a parent or guardian if you're travelling alone.'

'I'm not alone,' I repeat.

'I'm sorry, Miss Silva, but in Portugal you are classed as a minor if you are younger than eighteen. Minors need permission from a parent or guardian if they are travelling alone.'

*I'm not travelling alone.* I can't say it again, I'll look stupid. Mum obviously overlooked this rather important detail of Portuguese bureaucracy.

'I have a ticket,' I say, my voice rising. 'I have to go back to London, my mum is expecting me. Get the lady who just went on before me, Annabel Swinton, she'll tell you I'm flying home with her.'

The attendant is as interested as mud. 'I'm sorry, Miss Silva, but we need—'

'What on earth is the delay?' demands Mrs Swinton, reappearing by the gate.

I'm so relieved to see her that I beam like a lunatic. I was starting to think I was going to be left behind. The attendant explains once again that I need written permission from a parent or a guardian to board the plane. Mrs Swinton looks exasperated.

'There's nothing I can do now, Precious,' she says, checking her watch. 'The airport people will look after you until you can contact your mother and have her get you on the next flight.'

I hear her words as if down a long, thin tunnel.

'You're going to leave me here?' I ask in astonishment.

'Think of it as waiting for a bus,' says Mrs Swinton briskly.

I've never waited for a bus in my life. Nor, I imagine, has Mrs Swinton. Something tells me we're not missing much.

'But I'll be by myself,' I say.

'You'll be fine. Enjoy the rest of your summer.'

She taps away through the gate again. I feel like I have been punched.

Two men in dark shirts materialise in the departure lounge and start looking around. When you grow up like me, you can spot minders from a distance of half a mile. I feel a surge of hopeless anger. Dad always gets what he wants.

My plane is about to start trundling away from the gate. I think wildly of films where people flag down the pilot and do reckless stuff on those wheelie ladders. Think, Precious. *Think.*

'Permission,' I squeak. The attendant looks up from her computer screen. 'I'll call my mum if you give me a second, she can give permission over the line, can't she?'

'I'm afraid it's too late, Miss Silva—'

'It can't be too late,' I say, scrabbling for my phone, 'because I have to leave RIGHT NOW. My bags are on the flight, I have to be on it too.'

*'O voo BA507 para London Heathrow . . .'*

It turns out that Dad is still on the line.

'Precious? Are you there? I'm not hanging up until I know you are safe.'

I stare wonderingly out of the window at my taxiing plane. It is leaving without me on board. I am all by myself, hundreds of miles from home.

'My men will be with you in ten minutes, bad traffic on the coast road,' Dad is thundering. 'Don't move. They'll find you.'

Alone. Just me.

'Talk to no one else!'

It is the strangest feeling. I'm *properly* alone. I could simply detach and float away, out of view. No one is watching me, no one knows where I am or what I'm doing. Apart from the men in dark shirts looking straight at me.

In the midst of my brain-freeze, I suddenly feel puzzled.

If Dad's men are stuck in traffic, then who are these guys?

# HARRY

There are only six weeks until I have to be in Birmingham, and I'm about as far away from the UK as it's possible to be while still in Europe. It's time to get a grip.

I took the beard off last night, in the hostel Bacofoil Girl so kindly paid for. I look even madder, to be honest. But I've got more to worry about right now than a pale chin at the bottom of a brown face. I need to get on a train. Dad has to understand that I can't stay with him for ever. But I could never make him listen to me when he was alive, so how am I supposed to do it now he's dead?

The station in Faro is so close to the shore, it's practically in the water. Little terns with black heads and snow-white wings are squeaking at me overhead, and the stink of fish is everywhere. The sea runs alongside the tracks if you go east. Only I'm not going east. I'm going north, into a sea-free zone. A Dad-free zone.

Breathe. Breathe. Breathe.

There's some kind of commotion outside the station house. Keen for distraction, I leave my rucksack and my guitar beside a bench and head out on to the road.

'*Dez euros só, menina. Não tem moedas?*'

I watch the baffled cabbie gesturing at the fifty-euro note the girl is pushing at him. I recognise her at once, on account of both her height and her dismal accounting skills. No Bacofoil frock this time. She's wearing strappy brown sandals with laces that tie halfway up her elongated calves, and a short, khaki-coloured rompersuit thing. If I needed a distraction, I just got it.

'We meet again, Bond,' I say, feeling strangely pleased to see her.

There's no recognition on her face at all. I feel like an idiot. The cabbie is eyeing the fifty in her hand. I'm guessing that at any minute, his scruples are going to fail and he'll take the lot.

'You're giving him too much money,' I say. 'Again.'

I peer at the dash display, dig around in my pocket and fish out ten euros left over from last night. 'That do you, mate?' I say, pressing the money into his hand. He looks about a quarter relieved, three-quarters disappointed.

'You should have let him keep it,' she says as the cabbie drives off sadly. Then she frowns. 'What do you mean, again?'

'The hostel and hot dogs came to twenty-six euros,' I say.

She stares at the rest of her change as I pour it into her hands and her face clears. 'You're the guy at the beach,' she says.

71

The station tannoy starts mumbling something about doom and destruction behind me. *The train now approaching the platform will rip your soul from your body and ensure that you puke.* I feel the sweat creeping up my neck. All desire for distraction departs.

'I have to go,' I say abruptly.

I head into the station house again, my fists clenched by my sides. My rucksack and guitar are still waiting for me. I can't decide if I'm relieved that no one's nicked the guitar. It's four hours from Faro to Lisbon, across the dust-dry plains of the Alentejo. Dad was never like this before, but death has done something to him and now all I can hear is his voice begging me not to go. Perhaps I have been avoiding the sea all these years because I knew the moment I heard his loneliness, I would be lost.

'Where are you going?'

She's followed me in to the station like some kind of expensive dog. I moisten my lips and try to keep my heart rate under control.

'None of your business,' I say.

She's trembling, clutching her strappy little bag close. 'This is going to sound really weird, but hear me out,' she begins. 'There were these two men. I missed my flight and they were in the departure lounge and I got a bad feeling about them. So I left the airport and I got a cab and I don't know what I'm going to do next.'

I'm in no mood for this. 'Call Daddy and tell him to send a rescue limo.'

She bites her lip. 'Can I stay with you? I won't be any trouble, I just need to figure out how to catch another flight. I'll pay you. You know that I have money.'

The train is approaching, a great metal coffin clacking towards me on pitiless, bony wheels.

'Pay someone else,' I say.

'I don't know anyone else.'

'You don't know me, either.'

Grabbing my rucksack, I take a run at the train. Dad is calling frantically over the noise of the train and the sound of my crashing heart. Squealing air brakes. People. The smell of dusty rucksacks, and unwashed feet, and sun and sweat. Forcing my heaving stomach into submission, I stride along the train until I find an empty seat halfway down a carriage. Halfway so that if I flip and try to lunge for the doors again, I won't get there before the train—

'You forgot this.'

Dimly I see the girl standing in front of me again. She is holding out my guitar.

'Jesus,' I say. The train lurches and I grip tightly on to the arms of my seat. 'Are you on elastic? I *said* I couldn't help you.'

She puts the guitar down on the floor and sits on the seat opposite me. Hauling her feet up, she wraps her arms round her endless legs and rests her head on her brown knees. Her black hair flops over her shins in a long thick curtain.

The train is moving. My eyes dart to the doors. Closed. Outside the window, the scene is starting to slide away from me.

'What do you want?' I demand helplessly.

'I don't know,' she tells her kneecaps, somewhere underneath all that hair. 'Not to be alone, I guess.'

The snaky body of the train bucks and squirms. It's getting faster. I wipe my face in a useless attempt to cope with the sweat pouring into my eyes.

'Everyone's alone,' I say. 'Get used to it.'

'You sound like this dog I met yesterday.'

It's such a peculiar thing to say that for a moment I forget the grief and the nausea and the sheer, blinding terror.

'What?'

'Just this dog.' She tucks a piece of long black hair behind one ear. 'In my head, dogs always have American accents and say things like "How you doin'?" Like Joey off *Friends*.'

What the hell is she talking about?

I'm about to smash open the window beside my head and leap out but I can't let myself. Instead I snatch up the English-language newspaper lying on the seat beside me and stare at the front page. There's a story about the boat that blew up in Vilamoura and its local owner: his acrimonious divorce, his hotels spread across half the Algarve. He looks like a real charmer.

We're properly gathering speed now. My eyeballs feel like they're sweating, or maybe crying. Damned if I know the difference.

'You look terrible,' Bacofoil Girl observes. 'Do you get travel sick?'

The ticket guy is coming down the carriage towards us. I force myself to stop rocking. The sea is still there out of the window, but only just.

'*Bilhetes, senhores e senhoras*,' the inspector says, cheerily unaware that I am collapsing like a sandcastle at high tide. '*Bilhetes*.'

'I don't have a ticket,' says the girl. 'Do you think I can buy one from this guy?'

'How should I know?'

I grope for my pass, unable to look away from the window. The shoreline is receding, fading to a thin, bright line on the horizon. *Stay,* Dad implores in my ear.

'You don't have a ticket?' I say. 'Take mine.'

I thrust my pass at her, grab my bag and guitar and rush towards the doors. There might be a chance the train will slow down when it reaches a bend. And there will be a bend. There has to be, geographically speaking, to stop us travelling west and start us travelling north. A bend to send me round the bend.

The train slows, curves. Hovers for a moment. The rolling stock is old, and the doors have a failing rubber seal on them that I wiggle my fingers through and force apart. Surprised by the unexpected assault, they fly open and the carriage fills with air. Hardly able to believe my luck, I jump out.

Someone in a khaki rompersuit jumps out beside me.

For God's sake. Seriously?

# PRECIOUS

He must have thought I was crazy, talking about dogs with American accents. But he looked so empty when he said that thing about being alone that I just came out with it to fill the space.

There's quite a lot about this boy that reminds me of the dog at the villa. He's not ugly like the dog was. Far from it, actually. Apart from the stripy face and dodgy travel-stained clothes, he's tall and skinny and his eyes are a pale, intense blue. He is angry with me, but angry about something else too. And I don't think I've ever met anyone so sad.

Maybe I *have* gone crazy. Being stranded has pushed me over the edge. I've been so jumpy that I haven't been thinking straight, like those deer that run at oncoming cars. What if the Terminator Twins in the departure lounge weren't looking for me at all, and now I'm walking along a dusty railway verge with an angry-eyed boy for no reason? It's freaky to think that barely half an hour ago I was sitting in a VIP lounge with a complimentary Frappuccino.

This is the kind of thing I could post about if I wanted to turn my phone back on. I might even get a few likes. Lotta and Olivia would break the Internet if *they* did it. Thinking of them makes my stomach feel funny. I wonder if they even looked back when Mrs Swinton marched them to their seats.

'Why are you following me?' the boy demands.

'I'm not following you.' I wipe my eyes, which have grown wet, and point down the dusty, uneven road ahead of us. 'I'm following that, same as you are.'

I turned my phone off as soon as I got out of the departure lounge and I haven't dared turn it on again yet in case Dad reappears on the other end. I need to talk to Mum, to get permission to fly home. I decide to email her at the next town, and then turn the phone back off superfast the minute I press send. Only then I'd have to turn it back on again to get the permission up on my screen to show the airport people. Thinking about this is giving me a headache, although that could be the sun, which is directly overhead. Planes rumble through the blue sky above us as they take off from the airport on the horizon, reminding me how close I am to leaving, and yet how impossibly far.

He has picked up speed ahead of me.

'Why did you jump out of the train?' I ask, hurrying after him. Long legs can be useful sometimes. 'Where are we going?'

Silence.

'Do you want your ticket back? Why did you give it to me?'

Still nothing.

'Why were you crying back then?'

'Why are you following me?' he repeats.

'I jumped out of the crow's nest,' I say. 'But, like I always suspected, I can't actually fly.' I realise it's not much of an explanation.

We're passing rows of anodyne white buildings and bouffant, lime-green trees on sandy scrub now. No one is around at all. I wish I'd put on better shoes this morning but I was only expecting to go to the airport. Maybe we'll see shops soon, where I can buy some decent footwear. My stomach rumbles, and I fantasise for a moment about passing a pizza restaurant.

After half an hour of total silence, we hit a busier road. Hot air whisks at our legs every time a car or a truck hurtles past. I'm dying of thirst.

I suddenly have a bright idea.

'What are you doing?' he says as I stick out my thumb.

'What does it look like?' I return, trying to sound like I've done this before. I don't know which way my thumb should face. Up? Sideways? Down is something to do with killing gladiators so I don't do down.

'It's not safe, hitching.' His eyes are like icebergs in those Arctic nature programmes. 'You'd be better off calling a cab.'

I think longingly of a long cold drink at the club by the marina and a plate of nachos and a quick email to Mum. We can't be that far from civilisation. I even take out my phone, before my brain gets on that whole world-going-nuts-at-missed-calls thing.

'I don't think they have Uber in the Algarve,' I say.

# HARRY

Unbelievably, she is still following me, this lanky khaki shadow with anxious eyes. Her sandals probably cost more than my rail pass. I thought she'd have given up by now. Then again, once she made the decision to jump out of the train, I suppose she didn't have much choice. So you could say her well-being is now my responsibility.

Sod that.

A shiny red truck blunders by, spraying us with gravel. The tiny stones make *plink-plink* noises against the strings of my guitar as I turn away to shield my face. Cars packed with holiday gear, old trucks blasting black smoke, tour buses, motorbikes fly past, none of them giving a toss. A goshawk is shimmering on the tarmac up ahead, mantling its grey wings and gorging itself on roadkill.

'I don't think they have Uber in the Algarve,' she says.

'You'll have to use your legs then,' I say. 'God knows, they're long enough.'

Once again, I get the impression of her ears and neck changing colour while her heavily made-up face remains the same. I feel a squirming sense of guilt as I clamber up the pinkish rock incline that marks the right-hand side of the road, set my rucksack down under a tree and pull out my water bottle. She follows me, scrambling up the incline, and stands there shifting from foot to foot as I take a drink. Why is she here? I've been asking myself this since Faro station and am still no clearer on the answer. Her crow's nest comment didn't help. A plane explodes into view, a vast metal bird startled out of the undergrowth. We're opposite the airport runway.

'When was the last time you had a drink?' I say at last.

'We had mojitos in the villa last night. Lotta's mum makes them really strong. Lotta's my friend.' Something shifts and flickers across her face, but it's gone before I can make sense of it.

'Not a *drink* drink,' I say. 'Just a drink.'

'I had a Frappuccino at the airport about an hour ago.'

I eye her tiny handbag. 'Do you have any water in there? Like in a teensy bottle or something?'

She shakes her head. I hand her mine. She necks the lot.

'Great,' I say, irritation now overlaying guilt. 'I'll just fill it up again at the next Perrier fountain.'

She makes an apologetic face. 'I'll buy you some more at the next town.'

I snatch the empty bottle back from her and stuff it into my rucksack. After flattening out the scrubby grass and moving a few stones out of the way, she sits next to me, adjusting her spaghetti legs this way and that. Cars whip past monotonously. I fix my eyes on the sheeny horizon, at the drifts of gulls like smoke on the sky, past the planes bumbling around the runway in front of us. Calm descends, briefly.

'You still haven't said why you jumped off the train.'

'None of your business.'

'Or why you were crying.'

I don't answer that one.

'Can you play that guitar?'

'No.'

'Why do you carry it around then?'

'Sentimental reasons.'

I get more comfortable against my tree. It's shady here, around six feet above the cars as they shoot by. Out of the corner of my eye, I see her fiddling with her phone, her fingers drifting across the black screen. It's either been switched off or the battery's died. As she doesn't strike me as a girl who can live without social media stoking her insecurities, I'm guessing it's the battery.

'I've been on holiday with that friend I was telling you about,' she says. 'Lotta. She's on the plane home now, with her mum and stepdad and Olivia.'

I still know nothing about this girl, apart from the fact that she's tall and rich. Somehow we've missed the bit where you ask each other's names.

'I was supposed to be on the plane too, only Mum forgot to give permission and the airport went funny about it. And

I was trying to get away from Dad and these two guys who were following me, only they might not have been following me at all. It's a blur, if I'm honest.'

The cars have virtually all dropped off. Something to do with the time of day perhaps, with everyone heading home for lunch and a kip. I envy them. These pink rocks are hot and fumy and we have no water left thanks to a tall rich girl with *Bourne Identity* delusions.

'They couldn't have been Dad's people, you see, because he said they were running late. And even if they *were* his people, I wouldn't have gone with them anyway because that would have meant spending the rest of the summer with my father which I do not want to do. My parents are going through a bad divorce right now because of him so he's not my favourite person.'

'Your dad's your dad,' I say.

'You don't know anything about it.'

Make that tall, rich *and* a pain in the arse. I squint across at her. 'So they were following you, or they weren't?'

'I don't know,' she says. 'I was playing it safe.'

'Jumping out of a train with someone you don't know equals safe?'

'You probably think I'm paranoid.'

'Yes,' I agree. 'The only people who follow you in the Algarve are club reps trying to get you into their bars.'

A car comes into view. It's big, black and comfy-looking, and it's even going in the right direction, heading for the wide and glittering shore ahead. Two guys are riding up front with the driver's arm leaning on the windowsill, dark shirtsleeve pushed up a bestially hairy arm, heavy gold watch gleaming in the heat. I feel an urge to show this girl that I'm not scared of hitching after all.

'Time to go,' I say, getting up.

She gives a funny gasp. And then the world tips upside down as I stumble backwards over my rucksack and do a kind of flip that gets you points in gymnastic competitions. I realise as I roll helplessly away from the road, backwards down the pink rocks and into a weed-choked ditch behind us that I just got grabbed round the neck and pulled back like a tab on a can of beer.

# PRECIOUS

My clothes are a mess and my feet are wet where the water from the ditch has gone through the leather. From the smell, I think something might have died in there. I cheer myself up with the thought that at least it wasn't us.

I don't care if he's even madder with me than he was before. It was definitely the guys from the airport. Terminator One in the passenger seat had mirrored sunglasses on, but his hawk eyes were burning through the lenses and he was holding himself tight, coiled up, the way Mum coiled herself sometimes when she watched for Dad's car through the window in London. Terminator Two looked the way a large cat does when it hunts. They're hunting for me. I did the right thing, running away. So that's one thing straight, for me at least.

'You're certifiable,' he keeps shouting as we limp along the shimmering, heat-hazed road. 'Who half-drowns people they've only just met in stinking ditches? Who does that?'

The sky has opened above us, vast and pitiless. Stretches of water coil on either side of the road like rough aqua puddles after a rainstorm. There's hardly any passing traffic, and the sea glints ahead of us like a long thin slice of hairdresser foil.

'I didn't ask for any of this,' he repeats at intervals.

I follow him grimly onwards. My feet chafe against wet, spongy leather. Blisters are gathering beneath my toes. I haven't applied any SPF for two hours and my make-up is running down my cheeks faster than maple syrup down a hot fudge sundae. I should be sitting right now in an air-conditioned plane seat with a latte and a magazine and a view of lovely soft fluffy clouds, and *he's* mad? Does he think I've chosen to ruin his day on purpose? I need to talk to my mother, I need pizza. I need not to feel alone, scared and sweaty. Hot, angry tears bloat my eyes. Someone just blew up my father's boat. Doesn't that give me the tiniest right to feel paranoid?

He speeds up. I speed up too, matching him stride for stride. The water expands around us, sort of the sea and sort of not. There's a long wooden walkway on the left of the road, so for a while we're not directly in danger of being struck by a passing truck. But it doesn't last long and then we're back on the tarmac. We meet a narrow bridge, peeling green paintwork hemming us in, and I pray to all the gods that the Terminator Twins have already been this way. This isn't the Algarve I know, with its toffee-coloured cliffs and changeable water. This feels more like a very hot Norfolk.

We cross a large car park. The sea – I realise now that we've been crossing a great swampy lagoon – is dead ahead. There is a café to our right, shimmering in the heat. The Coke sign outside the door makes me want to faint with gratitude.

He lets the door swing back in my face. By the time I've wrestled it open, he's grabbing a bottle of sparkling water from the fridge cabinet beside the till. He doesn't offer to buy me one. Nor does he say anything when I sit down opposite him by the open window with its sea view, clutching my own beautiful, wonderful, ice-cold bottle. Instead he swigs half his bottle, then tips out a palmful and smears it across his face. I hear it fizzing against his dirty, tanned face with its weird white chin. On the wall above the bar, a TV blares out the news. I try not to look at it.

'I'll pay for your water,' I say.

I take out my purse and rummage around for some of the coins he gave me back at the railway station and push them across the table. Why am I still trying?

After a moment, he takes about half the coins and returns the rest.

'You're still paying too much for stuff,' he says.

As I silently scoop back what's left, my eyes snag the TV screen. It's too late to avoid the picture of the *Amalia* in broken black pieces, scattered around the Vilamoura marina. Now I'm looking, I can't look away. Not even when they pull up that awful picture of Dad in the Spanish hotel room. The newsreader isn't holding back. Alleged criminal contacts. Questionable legality. I suddenly wonder if the Terminator Twins are police officers, out to pull me in for interrogation. If they are police, am I breaking the law by running away?

'I read about this guy,' the boy says. 'Classic crook. You only have to look at him to—'

'He's my father,' I say.

The boy's eyes sharpen like pencils and his eyebrows climb towards his shaggy caramel hairline.

'His boat blew up,' I add unnecessarily.

'I know his boat blew up.' He leans forward. 'I heard it. I saw it. I read about it and now I just watched it again. That guy is your father?'

'Interested now, are you?' I ask a little acidly.

'What's your name?'

'Precious Silva.'

He snorts. 'Christ. Whose idea was that?'

I press my water bottle to my hot forehead and wish I could just melt away into the dry air. This is now officially the worst day of my life. I ought to leave. I ought to call a cab, or my mum. I ought to face a few consequences and get my life back under control. Wait, *back* under control? Who am I kidding? I've never had control over ANYTHING. I'm a blobfish in all but biology.

'I'm having a really bad day, and you're not helping,' he says. 'Will you go away?'

It turns out that when subjected to intense pressure, even the most boring landscape has lava underneath. I unscrew my bottle lid and tip half a litre of freezing, sparkling water over his head. It cascades, glittering and hissing, all over his tangled hair, fizzing in his eyes, exploding down the neck of his filthy T-shirt. He leaps to his feet, knocking over his chair with an awful clatter and clawing at himself. Two guys drinking coffee at the bar look over, then return their gaze to the TV.

'I should have drowned you in that ditch,' I say. I can't believe I have actually done this thing, and can only put it down to extreme and unusual stress. 'You think you've had a bad day? You have *no* idea.'

I march out of the hut, past the flapping ice-cream and Coke sign, past the lifeguard station with its curved red canopy and its orange-and-yellow-clad lifeguards, past the brown raffia beach umbrellas and on to the hot sand, making my way blindly down to the shore. I am aflame with embarrassment, anger and the tiniest bit of pride.

I am Precious Silva, hear me squeak.

# HARRY

Dad was many things, I think as shame rushes across my skin along with the bubbles, but he charmed everyone he met, big or small. Everyone was the same, he used to say, because everyone was born naked, bloody and bawling. But then we each got ideas above our naked, scrawny, bawling selves and began to cherish our own extra-special importance and that's when all the trouble began.

*Even the Queen had a shitty nappy once, Harry boy.*

The other people in the café return to their business while I rub my face and hair with my hands and try not to wince at how the rest of the water has already tickled its way to my bum and is pooling nicely in my crotch. I look like I've pissed myself.

The water has cleared a small part in the smeared windscreen of my brain. A man's boat has blown up and his daughter is loose in the Algarve. She's rich enough and clueless enough and looks sufficiently like the guy for what she just told me to be true. Therefore, it's not beyond the realms of possibility that two dodgy dudes in a tinted ride are out looking for her. I'm officially in a bad movie, in the front row with extra-large popcorn.

I pack up, buy two more bottles of water and squelch out of the café. I can't see her, but it's a big beach. There are people around, sprawling on bright towels and under even brighter beach umbrellas, roasting away like forgotten Christmas turkeys. I lift the guitar above my head to give me some shade as I pick my way down to the water's edge.

She's standing alone on the huge and open shore, up to her ankles in sea water. A few fat grey and white plovers scuttle about near where she's left her bag, their feathers ruffled in the breeze.

'You've still got your shoes on.' It's a hell of an opener.

'They were ruined anyway. What do you want?'

It's my turn to shift from foot to foot. 'To say sorry. I'm not normally like this.'

'Like what? Like a rude bastard shit?'

I blink. 'I'm having a hard summer.'

'I'm sure it's really hard. Sun, sea, suitcase.'

I decide to leave that one. 'I believe you,' I say instead. 'About the following thing.'

She walks a bit further into the sea. The waves push hungrily at her. I feel nauseous as they reach her thighs, and the water stains the bottom of her romper thing to a dark forest green.

'You're not trying to drown yourself or anything, are

you?' I check. 'Because I'm not coming in there after you.'

'I'm just swimming,' she says, sinking into the cold glitter.

She flips, making my stomach lurch, and ducks below the surface. I set my rucksack and guitar down on the powdery sand, sit a safe distance from the sucking line of surf and watch the plovers. Every now and again, I look over my shoulder for hairy arms sporting gold wristwatches. I wish I hadn't got rid of that paper on the train. There is a gentle breeze whiffling along the shore, and sailing boats bob and flit on the horizon on blinding white wings. A couple of idiots are whipping along on jet skis and there is at least one beach ball floating too far from land. I train my eyes on the horizon and don't allow myself to blink any more than necessary.

Six weeks till uni.

She pops up again like a seal.

'Do you have a towel?'

I consider the rag in my rucksack. 'Not exactly,' I say.

'Do you have anything? A T-shirt?'

'You probably should have thought about this before you went in,' I point out, and permit myself to enjoy the look on her face.

'Can you at least turn round while I get out?'

'You're not naked.' I get more comfortable where I'm sitting. 'Just walk out the same way you walked in.'

She looks down at herself. I can only see her shoulders, but the thing is clinging to her like you wouldn't believe.

If it shrinks after this, she will probably be arrested for gross indecency.

Dad nudges my conscience. Reluctantly unclasping the top of my rucksack, I study its contents for gallantry potential. One manky rag-towel. Stinking trainers, creased shorts. Boxers I don't want to study too closely, toothbrush. Three T-shirts. I pull out my Jimi Hendrix T-shirt and a pair of shorts and offer them up.

'Close your eyes,' she says.

As I dip my head, she sloshes out of the water and snatches the T-shirt from my hands. I hear a bit of wriggling. The end result, when she lets me look, is almost respectable.

'It's Jimi Hendrix,' I tell her. 'Guitar legend.'

She tugs at Jimi's hem and mops the smudgy make-up under her eyes.

'I know who Jimi Hendrix is, you patronising git,' she says.

# PRECIOUS

My plane touched down about an hour ago, and Ilynka will start wondering where I am and call Mum to ask if she fetched me from the airport after all and a fresh kind of hell will open at my feet.

I have to turn my phone on.

It feels like putting my hand in a box of snakes every time I think about doing it, but it's one of those things that have to be endured. A bush tucker trial of responsibility. I can't let Mum think I've been kidnapped, raped and dumped in a ditch. The only ditches around here I got into on purpose. I have no plans to contact Dad. He can screw himself.

The lava inside me is kind of fun.

My finger hovers over the on button. This is the longest I've ever been offline. Whole continents could have shifted, wars started, relatives died, for all I know. The world feels hazy and loose, reduced to sand and sea and sky, and me and a dirty boy with an unplayed guitar. And if I vanished right now, the sand and the sea and the sky wouldn't notice, leaving the dirty boy and his guitar to shoulder all proof of my existence. I put more faith in the guitar.

His manners have improved, although every time his eyes flick at the Hendrix T-shirt, it's clear that I'm not good enough to be inside its sacred seams. The shorts are on a belt, luckily. As for the romper, it's shrunk to something a slightly butch Barbie might wear. When it's dry, it might even fit in my handbag. Still no shop to sort out my footwear. My ruined sandals are hanging round my neck by their super-long laces, leaving my feet bare and roughened by the blazing sand. I feel odd, and reckless.

I hit the on button and assume the brace position.

There is a blast of missed calls, texts, notifications, even a few likes of the villa swimming pool shot I took half a lifetime ago. It rings even as I'm holding it, but I block the call. Dad. All the calls and half the texts are from Dad.

'I thought your phone was dead,' says the boy.

'Not dead. Just off.' I text Mum as fast as I can.

**Didnt leave coz 2 young!?! Send permission!! Will try 2 catch next flight home!!!**

'I didn't think girls like you turned your phone off.'

'Girls like what, exactly?' I close the phone down before it rings again. 'Girls on the run?'

He doesn't say anything.

'Have you met many girls on the run?' I enquire.

'Have you finished making your point?'

I am now feeling not just powerful but interesting as well. I'm on the run. I'm running. I look out at the vast and shining water, and briefly feel bigger than I've felt in my entire life. The feeling dips as I wonder a little anxiously if I should have found an Internet place and sent an email instead of a text. What if the Terminator Twins can trace a phone?

I tear my eyes from the sea. 'Are we heading back to the road?'

He's already almost a hundred metres away, following the frilled waterline down the beach. It's no bad thing to head *away* from the road, given how the Terminator Twins are roaming the tarmac, so I follow him once again.

'You still there?' he grunts after about ten minutes.

'You still an arsehole?'

I'm starting to enjoy myself.

We walk down the endless, endless beach, past the last trickles of tourists, the valiant few who made it this far with umbrellas and sun cream. The sun is relentless overhead. Soon the only sound is our feet squeaking through the sand and the grumbling of the sea on our left.

'Do you think text messages can be traced?' I ask, what feels like about half an hour later.

He gives a start, like he's forgotten I was there. 'Probably,' he says.

We trudge a bit further. There's no one here at all now. All I can see is sand, and those hard ridges you get when the tide goes out. I pull some wipes from my bag and attempt to repair my face as we move along. I've only got a bit of concealer, three mascara wands, some blusher, two eyeliners, a tube of foundation and a couple of brushes, so there's not a lot I can do, but it's better than nothing.

'Where are we going?' I say eventually.

'I don't know.'

I offer to carry the guitar for a bit. It provides me with a bit of shade as we walk with precisely nowhere dead ahead of us. I let him walk ahead, mainly so I don't have to talk to him. He's not a natural at conversation. His bum is nearly as bony as mine. His clothes are a wreck, his shoes almost worn through. His skin is burned and his hair is like the dried seaweed you get in Chinese restaurants beside your prawn toast. It would work in a man bun, maybe. All he'd have to do would be to wind it up and it would stay there like a very obedient, very dirty dog. If you shaved it off, his head would be long and thin like a smoked almond. He walks like someone carrying a very heavy load. In a funny way, he reminds me a bit of—

'Nathan Payne,' I say suddenly.

Nathan Payne, panthering around his eighteenth birthday party, all legs and dreadlocks and making out with Lotta. It was *him* I saw at the marina table. The dreadlocks were gone, but it was definitely him. Cumberbatch cheekbones, sea-green eyes.

'Nathan bloody *Payne*,' I repeat in wonder.

'Who the hell is Nathan Payne?'

97

Nathan Payne. God! Nathan Payne is on my patch.

'But the Paynes go to Spain!' I say.

'Is this some kind of riddle?'

'Nathan Payne!'

'I don't know why I bother asking questions,' he mutters. 'The answers only confuse me further.'

'Nathan Payne has your hair.' I recalibrate. '*Had* your hair. He's cut it. That's what confused me, you see?'

'Honest answer?'

Lotta will be pleased with Nathan's new look. The whole female population will be pleased with Nathan Payne's new look. Nathan Payne's look transcends five hundred likes.

'Nathan Payne lives on the edge,' I tell him. 'Of Primrose Hill. He's an incredible artist and he takes drugs he shouldn't. I think my father knows his dad through business or something.'

'Bully for Nathan Payne.'

It's probably time to change the subject. I twist my toes into the glittering powder under my sand-scoured feet.

'Are you ever going to tell me your name?' I ask.

He grunts.

'*Barry?*' I say, startled. And there was me, thinking *I* had it bad.

'HARRY,' he repeats more loudly. 'Temple.'

'Precious Silva.' *Girl on the run*, I think, as I set my shoulders a little straighter. 'But you know that already.'

# NATHAN

Not drugs then.

I have been feeling sick ever since the harbour. A sort of boiling, burning sensation in my guts which I'd like to put down to last night's clams but can't. Dad keeps telling me to toughen up but it's harder than it looks.

He selects a club from the bag and takes a couple of swings with it. 'You're acting like we boiled a litter of kittens alive.'

I shake my head.

'No one ever got rich playing it straight, Nathan. Ricky Silva didn't, that's for sure. And, on the subject of playing it straight, watch and learn.'

He tees up and clouts the ball. In a flash of dimpled white, it soars into the air, curves to one side and vanishes into a waving patch of rough ground. Dad mutters, thrusting the club back into the bag. I know better than to point out the irony as I choose my own club and tee up. I don't really like golf, too full of tossers in bad trousers. But when the sky is blue and the grass is green and your father screws up, it's not all bad.

My own drive is straight as an arrow. As I slot my club away, Dad chucks his bag into the buggy and drives off, forcing me to chase him down the fairway with my own bag bumping against my back. By the time I catch up, he's already cueing up his next shot.

'Isn't that my ball?' I say, gasping a little in the heat.

Dad takes a swipe, sending the ball soaring clean towards the green. 'Like I say, no one wins by playing straight.' He indicates the rough. 'You'll find yours in there.'

I hack my way through the rough, black thoughts swarming. By the time I make it to the green, Dad has marked his card and is sliding his phone into the back pocket of his red golfing trousers.

'Well, now,' he says, sitting in the shade of the buggy as I line up my shot. 'It turns out that Ricky Silva's daughter has gone missing.'

My putt shoots wide of the hole. 'Who, Precious?'

'There's only one daughter, the last time I checked. She was on holiday with a friend near Vilamoura, missed her flight and no one's seen her since.' Dad pulls a driver from the bag and weighs it in his hand. 'She's either got a local boyfriend, or someone's taken her.'

'Why would someone take her?' I say incredulously. 'No one in London ever wanted her.'

Dad strokes the shining edge of the driver and holds out

the club so that the fat end is under my chin. 'Use your tiny little brain,' he suggests.

I flush. 'Because of Ricky?'

Dad tilts the club, pushing my chin a little higher. 'The whole world knows Ricky's in trouble since his boat blew up. Where there's blood, there's sharks.' He considers me. 'Am I right in thinking you know her?'

'We go to the same parties, if that's what you mean,' I tell the sky.

'Was she at your party?'

I nod the best I can in the circumstances.

'The party you are doing your very best to make up for?'

I nod again.

He lowers the club. 'You're going to find her and keep her safe until this land deal goes through. A local boyfriend shouldn't be a problem. You're a handsome boy, you can handle that. Take the car. Girls like good cars.'

I feel a rush of wonder. My father's going to let me drive his car? He hardly lets me *touch* his car.

'Treat it well,' Dad adds mildly.

'Local boyfriend, no worries,' I say, trying not to snatch the keys from Dad's long fingers. 'But what if it's sharks?'

Dad feints at me with the club. I take an instinctive step back.

'I'd leave the sharks well alone,' he says. 'If I were you.'

'But—'

'You'll work it out, Nathan,' he says. 'You're my son.'

101

# HARRY

She keeps looking at me like I have all the answers and I want to tell her not to expect miracles. Except there's something nice about having a person staring at me like I'm worth staring at. And it's an improvement on water bottles and scorn. Talking of water, we've drunk two one-litre bottles since arriving in Quarteira. I can't speak for her, but walking on sand for three hours in the afternoon sun dried me out like a piece of biltong.

'Should I get them?' she asks for the second time.

'You can't spend that kind of money on a pair of shoes,' I say.

'Believe me, Barry,' she says, 'I can.'

She thinks the whole Barry thing is hilarious. To look at her now, turning her feet this way and that in the long mirror, you'd think our Sahara-like three-hour beach walk was a hallucination. The boutique assistant is watching me very carefully, like I might try to nick the gold trainers in the window.

'People on the run don't buy expensive shoes,' I say, keeping my voice low. 'They save their money for emergencies. And by emergencies, I mean plane tickets and firearms.'

'This is an emergency,' she insists. 'Have you seen my blisters?'

What in God's name am I doing here? Has this whole day been the result of too much cheese?

A flicking electric advert hooks at the corner of my eye.

'Precious,' I say.

Halfway through entering her PIN, Precious turns her head. We both gaze at the image on the moving billboard outside the shop. It's a recent photo. She's even wearing the romper thing, her hair pouring over her shoulders like thick black treacle. Taken in the past few days, I'm guessing. Portuguese words scroll along underneath her. *Você viu esta menina?* And then in English: *Have you seen this girl?*

Precious snatches her card out of the machine, slams down a fistful of money, grabs the shoes. We're out of the door before the assistant has finished asking if we want a bag.

'Shit,' Precious hisses, winding her thick hair tightly around her fist and holding that fist to her shoulder like the Black Power sign.

'Bad guys don't run billboards,' I say, hardly able to believe I'm even speaking these words out loud.

'So?'

'So, logically, the billboard thing must be a good guy,' I say. 'Like your dad. Which means you can stop running. Call the number, or maybe go into a police station.'

She bends her knees in a bid to blend in with the more normal-sized women walking around. She looks like she's about to take a dump on the pavement. 'In which part of your universe is my dad not a bad guy?'

'He's your dad,' I say, unable to think of any other response.

'He cheated on my mother and ran out on us. He just wants me where he can see me. I'm not spending any part of this summer with him.'

Is she enjoying this? 'Your mother then,' I say.

'Billboards aren't her style. She's all about Twitter campaigns and social media. This is definitely my father.' She sticks out her chin. 'I'm not calling the number and I'm not turning myself in. Do you have a hat?'

Am I going to get done for kidnap, or collusion? Depends who gets me first, I suppose. All anyone has to do now is look our way, recognise Precious, call the number and that will be that. I think about calling the number myself.

I pull her into a side street beside the boutique.

'You need more than a bloody hat.'

Somehow this has become my problem as well as hers.

'What are we going to do?' she asks.

The gold chains on the shoes she's holding clink together like tiny bells of foreboding. I pull my rucksack open and drag out a knackered baseball cap, complete with a band of head sweat.

'Put this on,' I say. 'It's that or cut your hair off.'

'I shouldn't have bought the shoes,' she mutters as she reluctantly grabs the cap and stuffs her hair under it. 'When I don't turn myself in, Dad will stop my credit card and then I'll only have a few hundred euros to live on until I can contact Mum and catch the next flight home.'

'Only a few hundred?' I say sympathetically. I peer out of the side street and study the billboard. 'OK. Six ads are running, at around ten seconds each. That gives you fifty seconds between ads. If you time this right . . .'

I realise she's not beside me. She is, in fact, back in the boutique, putting the shoes on the counter and asking the assistant for her money back. I can see her plain as day through the plate-glass window. The assistant looks massively pissed off.

The billboard broadcasts Precious Silva to the street again. It's three extremely long minutes before she returns. Three more rounds of pixelated long black hair, romper and agonising hellfire.

'I got a refund,' she says. 'And these,' she adds, pausing to lean against a whitewashed wall and slip on a pair of blue deck shoes with embroidered flowers on them. 'They're better than those shoes in this situation, and they were only sixty euros, can you believe it? That billboard picture is horrific. I can't believe the whole of Quarteira has seen it. Probably the whole of the Algarve.'

'You're crazy,' I say as she sets off up the side street.

'You told me that when I pushed you in the ditch.'

We move towards a more residential area, with apartments and balconies covered in flowers that nod their fat pink heads at us. I'd almost go as far as to say this place had a holiday vibe. The sun is getting lower, preparing for a slow and beautiful evening. The shadows in this street don't give much sense of that, though: just cobbles under our feet and cars parked haphazardly along the pavement.

'Oh, and I got these too,' she adds, rummaging in her bag. She presses a pair of scissors into my hand. 'They were just sitting by the till.'

Why has she given me scissors?

'You said it was either the cap or the hair,' she says. 'Well, I can't keep wearing the cap. It stinks. So that leaves option two.'

I wanted distraction. I have got distraction.

Be careful what you wish for.

# PRECIOUS

'It's not open-heart surgery,' I prompt as he stares at the scissors. 'It's a haircut.'

Every single girl in my school has long hair. Boys prefer it, apparently: a crap excuse in a so-called feminist age. That said, it's never worked for me. Being freakishly tall and flat-chested weights the scales, no matter how long or lustrous the locks. Having short hair might end up making me even *more* unattractive to the likes of Nathan Payne, but what if you're starting from zero anyway? I think hopefully of Audrey Hepburn, Carey Mulligan, that sixties model Mum loves with the spider eyelashes: Sticky. This could work out.

'It'll be like casting off into the great and glorious unknown,' I say, with mounting excitement. Why have I never felt this molten power inside me before? This is my Samson and Delilah moment, only the short hair will make me stronger. 'Severing the ropes that tie me to the shore of my previous life.'

If anything he looks a bit sicker.

'The person in that awful billboard picture has long hair,' I say, as persuasively as I can. 'If you give me short hair, you can have your cap back. And, frankly, not before time. I think there's something living in it.'

He braces himself, opening and closing the blades a couple of times. The yellow plastic handles are a bit weeny for his knobbly fingers.

'Makes sense,' he says finally. 'As far as anything today makes sense.'

At the exact moment I pull the cap off and Harry raises the blades, two men appear at the bottom of the road. Big. Dark shirts. The sun flashes on a pair of mirrored sunglasses and my heart stops.

Terminator One breaks into a sprint, straight up the street towards us. I lock eyes with Harry for a total of half a second. Enough time to gather that they are very, *very* blue. Then we are both on our feet, arms pumping, hair everywhere. The scissors glint in Harry's clenched fist and I think: at least we have a weapon, and Terminator Two has a belly.

'Why are *you* running?' I shout, momentarily struck by the comradeship Harry is showing.

He either doesn't hear or chooses to ignore me. I try to run faster, to keep up with him, weaving along the uneven road with its pocked tarmac and occasional cat. It feels like the least I can do.

'Go right!' I yell as we approach a nondescript junction.

But Harry belts left, back towards the seafront. I almost dislocate my ankle taking the turn after him. This street is like the one we just took, but heading in the other direction. I hope the Terminator Twins think we've gone further inland, not back towards the shore.

We run and we run. I daren't look back. We are on a cobbled road now, the cobbles laid in straight lines unnervingly like a racetrack, passing a pedestrianised street on the right with postcard racks and café tables and tourists *passear*ing up and down, and my hair is flying behind me like a big black flag. Left now, past a supermarket and a copy shop, hoardings for cars and supermarkets, a bright yellow digger. We career through a vast open space next, with scrub and more diggers standing between us and the beach, and I think to myself: *wow, this town needs a makeover*. I guess that's what the diggers are doing.

I risk a glance over my shoulder and immediately wish I hadn't. Terminator Two's belly is bouncing from side to side like a wrecking ball, his watch flaring every time it catches the sun. Terminator One is cruising along in his fat mate's slipstream like he's got all the time in the world, his eyes inscrutable behind their mirrors. I'm pleased to see the large sweat patches under their dark blue arms.

I don't think they are police officers.

Harry pelts on towards the beach, running hard on his special brand of angry diesel. If we get out of this, I will find out more about him. The only thing I have right now is his name, which feels kind of – weak.

'Stop,' I beg, although stopping is the worst thing we could do.

Sand now, slewing and twisting treacherously under our feet like those dreams I had when Mum and Dad were at their worst. Shifting, changing. Still hot. Some part of my brain wonders if I've ever been to this beach before. We've done so much of this coastline down the years that the answer is probably yes. It doesn't seem familiar, but it probably looks different from the deck of a yacht. My sandals are bouncing in my face so I hurl them from my neck before they give me a black eye. Perhaps they'll turn into a useful obstacle like in that fairy tale.

'Do you know the story about a witch and the comb that turns into a forest?' I pant as Harry hurdles a line of beach towels and avoids a thatched beach umbrella.

'What are you on about now?'

'Everyone needs something to talk about during dark moments,' I gasp.

He doesn't have his guitar any more. Or his rucksack. I wonder where they went as a particularly uneven bit of sand nearly tips me sideways. I blink away the stinging sweat and clutch at my ribs. This is too real and I want it to stop. I'll call the number on the billboards and tell Dad that he's won and I'll spend as much of this summer with him and his girlfriends as he wants. I just want to breathe normally. And yet . . .

I don't reach for my phone.

We slalom through the beach crowds slowly packing up their stuff. We explode sandcastles, we machine-gun grit over oiled bodies, we shatter games of volleyball. My blisters scream in my new shoes. My make-up – don't let's even talk about my make-up. The Terminator Twins are still there, but we have pulled away so they are small running bastards rather than big ones up close and personal. I'm going to puke. I've never run this far, this fast, for this long.

And now, suddenly, there's nowhere else left to run to. There's just sea to our left, huge and shiny and wet, and a long stone jetty ahead with a familiar green-and-white lighthouse on the end. A fishing boat buzzes past, its painted eye staring dead ahead. We have reached a little walled-in river mouth which separates this beach from the next one along. I realise with a jolt that we're back in Vilamoura, beside the beachside club from two nights ago.

I bend down with my hands on my knees and gasp for breath and peer between my thighs for the Terminator Twins. I can't see them but I know they're there. Where else would they be?

Harry has thrown himself down on the sand. I think for a very weird moment that he's praying. Then I realise that he's digging.

'This is no time for sandcastles,' I say.

He ignores me. I stare at him through the waterfall of sweat blinding my eyes. Is he genuinely trying to dig us out of this? Crowds sway and part around us like seaweed in a current. Gulls wheel overhead, crying with glee as any advantage we might have had starts leaking away.

'Why don't we swim?' I suggest. I crane my head to peer over the stone jetty, point across the little estuary. 'It's not far to the other side.'

He digs harder.

'There's only one deep bit, from what I can see.'

'Stop talking and dig.'

'Harry—'

'We're not swimming,' he pants. 'We're digging. We'll cover ourselves. It'll be fine.'

I glance back. Catch a flash of sunlight on a fast approaching wristwatch. I stamp my foot in frustration, and there's a little puff of sand. We're losing time.

'We have to swim,' I shout.

'NO.'

'But why n—'

'I CAN'T SWIM, OK?' he roars. 'I CAN'T BLOODY SWIM.'

# HARRY

It's all about breathing through the mouth. In, out. Simple and yet surprisingly difficult to do. I'm shivering violently, and not because the water is cold – which it is – but because this . . . this . . .

In, out.

Something hard and bony wraps itself around my fingers and squeezes. I want to scream like a kid at a Harry Styles gig but I can't because then I will drown. My eyes burn with salt. I can't open them for more than half a second at a time but I need to see where I'm going. Precious's face looms at me, blue and dead, her hair an inky cloud around her. Her eyes are even bigger under the water. Her fingers squeeze tighter. I close my eyes again and let her pull me, and I move a few more steps, and I somehow keep breathing.

In, out.

One violent shiver too many and my mouth slips from the scissored gash in the bottom of my water bottle and I get a mouthful of seawater and dead things. It's amazing how you can gag and stay underwater at the same time when you have to. I try not to think about how the only thing between me and the end of everything is the top of a branded plastic cylinder.

In, out.

In, out.


*I eye my towel, draped over one of the blue flip-up seats that line the side of the pool, and shrug. The swimming teacher's boobs bounce about under her standard-issue swimsuit. Her hair curls damply on her shoulders, like a spaniel's ears.*

*'He did brilliantly!' she says. 'He kept his feet off the bottom the whole time!'*

*I burn beneath Dad's gaze.*

*'I learned to swim when my dad threw me in a river,' he tells my teacher. His hand is warm on my cold-pimpled shoulder. 'I was five years old. Sink or swim. Didn't work with you, though, did it, Harry boy?'*

*I let my eyes rest on the long, blue pool.*

*'Make it a length next week, eh? Tell you what, we'll come down here on Sunday morning, get in a bit of practice.'*

*My cold fingers are sluggish as I battle with the buttons on my shirt.*

*'We'll get you there,' Dad promises.*


Precious is still pulling me along, step by tiny step. I burn with humiliation as I feel how my hand is shaking in hers. I grip my water-bottle snorkel more tightly, pressing my lips hard against the ridged plastic. It's as unresponsive as Sasha the last time I kissed her.

*I choke, reaching for the surface like the drowning rat that I am.*

*'Swim,' Dad encourages, a colossus on the tiled edge. 'Pull at the water. Harder. Use your feet!'*

*I gasp and reach for the side. Try to stop myself because Dad's shadow is lying right over the place where I want to give up. I know that the shame will scald me but it's no good. I watch my hands reach for safety and I want to snip them off at the wrists.*

*'Harry boy,' says Dad. 'It's not even seven feet deep.'*

I open my eyes again, just a fraction. I can just see the sand through the sting. It's cool, hard and ridged, like the fingers that won't let go of me. The ridges feel like snakes beneath my outstretched toes. I can't look to my left, out into the darkness where the sand sinks away into whirlpools and caverns and quicksand, and trenches two miles deep where the pressure will crush your bones to powder. In my near-catatonic state I look at Precious instead, with her long, distorted, blue legs. Inhale another slug of plastic salt-tinged air.

In, out.

*'He'll do it when he's ready, love,' says Mum. 'Not everyone is like you.'*

*I study the tips of my fingers. They are still crumpled from the chlorine.*

*Dad claps a couple of chapattis on his tikka masala. 'Don't worry, Harry boy,' he tells me as he tears into a great man-sized mouthful. 'We'll get there if it kills us, eh?'*

My whole foot is suddenly, wonderfully, flush with the sand. I'm curving my back to keep myself below the surface. Hands and knees now. I crawl up the rocks, stacked neatly together to form the harbour wall, and flop over the top, feeling the sand on my belly, gasping like a prehistoric fish.

A long, empty beach lies before us, rumpled as an unmade bed, glowing red and orange in the low sun. The bottle-snorkel rolls out of my numb fingers. My mouth is touching air and sand, not plastic. The luxury is unspeakable.

I roll weakly on to my side. Sand coats me all over like breadcrumbs on a fish finger. I smile stupidly at Precious because I'm alive and nothing else matters.

'A bit more effective than bloody digging,' she says.

# NATHAN

'Good car, *senhor*.'

I rouse myself from staring at the satnav. A couple of kids are loitering on the pavement beside the Boxster in low-slung shorts and snapback caps. They're around ten, snot on their faces and black stuff ground into the seams on their palms.

'Don't touch the paintwork,' I say.

The kids grin and circle the car. When one of them gets too close, reaching out a skinny arm to stroke the bonnet, I hit the horn. That makes the little shits jump.

The places all run into each other along this part of the coast: Quarteira, Vilamoura, Olhos something. It's all cartoon blocks, and bad roads pimpled with potholes, and crazy drivers swinging too close to me. How am I supposed to know where Precious is hiding? I'm not even sure I can remember what she looks like.

I find her and Lotta Cooper on my Insta feed, doing the duck-face thing in a school corridor. The angle works for

Lotta. Most things work for Lotta. For Precious Metal, not so much.

Dad was frowning in the rear-view mirror when I left him at the club, like he regretted handing over the keys. The responsibility presses down on me like a block of stone.

'Is fast car, *senhor*?' says one of the kids. 'How fast?'

The other one is trying to sneak round the back, out of sight. I can't see his dirty fingers, but I know they are reaching for a wheel arch.

*My tips of my toes are barely touching the smooth black driveway as Dad holds me by the scruff of my jumper and shakes me like a rat. I try to fix my eyes on something. I feel less sick that way.*

*'I told you NOT to touch with suncream on your hands. Are you stupid? Are you deaf?'*

*With the shaking, it's hard to focus on anything at all. The handprint is there, lurking on my conscience, but the shape of it is nothing but a blur: sometimes with five fingers, sometimes not.*

*'How many times?'*

*I almost welcome the slap to the side of my head because it means the shaking stops. When he drops me, I fall over because my brain is still rolling around inside my skull and I can't find my balance. The new-laid driveway looks smooth, but there are jagged parts that claw through the skin on my knee. Ruby-red drops of blood bloom as I watch.*

'Piss OFF,' I yell, half rising in the driving seat.

The kids leap backwards, under the awning of a nearby street café. It's like trying to keep wasps away from a can of Coke. I key the next identifiable town into the satnav and pull away angrily, before they try again.

# PRECIOUS

I was hoping for a sunset over the sea, but it's just set behind some cliffs off to our right. The air is warm and still. I try not to worry at the heavy sensation of the scissors sliding across my scalp, or the soft flopping sound of my hair dropping around me like black ash.

The Terminator Twins are still out there. I wonder how long it will take them to realise that we didn't double back. Now they know I'm with someone, they will be hunting him too. I feel awkward about this, but no longer so scared.

Harry doesn't seem worried. In fact, he's almost cheerful. He hasn't stopped talking since we crawled out of the water an hour ago and walked along to this sandy stretch with its cliffs and silence. It's taking a bit of getting used to. I like it, though. It saves me from thinking too hard about what on earth I'm doing, and what the hell is going to happen next.

'. . . honestly thought I was going to die about halfway across. That was good thinking, the bottles. I'd never have made it across without mine. I still can't believe we did that. It was like James Bond or something. My dad—'

He closes down suddenly, like a crocus on a cloudy day.

'Do you have a problem with your dad?' I ask, twisting round to look at him.

There is a long silence.

'Depends on whether him being dead is a problem,' he says finally.

Oh my God. That explains the sad thing. And the grumpy thing. And most of Harry Temple in one go, now I think about it.

'I'm sorry,' I say, feeling a bit choked. 'When?'

'Five years ago.' Harry lifts a heavy hank of hair off my shoulders and saws at it. 'Don't move, I'll cut it wrong. Well, more wrong than I've cut it already.'

Five years seems a long time for him to be this raw. But what do I know about grief? The only thing that's died in my life is my parents' marriage.

'I really am sorry,' I repeat.

'I'm over it.'

He's clearly not over it at all, but I don't press him. So far, he hasn't reacted kindly to direct questions. Anyway, I'm enjoying chatty Harry and I'm not so keen on getting gloomy Harry back. As he snips, I think about my dad and the shattered *Amalia*. How would I be feeling right now if he *had* been on board when it blew up?

I risk a question after all.

'Did you like him?'

His hands tighten on my hair. 'He was my father. Of course I bloody liked him.'

I'm clearly not destined for a life in the diplomatic service.

'You don't have to like your father,' I offer up. 'I don't like mine. I used to like him, though. A lot. It makes the not-liking thing harder, somehow.'

'At least you've still got him.'

I feel bad and let him cut for a bit in silence. We listen to the sighing of the sea.

'I can't believe you didn't lose the scissors on the way across,' I say eventually. 'How come you never learned to swim?'

'My dad chucked me into a river when I was five. I sank. I never liked the water after that.'

I remember the feel of his shaking hand in mine on our underwater walk. He snips harder. I can't think of any more awkward questions to further kill the mood, so I shut up.

After what feels like an hour of tension, he's done. I put my hand up, and feel the unfamiliar shape of my skull and the ragged fringe of hair that remains. It's strange. Promising, perhaps.

Unfortunately it's hard to miss his expression as I face him.

'Not Carey Mulligan then?' There's nowhere to go from zero, I remind myself.

His own hair is still drying after our underwater walk, springing away from his head. 'It's a bit more shit from the front than the back,' he admits, 'but I can confirm that you look like a different person. Which was the point of the exercise.'

I ought to gather up all the hair and send it to a cancer charity for wigs like a girl at school once did for her Duke of Edinburgh award. Mum's always going on about social responsibility with her committees and charity auctions. Only I don't know the address of any cancer charities and I'm nowhere near a post office. I'm not sure they'd want my hair anyway, stiff as it is with salt and sand. I scrape it all together into my arms and head down to the water.

'What are you doing?' Harry asks.

'Tidying up.'

I feel like I'm enacting some kind of ritual. It's like I said to Harry earlier, about severing ties with what's gone before. Every strand could represent something I don't like about myself, something I'm getting rid of. It's basically what Lotta's mum's therapist makes her do with bits of paper and a candle, only with hair. Burn the past and start again.

The sea is beautiful in the darkness, with its badger-stripe of moonlight glinting and glowing and never staying still. The lights of Vilamoura are off to our left, surprisingly far away already, and the deep red cliffs at our back are high. I start wading in, holding my armful of hair close to my chest and feeling the strands tickling my face while the evening breeze cools the back of my neck.

'Don't go too deep,' says Harry behind me.

It's strange not feeling my hair on my shoulders. Like I'm not me any more. I'm fine with that, to be honest.

'It's so lovely,' I say as I wade in further. 'They say that about danger, don't they? It brings out the colour in things.'

'I'm happy in black and white, thanks.'

'You don't like the sea much, do you?'

'I explained my feelings about water.'

'But this is the sea,' I say. 'How can you not be moved by the sea?'

'Call me a freak of nature.'

'You're a freak of nature,' I oblige.

The water is around my waist now. I've never felt more alive, or in the moment. It's just me and the moon and the sea all around. And Harry pacing the beach behind me.

'Do you know how quickly a riptide can take you?'

The water tickles and sighs around my shoulder blades.

'You can't see what you're treading on. Doesn't that freak you out?'

It doesn't. Not even close. I feel more grounded here, up to my neck in the sea, than I do back home. Maybe it's the stories. Dick Whittington never meant as much to me as the Barcelos rooster or Bartolomeu Dias sailing the Indian Ocean.

'Dad's family came from this coast,' I explain, trying to make him understand. 'They worked around the tides, and the moons, and the currents, and everything we're looking at. All those generations with all that knowledge stretching back forever. The sea is inside me.'

'It's inside me too,' says Harry. 'I swallowed half of it today.'

A thousand generations gather around me in the moonlit water, in a vast flotilla painted yellow and red and blue like the boat that passed us on the estuary earlier. All smiling at me, understanding me. I feel dizzy with belonging as I throw my hair into the waves.

# HARRY

'So,' I say, 'just to be clear, you threw your money in the sea?'

'I didn't *mean* to throw it in the sea!'

'And that makes it OK?'

'Maybe I didn't lose it when I threw the hair in the sea,' she says unhappily. 'Maybe I dropped it when we crossed the estuary or were running down the beach or something.'

'And it's now dark and we have no money,' I say. My voice is rising. 'I've lost my rucksack. I've lost my guitar. I've almost drowned. We have no money, no food, no shelter, and I still have no idea why any of this has happened. This is over, Precious. Call your dad. Make him come and bail us out.'

She shakes her head. We both stare into the huge black night with the waves rumbling away like a huge sodding tiger just waiting to eat us.

'What is so bad about your father that you can't ask for his help even now?' I demand. 'Do you hate him that much? *Call your dad.*'

'I can't.'

'Precious, even I would call my dad on this one, and he's dead.'

'My phone isn't waterproof,' she says.

I squint at her blank, fogged-up screen in the moonlight. Several heavy stones settle in my stomach as I realise that mine will have the same problem.

*Get it together, Harry boy. The world doesn't need panickers. It needs managers.*

'We are going to walk up this beach right now,' I say, 'and we are going to go to the first place we see with a light on, and we are going to ask very politely if we can use their phone.'

'I don't know my dad's number.'

'Call your mum then.'

'I don't know her number either.'

I'm really trying to be patient. 'How about your home number?'

'My phone has everything on it,' Precious says. 'You'll have to call someone instead.'

I'm about to say something sarcastic when it occurs to me that Mum took out our landline last year and I have no idea what her mobile number is. I don't really do friends, or friends' numbers. The only digits I can dredge up are for my local Indian takeaway and I don't think they'll be able to help.

'I don't know any numbers either,' I admit reluctantly.

Precious is shivering. Half of me considers this fair. The rest starts worrying about hypothermia.

'We need to light a fire,' I say.

'What with?'

I try to sound like I know what I'm doing. 'There's dry wood washed up all along this beach. Dry seaweed too. Lots of flammable material.'

'Any dry matches?' she says. Dryly.

My father is standing up to his ankles in the midnight waves and shaking his head at me. He could probably fart and click his fingers and a fire would leap from his arse, I think hopelessly, all bright and life-giving and perfect. Nothing went wrong for Dad, ever. Except when his boat sank, obviously.

Two hours ago we had money and phones and belongings. Everything was fine apart from the two goons chasing us. Peachy, even. Why do we only know what we've got when it's gone?

'We'll have to walk then,' I say finally. 'Find help.'

We both gaze down the long, empty beach. The cliffs are so dark that it's impossible to tell whether there are any paths to the top. Precious's teeth clack lightly together in the gloom.

'This is real now, isn't it?' she says.

'It's always been real, rich girl,' I snap. 'You've just never done real before.'

She takes a short, gasping breath. 'Everyone's life is real. Being rich doesn't make me fake.'

'You solve a problem by flashing around a fifty-euro note,' I say, hot with misery.

128

She pulls herself back and up, like a cobra flaring its hood and aiming for a rat it's just seen in the undergrowth. 'And you're so poor and real, are you? Tossing around Europe for the summer, off to uni in September, isn't your life shit?'

*I'm not tossing around Europe for the summer*, I think, enraged. *I'm . . . what am I doing? Exactly? I'm . . .*

'When my dad was eighteen, he was sifting sand on the beach for all the tiny fish. The ones that slid through the fishing nets, the ones no one else wanted because they wouldn't feed a bloody flea!'

'And I'm sure he took them home to feed his aged parents and twelve hungry siblings in their charming, weather-beaten beach shack before heading out again to make a real wage flogging pills in nightclubs,' I fire back, doing my best to recover. 'You say you don't like him, but right now you're making him out as some kind of hero. What's that about?'

Either the moonlight is turning her skin blue or the hypothermia is setting in for real. The cobra hood is still there. 'And you won't say you hate yours even though it's obvious that you couldn't stand him.'

How have we got this deep, this quickly? 'We're not talking about our fathers,' I say, trying to wrest back some kind of control. 'We're talking about you and your bountiful credit-card existence.'

'Fine, let's talk about me.' Her voice has gone quiet, though it's hard to tell whether that's from cold or rage.

'Let's talk about being stuck in the middle of a shitty divorce. Let's discuss at length the fact that I have no friends, no idea what to do with my future – or my present, in all honesty – no imagination and really not much of anything at all apart from two creeps chasing me and an idiot with a father fixation who can't swim. Believe me, I'm fully aware of my deficiencies. My reality may be pathetic, but it's NOT fake.'

Wow. That's . . . direct.

'You think your life's real?' I try, going after her as she starts walking away. 'You want to try losing your dad when you're fourteen. You want to try being a disappointment to a guy even after he's dead.'

'You can't disappoint someone who's dead, *Barry*.' She's still walking, sliding on grimly through the pale, moonlit sand.

'Where are you going?'

'Away from you!'

So I'm tossing around Europe. I'm avoiding big questions about my feelings towards the most important person in my life who is no longer in my life. Big deal. More of an issue is how I'm not enjoying it much.

I stub my toe on something in the sand and swear. The offender is a small plastic canister with a metal top and sharp edges. Hopping around on one foot and dusting off the powdery grit, I study it for a moment, squinting in the moonlight, half in hope and half in disbelief. I press the black plastic lever – and see a spark.

'Stop!' I shout a bit louder. 'Will you bloody *stop*?'

Her voice bounces towards me over the dark sand. 'Why should I?'

I hold the lighter aloft like an Olympic torch bearer.

'Because I just made fire!'

# PRECIOUS

With the success of his fire, Harry is cheerful again. Lucky him.

'All we need is something to barbecue now,' he says as the flames jump and crackle in Gothic shades of blue and purple. Driftwood smoke stinks.

'How about your mouth?' I say sulkily.

He prods the little mound of glowing twigs and ash. 'Are you warmer?'

I give him the look of death. If that's an apology, it needs work.

'Your hair looks better by firelight,' he offers next.

'Better than what, exactly?'

'Just . . . better,' he says.

I'm so hungry. I'd barbecue one of my shoes if I thought it was worthwhile. Shortly after barbecuing Harry Temple's head.

He clears his throat. 'I'm sorry about having a go at you like that. You see, my dad . . .'

It's like he hits a wall every time he mentions his father. It's interesting to watch.

'I get it,' I say, relenting a bit. 'You were scared. I was scared too.'

Harry makes a face. 'You probably wish you'd jumped out of that train with someone else.'

I cast my mind back to this morning's passengers. 'Like the nun?'

'There was a nun?'

'Or the snoggers across the aisle?' I suggest. 'They could have coated the Terminator Twins in saliva.'

'Superpower saliva,' says Harry after a moment.

'I'm sorry too,' I say, a little nervously. 'About the father fixation thing.'

'I can't get him out of my head.' Harry's eyes are haunted in the purple flamelight. He rubs his forehead, smearing bonfire ash above his eyebrows. 'I feel him all the time now I'm by the sea. God, I bloody *hate* the sea.'

'I worked that out,' I say.

'I owe him,' Harry says. 'I have to stay by the sea so he isn't alone. I avoided the sea for years after the accident. I think I knew he'd give me a hard time if I ever did show up, and I was right. Now I'm finally here, he's all, *Don't go, don't leave*. And so I don't. I literally can't. Does that make any kind of sense?'

'Maybe,' I say, considering.

'What was your dad like when you were younger?' he asks after we've been staring at the flames for a while.

I don't want to think about the times my dad made me happy. But Harry's doing his best, so I do my best as well. 'He was fun, I guess.' And there I am in the crow's nest again, with the sound of leaves whispering around my ears. *Find the end of the world.* 'He told me stories. And built me a ship.'

'An actual ship?'

'A treehouse, in ship form. It had masts and everything. If you want to get technical, it was a caravel.'

'Caravel,' Harry repeats.

'Caravels were really fast ships that the Portuguese explorers invented so they could sail close to coastlines,' I tell him. 'They had triangular sails and shallow hulls. Caravels were how they discovered everything. Well, not *discovered* like there was no one there to begin with, but – found for trade and general . . .'

'Exploitation?'

I can't deny that. 'Vasco da Gama followed Africa all the way around its coast until he reached India. Pedro Cabral found Brazil when they went off-course. Dad was always telling me stories of the Portuguese explorers sailing around the end of the world, bringing back gold and treasure. I sailed with them all in my ship. Mostly when he wasn't there.'

Harry's eyes reflect the purply colour of the driftwood flames. 'I couldn't get rid of my dad,' he says. 'He was always breathing down my neck.'

'That must have been nice.' Reaching for a driftwood stick, I start prodding the flames too. Their bubble-bath colours are very pleasing.

'He was always expecting me to be building a rocket, or rewiring a plug. Something useful or interesting to prove that I wasn't a waste of his time.'

'And what were you doing?'

'Watching the birds in the garden. Throwing playing cards into a hat.'

With the ash on his head, Harry reminds me of those mad-eyed Indian gurus who live beside the Ganges. He's quite guru-like, with the hair and the skinny thing.

I prod the flames, assembling my thoughts. 'Harry,' I say. 'I'm going to ask you something. You don't have to answer if you don't want to.'

'Thanks for the get-out clause.'

'How did your father die?'

'Heroically.'

The bonfire does a little *whoosh*, and a shower of bright colours rushes up into the night sky.

'My father did everything heroically,' Harry continues.

'Was he rescuing someone?'

'Himself, I think. From the interminable boredom of family life.'

Maybe the women in Spain was Dad rescuing himself. From Mum. From me.

'You've probably worked it out by now,' Harry is saying. 'With the sea and everything.'

The answer clicks into my brain like it's always been there.

'He drowned,' I say. 'Didn't he?'

'He was trying to sail round the world like your explorers.'

We share a moment of understanding, of driftwood sparks, of . . . something. Harry waves his prodding stick in the air.

'I'll dig us some beds,' he says.

The flames are dying down. My stomach rumbles wanly.

'I don't suppose you can dig us a couple of burgers too?' I say.

The world is white when I wake, and it's like that scene at King's Cross with Dumbledore coming towards me. Only it's not Dumbledore, because he doesn't have a beard and he is quite a lot younger. He's also naked. He sort of slides into view, as though the sea mist is a set of theatre curtains and he's the main act. Sea mists along this coast are known to come in quickly and silently and cloak everything like damp white assassins, although I didn't think they came in the summer.

'Harry,' I say in a low voice.

Harry sits up from the furrow he dug himself last night. His hair is like candy floss that someone dropped in a sandpit. My hand automatically goes to my own hair, only to remember with a pang of anxiety – which could also be hunger – that it is entirely missing, lost at sea together with credit cards and approximately five hundred euros.

The guy is a little distance away, walking calmly and casually through the fleecy mist like he rambles naked on dawn beaches most days. He's pale, like the mist has leached the colour from his skin, and his hair is blond and cropped close to his head. He doesn't *look* like a ghost. Too muscular. I find myself hoping that Harry's haircut turned out more Carey Mulligan than Juvenile Detention Centre after all.

'He's *naked*,' I hiss.

'Who?' says Harry.

The rambler is already part cloud and part skin again, the shape of him just a whisper in the white. I feel a sudden urge to follow him.

'Precious, what are you doing?'

'Aren't you curious?' I say, moving away from the ashy remains of our fire. 'He came out of nowhere.'

'I have no idea what—'

The mist swallows Harry's voice. It really is extraordinarily thick, I think, as I walk through its lambent brightness. I can hear the sea somewhere ahead. I'm guessing it's low tide. The mist clings to me, damp and salty and disorientating. Beautiful too, and so white. It could just be me and him out here, I think as I walk, as if we've stepped off the world and on to our own personal cloud.

The sound of the sea has disappeared. Perhaps I'm not walking towards the shore at all. I stop where I am, confused. The first inklings of what I'm doing start to itch at my neck. Spontaneity is one thing, but stupidity is something else.

'Harry?' I say a bit weakly.

The mist pushes the words back into my mouth.

'Harry, are you there?'

I turn around where I stand, trying to find my own footprints. There's something truly freaky about the way

137

this whiteness swirls about my ankles, obscuring the beach so that I could almost believe I'm walking on mist and not on sand at all.

'Harry? Harry? HARRY!'

A figure looms up on my right, its shape indistinct in the pressing whiteness. Arms come round me. I'm incoherently, totally terrified, and start karate-chopping the space around me like a crazed ninja.

'STOP HITTING ME!' shouts Harry.

I calm down, hiccupping, unnerved at how blindly I just did what I did. Like I was hypnotised or something. But now no one is going to find my body hacked to pieces, no one will whisper questions about what I thought I was doing, following a naked stranger to my horrible and doubtless prolonged death. I am simply standing on a beach in Harry Temple's brown arms.

His shoulder blades are sharp beneath his T-shirt and his body is hard, and I realise with a sudden shock that I've never hugged a boy before, not like this. Disconnected thoughts dart like minnows round my brain. I want to feel his skin.

I step back, trying to adjust my focus. My foot knocks against an old guitar lying on the sand. Tucked beneath its peeling brown veneer, something flutters.

# HARRY

Precious helps herself to another salt-cod croquette. 'I've had a few issues with impulse control lately. It's all been under the surface for a long time, and now it's starting to come out.'

'No kidding.'

I have revised my opinion of her haircut looking rough from the front. She gets away with it, in a Joan of Arc kind of way. I can still feel her in my arms the way she was on the beach earlier, and it's unnerving me a bit.

Thanks to the fifty-euro note we found lodged under the guitar, we have covered a reasonable distance today. We even caught a bus for a short while: something Precious told me she'd never done before. Never let it be said that I can't show a girl a good time. And now we're in Albufeira, home of stag parties and all-night vomiting. It's about as anonymous as anywhere along this coast, apart from the billboards scattered through the town centre plastered with her face. Even with the new hair, she's still painfully noticeable, the way a giraffe would be noticeable in a field of cows. If I could just chop six inches off her height and make her face a bit less . . . unusual, we'd be laughing.

I've chosen a quiet table in an even quieter café and made her sit with her back to the window, beside a small printed poster shouting something about 'NO TO THE OILGARVE!' Memories of sitting with my back to the sea in the café in Nice kick at my ankles like a grumpy kid.

'It's probably because my dad always got me everything I wanted the minute I asked for it.'

'No wonder you hate him,' I say.

She looks irritable. 'Are you saying your dad gave you nothing, ever, not even on your birthday?'

'Of course he gave me stuff.'

'Like screwdrivers, rocket-building kits and a painful sense of failure?' She finishes her croquette and raises her hand for the waiter. I grab her hand and pull it down again.

'Don't draw attention to yourself.' I'm interested to note that my fingers are lacing through hers. 'And we can't afford any more.'

'Come on! *Pasteis de bacalhau* cost what, one euro each?'

'I'm in charge of finances since you threw your money in the sea. And you pay fifty euros for everything.'

She rewards me with a glare to strip paint and removes her hand.

'I'm just looking out for you,' I say.

'You're bossing me around,' she replies crossly. 'I'm *hungry*.'

I thumb the billboards out of the café window in exasperation. 'You want to get caught? Go right ahead. Then I can get back to tossing around Europe by myself, the way I like it.'

'But you *don't* like it,' says Precious.

I realise with a shock that I'd like to kiss her. Could I kiss her? The table's in the way. If I try and fail, there will be a furniture situation that will kill the moment. Does she want me to kiss her?

'Where did the naked rambler go, do you think?' she says into the void. 'He seemed to just . . .' She flicks open her fist, splaying out her fingers. Vanished, says her hand. Vaporised.

'Probably a hallucination,' I say. I hadn't seen anything. 'Mist can do that.'

We both contemplate my guitar, drying out against the sunny window. It'll never sound the same again. I realise I don't actually know how it sounded to begin with, which is quite cheering.

'Nathan Payne,' Precious says suddenly.

I rest my chin on my hand because I like looking at her.

'Is this the Nathan Payne game again?' I say.

# NATHAN

Oh my God. She's here.

Not just on one of the hundred billboards I've seen in the past twenty-four hours, but here in the window of a shitty little café in this arsehole of a town, head bent towards a hairy dude who hasn't had a shower in a while. She looks like she's been in a fight with a lawnmower, but she's unmissable. The hairy guy has a definite air of local boyfriend about him.

My hands shake as I plip the locks on the Boxster. Part excitement, part relief. I've been avoiding Dad's calls all night because I didn't want to tell him how hard I was failing.

The café door is open, and Precious is already staring. I remember her now. Those buggy brown eyes on the stairs at the party, looking into mine before . . . well. Before.

'Hello, Precious Metal,' I say, trying not to grin too much. 'What are you doing here? I'd offer an excuse for being in this armpit, but I don't have one.'

'You don't have an armpit?' says the hairy guy.

I lower my sunglasses and assess him. His clothes are in tatters, his shoes practically non-existent. Brown, ropy arms protrude from T-shirt sleeves held together with sand and optimism. I had no idea Precious was so desperate.

'Nathan Payne,' says Precious with a funny sort of squeak.

'You must be Nathan Payne,' says the hairy guy.

I take off my jacket so that I can share the tanned guns beneath. Then I pull out the chair nearest to me and straddle it, in order to take up extra space. Leaning my hands on the back of the chair and my chin on the back of my hands, I'm heartened by the little gasp that escapes Precious Silva's throat. This won't be difficult.

'Not interrupting anything, am I?' I say.

'Why aren't you in Spain?' Precious's hands flutter round her car-crash head like bony brown butterflies. 'You always go to Spain.'

'Dad has business this side of the Guadiana,' I say, hoping I sound suitably mysterious. 'What the hell happened to your hair?'

'Harry cut it for me. '

Harry, is it? Hairy Harry.

'Mate, did you even get the NVQ?' I ask, grinning. I notice a guitar propped up in the window. It's as brown and decrepit as he is. 'You play that?'

'Yes,' he says.

Precious unglues her gaze from mine and stares at him in unflattering surprise. 'You told me you couldn't,' she says.

143

Hairy Harry flushes. Classic.

'Precious Metal, well, well, well,' I say, when I've stopped laughing. 'What are you doing on half the billboards in the Algarve?'

'I'm running away.' Precious's eyes are bright. Her hands can't leave her hair alone. I get a whiff of those rank fish balls they eat around here.

I can feel Hairy Harry eyeing my jacket, my shirt, my tan and pretty much everything else about me. I wonder how long it'll take him to quit.

'Anyone want a drink?' I say.

'Yes please,' says Precious.

I turn to Harry. 'Get them in, will you?'

Like an obedient dog, he heads for the bar. I shift the chair slightly, blocking his line of sight with my elbow.

'Where did you find him?' I say, winking. 'In a beachfront skip?'

Her eyes darken. For a moment, she looks like Ricky when he read whatever it was Dad had written on that piece of paper.

'He helped me out,' she says.

Small misjudgement. I retreat and revise. 'Are you running away because of him?'

She shakes her head, keeps fiddling with her hair. What is it with girls and hair? 'I'm running away because I missed my flight and it seemed like the right thing to do. You know when things get too much and you want to hide?'

There's a cupboard in the utility room at home. Big, cool,

used for storing mops and cleaning equipment. About the right size when you're ten and developing tactics. Too small when you've smashed your parents' house to splinters during your eighteenth birthday party.

'Dad's being such a bastard about the divorce, he won't . . .' She stops. 'Why are you interested?'

I pull myself back from the utility cupboard. 'You've always interested me, Precious Metal,' I say, in my most sincere voice.

She looks disbelieving. 'You were never interested before.'

'You never ran away before,' I point out.

Hairy Harry doesn't have much in the way of bar presence. He is still waiting for someone to notice him. Story of his life, I imagine. And then Precious comes along and – boom. Noticed.

Not for much longer.

I smile one more time at Precious and saunter over to lend him a hand.

'I never thought I'd say this,' I tell him, leaning on the bar top, 'but Precious Metal looks totally hot with that hair. She used to be a bit of a dog, all hair and bones. You known her long?'

'Years,' he says.

He's lying.

'Banged her yet?' I enquire. "'Cos you know, if you haven't, I don't mind if I do. Hey, beers over here!' I flick my fingers at the waitress, who flips up to me like a yo-yo. That, my hairy little friend, is how you do it.

'You know you're a tosser?' Harry says.

'Precious not giving you any?' I eye his torn, dirty T-shirt. 'Can't imagine why. You don't mind carrying the drinks, right?'

He gapes at me.

'Kidding. The bar chick will bring them over if she wants a tip.'

Harry slides up the bar and out of the waitress's way so she can get past with the tray. Naturally enough, his bony elbow lands in a small, sad puddle of beer. He lifts his arm, startled, and I see an opportunity.

'You'll probably want to wash that off,' I say.

He meets my gaze. 'I'm good, thanks.'

It's laughably easy to nudge one of the beer glasses on the tray as the waitress is squeezing past us. The amber contents pour straight down his grubby T-shirt, soaking him from collarbone to crotch. The waitress is all apologies as she rushes back behind the bar for a refill.

'That's a little more serious, wouldn't you say?' I pat him on the shoulder, nod at the back of the bar. 'Bathroom's that way. Don't rush back.'

# PRECIOUS

I pause, appalled, my beer halfway to my lips. 'He *said* that?'

Nathan leans closer, his cut-glass chin resting on his hands. His eyes are even greener than on his Instagram account, excluding filters, and he is tanned and healthy and perky-looking with his muscles and his chinos and his deck shoes. There's a bump on his nose that wasn't there before, but it doesn't outweigh his many other perfections. I don't know what happened to the previously permanent paint smears on the back of his hands or the long hair. He obviously took the dreads off the minute his exams were over, in celebration. A new haircut to mark a break from the past is something that we have in common.

'Guys like that are lone wolves, Precious Metal,' he is saying. 'Not designed to travel in pairs. He practically begged me to look after you so he could get back to his own life. He was perfectly nice about it, but you know how it goes.'

My stomach collapses like a badly baked cake. I thought Harry had been enjoying my company. Not at first, admittedly, but . . . later? On the beach, poking the purple flames, hugging me in the mist. Holding my hand only five minutes ago. Maybe.

What, says a mocking voice in my head, enjoying your company when you pushed him into a stinking ditch, and poured water over his head, and made him run for his life through a holiday town? Took the piss out of him for trying to dig you out of trouble? Forced him to cross an estuary like a terrified scuba-diving Moses, demanded that he style you up with a pair of stolen yellow scissors, yelled at him about his dead father, told Nathan he couldn't play the guitar?

*You want to get caught? Go right ahead. Then I can get back to tossing around Europe by myself, the way I like it.*

Mortification burns hot. Nathan Payne's appearance must feel like some form of angelic deliverance. I take a long and trembling gulp of my beer.

'Try not to take it personally,' Nathan says.

'How can I not take it personally?' I say, setting the beer down. 'I've just spent twenty-four hours with the guy. I didn't *mean* to ruin his holiday. I didn't *ask* to get chased down the coast by a pair of unidentified kidnappers. I could have sworn he hated his own company but clearly I had that totally wrong.'

'Kidnappers?' Nathan says sharply. 'What kind of kidnappers?'

Normally this level of proximity to Nathan Payne would

make me a gawping fool. But I've got more on my mind right now than Nathan's jawline. A hot knot of tears is gathering at the base of my throat.

'I don't know, I've never met kidnappers before,' I say. 'I thought Harry liked me. I know we only spent twenty-four hours together, but there was a lot going on and . . . I thought maybe we bonded a bit.'

'I'm sure you did,' Nathan soothes. 'As far as guys like that bond with anyone.'

I gaze down the length of the café, hoping to see Harry looking at me and doing his half-smile thing. Forgiving me for dumping him in it about the guitar. Anything to disprove what Nathan is saying. But he's not at the bar, not by the door, not at the jukebox. He's nowhere to be seen.

'Unbelievable,' I say, rising to my feet. 'He's skipped out the back. He's not even going to say goodbye!'

Nathan lounges backwards, hooking his arms over the chair back. It makes his chest look extra-wide, and for a moment I stop dwelling on my burning sense of injustice.

'It's probably easier this way,' he says, looking up at me. 'He didn't strike me as someone big on social niceties.'

Harry didn't like me at all, at any point. I sniff fiercely and stare at the ceiling and rain curses on Harry Temple's matted man-bun head as I let Nathan lead me out of the café like a lamb on a string.

'It's really incredible that we ran into each other like this,' he says as we turn off the square and up a small pedestrianised street.

I make an effort to blink back the angry moisture in the corners of my eyes and think back to that moment of paralysis when, for the second time in as many days, Nathan Payne imprinted himself on my eyeballs.

'Yes, it is kind of amazing,' I say. 'Especially as you're never in Portugal and I only reached Albufeira this morning. I knew I'd seen you in Vilamoura.'

He sounds a little shocked. 'You saw me? When?'

'A couple of days ago. I think it was you, anyway.'

To my intense surprise, he puts his arm round my shoulders. Nathan Payne has never given me a second glance at home. I'm not sure what's happened to change this. He smells warm and spicy. Clean. Gazing at him is soothing.

'Do you want to go for a drive?' he says. 'You look like you need cheering up. Dad lent me his Boxster for a couple of days.'

I have a sudden and extremely pleasant vision of whipping along in the sunshine in a Boxster with Nathan, the salt-scented Atlantic wind whipping through what's left of my hair. Harry can piss off if he wants to. I have *options*.

'Your dad's on business here doing what?'

His thumb strokes my shoulder. 'Buying land.'

'It probably belongs to my dad.' I'm hyper-aware of his thumb.

Nathan's staring ahead with this distant look on his face. He still has his arm round my shoulders. It's surreal.

'I thought your dad's business was in Spain,' I say after a bit.

'He's branching out.' He squints at the sun-faded poster stuck in the door of a tiny hair salon beside another one of the anti-oil-drilling posters that are everywhere. 'Before our little drive, let's tidy up the mess Hairy Harry made of your head, shall we?'

I put a hand self-consciously up to my head. 'I thought it would be a good way to disguise myself, look a bit less like all these billboards.'

He runs his fingers through the hacked black edges of my new look. 'It's awesome,' he says. 'I'd draw you in a heartbeat.'

I am not very good at reading boys' intentions, but this is definitely flirting. There is no other reason for a boy randomly to stroke a girl's head.

Nathan is flirting with me.

'You can if you want,' I say, doing my absolute best to flirt back.

I suddenly remember that Harry has what's left of my cash. A fresh wave of outrage hits me, followed by confusion. I'm pretty sure he isn't a thief. The first two times we met, he actually tried to *save* me money. And now I think about it, wasn't his guitar still by the window in the café when we left?

I glance back down the street. The café is around the corner, out of sight. 'Are you sure Harry left?' I say.

Nathan checks his watch. 'Does it matter?'

'Well, he looked after me when I needed it, and I'd feel pretty bad if he was in there and wondering where I went.'

'I don't think he feels the same way,' Nathan says. 'Not from what I saw.'

I feel a bit crushed. While I may not be able to do much about Harry's feelings, I can't leave without checking that he's definitely gone.

I reluctantly slide out from underneath Nathan's linen arm.

'I won't be long,' I say.

# HARRY

The hand dryer in the bathroom has about as much power as an old man with lung disease. I dry my T-shirt as best I can, half a square centimetre at a time, cursing Nathan Payne all the way back to Spain.

When I finally return, no one is sitting at the table. I stop, confused. Two beers, one partially drunk. One guitar, noted with a fresh level of irritation. Zero people, wankers or otherwise.

I pick up the guitar and leave the café to peer around the sunny street. I don't think the rising unease in my stomach is down to the croquettes. Precious wouldn't have gone off with that guy and left me without saying anything, would she? Would she?

I walk the perimeter of the square, dodging the milling crowds, scrutinising the shops. Every now and again her picture pops up on a billboard, making me think she's standing on the edge of my vision with an unaccountably enormous face.

Why *wouldn't* she go off with Nathan Payne? She doesn't know me like she apparently knows him. He has nice clothes and doesn't smell of beer. She's clearly into him, and he made it clear that he'd be open to extending that acquaintance. Nathan Payne with his perfect hair and fat wallet. Nathan Payne, whose dad has business this side of the Guadiana. *I'd* probably go off with Nathan Payne, if I were female and not too particular about a personality. But I can't help feeling put out. I gave Precious a rail ticket, and clothes, and a haircut, and something resembling emotional honesty. I found her in the mist, and kept her company, and reminded her that she was lucky her father was still alive. I went *underwater* for her, and lost my rucksack. I should at least qualify for a goodbye.

What the hell is the Guadiana anyway? It sounds like a star system.

I settle down a little bitterly under a sparrow-rich tree on a hot scratched-up bench beside a guy with a bulldog tattoo on his roasted belly, swing my guitar round and study it with loathing. It's the same busted brown thing it always was. I press a few strings to the fretboard and stroke the result with the tips of my fingers. Something chord-like emerges. When I absently pull out my phone to ask Siri about tuning guitars, I am faced by a screen thick with condensation and self-pity.

'Know any Metallica?' asks Bulldog Tat with a belch.

I don't have time to tighten my grip before the guitar is whipped away from me. The guy's fingers might be pudgy, but they seem to know how to twist the tuning pegs. He plays a series of chords that rise one after the other. The tune is familiar. He repeats it a couple of times, then changes it a bit to wrap up the riff.

I take the guitar back and try to copy what he just did. Three proper chords emerge. Curiously, I play them again. Get them wrong, but discover that there are worse ways of wasting time than bending my fingers around a set of gut strings and making noises. I also realise with a sudden pleasurable shock that playing a guitar was something Dad never did.

'I wouldn't say Jonny Buckland should start panicking any time soon.'

Cool as an ice cube, I squint at Nathan Payne. 'Could have guessed you like Coldplay. What have you done with Precious?'

'She went looking for you.'

Ice cubes are emotionless when faced by wankers.

'I haven't seen her since you bunked out of the café together,' I say. 'Thanks for that.'

Nathan polishes his sunglasses on a cleaning cloth, slips them back on over the little bump on the bridge of his unburned, unpeeling nose. 'We had some catching up to do,' he says. 'Turns out you only just met. I can't say I'm surprised. I know all the dogs round my lamp post, you see, and I don't recognise the smell of you. Too suburban.'

I wrap my fingers around the neck of my guitar, imagining it's Nathan Payne's windpipe. Something about this guy is bringing out a competitive streak in me that I never knew I had. Dad would be amazed.

'When I said years, I meant on an emotional level,' I say. 'We've been through a lot in twenty-four hours. Stuff you can only imagine.'

'And yet she hasn't found you,' he points out, 'despite your unmissable guitar playing. Why is that?'

There's a sudden rush of blood to my head. I stand up from the bench.

'When did you last see her?' I say.

We both register a black car with tinted windows, the flash of a wristwatch. Jimi stretched almost past recognition. The soft thud of the car door cuts Precious off mid-scream.

I'd like to say a hundred things shoot through my mind. Plans to throw myself under the wheels of the car, to hurl a civic dustbin into the road, to climb a tree and shout for attention. But the honest truth is that the hamster wheel isn't even turning. It's iced up, fixed tight. The hamster, basically, is dead.

'Shit,' says Nathan, wide-eyed.

Square life continues. The gypsy ladies sell scarves, the old men play cards, the drunken stags sleep off Jägerbombs beside the bins. I am fixed to the spot as the car cruises away with hardly a rev to show for its efforts, just the glint of blistering sun on its chrome hubcaps and a streak of light on its shiny black flank. Its number plate is smeared with dust and impossible to read. I see Precious's face, her hands

156

pressed to the back windscreen, her mouth a perfect O. The car takes a corner and heads up the hill, away from the centre.

Away from the sea.

# PRECIOUS

Terminator One is driving this time. Terminator Two is sitting on the burning black leather seat beside me and holding on to my arm. I have tried every karate move I know and screamed myself hoarse but he's not letting go. He smells sour, and the patches under his arms have spread halfway across his back. I get the impression he's not too pleased at having had to chase me for twenty-four hours straight beneath the blazing Algarve sun.

'Get OFF me,' I shout, trying to wrench my arm free.

He just holds on tighter. I want to sob with frustration. I can't stop thinking about Harry's face as I drove away, his fingers clutching his toasted seaweed hair. For someone who wanted nothing more to do with me, he looked pretty cut up. I take comfort in that. Then I think about Dad's exploded boat and start shivering.

'Are you going to kill me?' I hiccup.

They don't answer.

'Who are you? What do you want?'

That doesn't get a reaction either. I try both questions in Portuguese, and then wish I hadn't because now they know I speak Portuguese. But still nothing. Leaning as far away from Terminator Two's spreading belly as I can, I pull my legs up on to the car seat and hug my knees. A memory rushes into my head, of doing the same thing on the train with Harry. Twenty-four hours has never felt so long. It's stupid, but it feels rude to have been kidnapped without saying goodbye.

The radio in the front of the car is playing that song from last year, the Eurovision winner. The words are so sad, about how love needs two people and two hearts, although one heart will do its best to cover both bases until the other is up to it. Something like that. Portuguese is hard to translate. So much of it is about feelings.

I can't help thinking that if I'd stayed with Harry, they wouldn't have got me. It's irrational to give him what amount to superpowers, but that's hard to translate too.

I press my forehead to the tinted glass window as the car purrs along, to cool the panic raging through my skin. We're out of Albufeira, heading west, avoiding the motorway. Tolls mean cameras. Cameras mean witnesses.

All I did was miss a plane.

I force myself to think rationally. It's been hours since I sent Mum that text. Knowing her and social media, my disappearance is probably all over Twitter. I might even have my own hashtag. #findprecious, #precioustome. Something to tug at the heartstrings. Then I remember the day Mum thought I'd got out of the car when I hadn't, and suddenly I'm not so sure. It's entirely possible that she's too engrossed in Bacon and the divorce proceedings to notice that I still haven't made it home.

Dad used to be the fixer in my life, the one who bandaged my dolls when they walked the tree-ship plank a little too heavily, and took me to Nando's when I failed Mandarin exams. Could he fix this? Surely he's out of chances now.

*At least he's still alive*, Harry says, somewhere deep inside my dulled head.

The landscape through the tinted window isn't exactly a postcard a minute. Shopping malls, petrol stations. A waterpark with stripy snake slides, a huge billboard shouting 'NO TO THE OILGARVE!' Every now and again I toy with the idea of yanking the door open and throwing myself out at seventy miles an hour, but the door is locked and – you know. Seventy miles an hour. Mainly I sink into a kind of hopeless torpor as we whip along. The horizon is undulating in an attractive manner, offering up the Monchique mountains somewhere beyond the pottery outlets, scrubby vines and *VENDE-SE*s sprayed in jaunty colours on broken-down buildings. The Algarve isn't much of a looker until you reach her ankles, the place where she lifts her hem to reveal her clear water petticoats and golden sandstone kick-pleats. This bit is definitely around her shins.

The indicator ticks smoothly as we swing off the main road. Terminator Two's fingers are still clamped around my bicep like the guy with the metal claw in *Live and Let Die*. I immediately wish I hadn't thought of a film with the word 'die' in the title. All journeys have to end. What's going to happen when we stop?

Slower now, the road twisting in less predictable patterns. We pass a supermarket, a garden centre, the sign for a golf course. And that's when I see him on the side of the road.

Cropped hair. Bleached skin, what I can see of it. He's shining, dazzling in the sun.

But before I am sure of my sanity, everything twists.

Spidery lines explode across the windscreen as the golf ball hurtles like a white bullet through the glass. It glances off the temple of Terminator One, who falls forward like someone cut his strings, smashing his head into the steering wheel. There is a tinkling sound as his mirrored aviators shatter around the dashboard. Terminator Two flings himself sideways in shock, slamming the side of his skull so hard against the window that his eyes roll up in his head and he slumps beside me in a large, sweaty, insensible heap.

The next ten seconds stretch like a concertina. We slide and spin, the road before us impossible to see through the jagged diamonds that have replaced the windscreen. There is no time to think, no time to pray, no time to do anything but curl into a ball. Squealing tyres, the bruising thump of something smashing into the fender, the smell of burning rubber. The gentle hiss of a smashed-up radiator. Something ticks quietly, slows and stops altogether.

Seconds pass, masquerading as hours. There is no movement and no sound, apart from an urgent bird in the hedge beside the car. Very cautiously, I uncurl myself. I'm unhurt, apart from the bruise blooming nicely on my upper arm. Terminator One has a bump the size of a chicken's egg on his head, and is out cold, splayed across the driving wheel. Terminator Two is pale, twisted awkwardly in his seat and also somewhere in la-la land.

Almost as if I've been in this kind of situation before, I know what to do. Stretching across the taut, slumped back of Terminator One, I grab the keys from the ignition. They swing cool and heavy in my hand as I plip the locks, fling the door open and gulp at the air. With a sudden flash of foresight, I turn back and grab Terminator One's phone and charger and scoop up the wallet that's slid from his pocket on to the passenger seat, and put the keys back in the ignition. I'm too weak to pull two dead weights out of the car. They'll have to take their chances with the pooling petrol.

Now I've reached this point in the decision-making process, I can't get out fast enough. And so I slide free and stagger from the crumpled vehicle, stumbling on the rocky roadside, squinting uncertainly at the corner where I swear I saw . . . where . . .

A car approaching from the opposite direction is beginning to slow curiously at the sight of the black car smoking gently on the verge. Realising with relief that someone else can deal with the problem, I move off the road, across a field and behind some trees, where I feel reasonably confident no one can see me. I switch my attention to the wallet in my hand with its fat frill of fifty-euro notes. The hot shower, food and bed they represent almost makes me cry. Terminator One's phone is on, no passcode is required. Now all I need is to remember Mum's number. 44 79 . . . no, 44 76 . . . nope. 44 77 . . .

It comes to me in a sudden waterfall of numbers. Keying it in gratefully, I squeeze my eyes shut as the reality of the past twenty-four hours hits me. I'm exhausted, wrung out, alive and alone. But now everything's going to be all right.

Mum's number rings once, twice. I feel a rush of hope and love when she speaks.

'Where the hell are you?' she shouts.

I open my mouth to apologise.

'You should have been here yesterday! What have you done with my daughter?'

I pull the phone from my ear, and stare stupidly at the screen.

The Terminator Twins appear to have my mother on speed dial.

# HARRY

'Don't throw up on the upholstery, man. Do not even think about it.'

Nathan's linen jacket hangs over the back of the driver's seat. I cling miserably to the passenger door, the wind whirling my hair around my head, my eyes trained on the horizon. The sea isn't in my direct line of vision, but the sky glows with its presence. It's the best I've got. *Please understand. Please, Dad.*

Dimly I hear the Boxster growl and shift gears as we overtake a scooter with a box of oranges balanced on its back wheel. I can't look ahead, I can't look back and I definitely can't look at the driver. My hand flexes, preparing to wrench my way to freedom and quite possibly death the moment we swing inland.

'Jesus,' Nathan mutters.

It's not wholly clear whether his anxiety is on behalf of Precious or the car. Part of me would enjoy puking on the Boxster's expensive-smelling leather. The rest wishes to keep Nathan Payne's scorn at arm's length.

'If you produce even one speck of vomit, I'll kill you. You have a *serious* travel-sickness problem.'

The Boxster growls louder. My fingers tighten convulsively on the door handle. Ten kilometres from Albufeira and counting. Dad's fingers reach for me, clutching at nothing but air.

'I'm only doing this because I'm heading to Portimão anyway.'

'Keep telling yourself that,' I whisper.

'You're lucky I'm giving you a ride.'

'It's the least you can bloody do,' I say. 'If she'd stayed with me . . .'

'How do you know she's not headed back to Faro?'

I don't.

Big blue road signs loom, advertising Junction 7 of the A22. Nathan sets off the purring indicator, prepares to turn the wheel to the right.

'Straight on,' I croak.

'Motorway's quicker.'

'They won't go on the motorway, it's too obvious. Small roads. Coast . . . roads.'

He hesitates.

'I'll puke,' I groan. 'On purpose.'

Nathan flicks the indicator off again and stays on the smaller road. A truck behind us honks its disdain.

'What are we looking for?' he says every few minutes. 'Do you even know? Why don't we just call this in?'

'You know how to call emergency services, do you?' I say

from the depths of my nausea. 'Explain the problem, demand the Flying Squad?'

*Black car, tinted windows, shining wristwatch, dusty number plate.* I mentally recite the list, keeping my nerves steady and my stomach still.

'We don't know who these guys are,' says Nathan petulantly. 'What if they're dangerous?'

'Deal with that . . . when we have to,' I grunt.

Twenty kilometres from Albufeira. Thirty. No black car, no tinted windows. Nathan drives on, fingers drumming on the steering wheel. We approach a big white bridge, its spidery lines soaring above us with water, blessed water, on all sides, and the sea not far away. I twist myself so that I'm facing forward, and my whole body groans as muscles readjust.

'I need to make a call,' Nathan says as we reach the far side of the bridge.

I feel too sick to care that we're stopping while Precious is getting further away. We glide into the hard shoulder. Gratefully I pull open the door and stand by the railings of the bridge and breathe my father and the sea into every particle of my body. Nathan gets out on the other side. I'm drunk on the smell of ozone and the sight of spoonbills down in the marshy edges of the water and it's easy to tune out his conversation, peppered as it is with 'Don't . . .' and 'I can't . . .' and 'you know it's not . . .'

He ends the call. I peel my gaze from the sheet of water beneath the bridge.

'Who were you calling?' I say.

'My father.' He wipes his forehead, which is looking sweaty in spite of the brisk sea breeze.

'Why? Is he in the Portuguese police force?'

'Of course he's bloody not. He's in the oil business.'

It looks as if he's going to kick the wheel arch of the Boxster, but seems to think better of it. His face is grey. Maybe he cares about Precious after all. Maybe I've misjudged him.

'She'll be all right,' I say, even though I have nothing to back this up.

'You know anything about it.' Nathan runs his hands through his hair. 'She's Ricky Silva's kid.'

I think about boats that explode in harbours, headline news about hotels and golf courses and more money than I can imagine. He's right, I haven't got a bloody clue. My attempt at optimism – which was for me, I realise, as much as for Nathan – whimpers and dies inside. What if they kill her? How did I get to a point in my life when this question is even *slightly* relevant?

'What do you think they're they going to do to her?' I ask nervously.

'Use her as leverage, you pillock. It's what I'd do.'

He gets back into the Boxster. I hear the door shut with an expensive click. The engine flares into life. I move a fraction too late, my fingers barely grazing the door handle before the car is swinging out of the hard shoulder and back on to the road, and within a matter of blinks is little more than a faint line in the distance.

'Great,' I shout after him into the swirling dust. 'Terrific. Thanks. And YOU'VE GOT MY BLOODY GUITAR.'

I sink on to the tarmac and rest my head in my hands. The sound of gulls, the roar of the occasional car and the smell of faintly dank, salty water surround me. Surprisingly, I don't feel too bad. In comparison to how I was feeling in the passenger seat of the Boxster anyway.

Eventually I dust myself down, cross the road, climb over the railings and drop down to a smaller road on the other side. A red-sand path meanders through sweet-smelling thickets of pine trees full of birdsong, past several not so sweet-smelling chicken pens, towards apartments and boats and bridges and an orthodontic-looking railway. I squint in the heavy sunlight as the water runs away to my left, and wonder if it ever gets bored of flowing endlessly and unquestioningly into the sea. Without thinking, I lift my hands to adjust my rucksack, only to remember that it's lying on a seabed somewhere. Useless, dead and gone.

*Talk to me, Harry boy.*

'Oh, I'll talk,' I tell my father grimly. 'But will you listen?' He's quiet.

'Thought not,' I say.

It takes around forty minutes to skirt the estuary, past the Portimão Arena with its glitzy posters of dance competitions and Lego conventions and along the railway line until my feet are almost in the river. The luxury of the shade beneath the rusting blue and yellow railway bridge, past walls plastered with more 'NO TO THE OILGARVE!' lasts all of two seconds, and then I'm out the other side. There's something enjoyable about walking without the weight of a rucksack and guitar, if a bit inconvenient. A hat, or sunglasses, or a long shady tree-lined promenade where my brain can cool down would be good. Who has taken Precious? Where is she, what's going to happen next? And is there anything I can do about it?

An English-language paper flaps from a news kiosk peg on the waterfront. Fishing some change from my pocket, I send a silent apology to Precious for spending her money and buy myself a copy. Then I settle down on a bench occupied by two pigeons and a smouldering cigarette butt.

### TRIPLE TROUBLE FOR TYCOON

Infamous property tycoon Ricky Silva's daughter was reported missing two days ago. Precious Silva (16) was last seen in Faro airport, having failed to board her plane home. Taken alongside the destruction of Mr Silva's €6-million luxury yacht *Amalia* in Vilamoura marina two days ago and the increasing financial pressures on his property empire, Desejado Developments, it's clear that Mr Silva's problems are mounting.

'That man has dangerous enemies,' says Linda Silva (42), Mr Silva's estranged wife. 'People who'll stop at nothing to get what they want. I haven't slept for three days. If anyone has seen my daughter, please contact the police. I love her, and want her home safe.'

The rest of the article is a straight re-hash from the paper on the Faro train. I lay it in my lap and experience a rush of nausea that has nothing to do with the sea.

After a while, I fold and tuck the pages and place the end result on my head. I already look crazy. What with the way my life is heading, why not go the extra mile? At least I'll save myself sunstroke.

# PRECIOUS

**Ferragudo 40 minutes**

I press the send button and lean my head back so the girl can get the conditioner out. The water pressure is light but insistent, and tickles my ears. She massages my scalp and chatters about her boyfriend wanting to get married at the town hall instead of the church in her parents' village twenty minutes inland. I'm not in the mood for talk of parents or weddings, but there's not much I can do about it in my current position.

'Can I charge my phone in here?' I say.

As if hearing its name, the Terminator phone beeps.

**We agreed Portimão**

Portimão glimmers at me across the estuary. I don't especially want to catch a ferry across the water just because it will make my mother's life easier.

'*Linda*,' the girl murmurs as she blows my hair around my head.

The Portuguese word means beautiful. It's also, appropriately, my mother's name.

Returning my attention to the text message, I can't quite resist.

**Ferragudo or we cut her ears off**

The forty-minute walk of heat and questions down to the sea has done something interesting to me. Hardened me up, like a kiln hardens a pot.

**Don't you dare touch her!!!**

I put the phone down and consider myself in the mirror. One strip wash in the café on the Ferragudo square and I'm cleaner than I've been in days. The Terminator Twin funds have bought me a dress that is short and shoes that are high. The hair is . . . surprising.

'Do you do make-up?' I say. 'Manicures?'

The girl hurries to the back of the salon, returns with a trolley of sparkle and glitter. I move my head from side to side, studying the way the light falls on my freshly revealed cheekbones.

**1000 euros more for Portimão**
**DO NOT TOUCH HER!!!!**

'Is this for someone special?' the girl asks, painting my nails a deep and gorgeous aquamarine, the colour of the sea outside the salon window. I marvel at my strange, exotic reflection. A silver-dusted eye, an earring, a sharp red lip.

'Yes,' I say. 'Me.'

Everything I have ever thought was wrong.

### Jacaranda Hotel 40 minutes

Across the water, the blues and mauves of the Jacaranda Hotel glow like gas flames. Payment made, I zip the phone into my new bag and slide my new sunglasses from their case. Head for the waterfront and its charter boats. Men look up from café tables, coffee cups tilting. I know that they are looking at me. I walk on, holding my head higher, stepping with care over the cobbles.

Lava is nothing. I am steel. I am flint. I am gunpowder.

Bang.

# HARRY

I have no idea where to look for Precious. I'm so far out of my depth that I might as well be on the seabed with Dad's yacht. I just walk into Portimão. At least with walking, I'm moving forward.

Identical apartment blocks, buses, traffic, a stupidly large cruise ship. Not one marina but two. It looks nicer on the other bank, where a pink castle sits prettily with its feet in the water, all clustered about with older houses. Boats are puttering around between the banks, flashy ones and fishing boats, taking tourists one way and locals the other.

When a beach finally opens up before me, I take off my wilting paper hat and sit on the beach wall and squint into the light. A couple of tourists edge away from me. By way of explanation, the sharp sea breeze changes, directing the stink of my armpits straight up my own nostrils.

The Atlantic was Dad's favourite ocean, its depths and winds and unpredictability all part of its charm. I suppose it's attractive enough just here, the gulls and petrels shooting the breeze overhead, the water clear and the colour of empty wine bottles. It helps to picture Precious taking my hand as I wade in. I'm breathing fine until its cold fingers reach the tops of my legs, and then I have to fight the urge to return to shore. She holds my hand a little tighter. I hope she's OK. I really hope she is.

The T-shirt comes off first, followed by the shorts. I peel off my boxers, first checking to make sure there are no impressionable children in the vicinity, and walk in further, holding my clothes above my head, teeth gritted, until the sea sluices at my offending armpits. The sand mists around my ankles and something small and silvery darts past what's left of my shoes. I heel them off to let the water slip between my toes.

The head is the hardest part. I tip my head backwards until the water snakes around my scalp and then I stand quite still, feeling the gentle pull of the waves as they rise and fall around my ears, my arms held out to the sides and the sun on my eyelids. This is how I'll do it, if I ever have kids. Take them into a quiet sea a step at a time.

A rather larger wave smacks me in the face, waking me from my trance, and I wade hastily back up the beach, dressing each part of myself as I emerge, until I can cough and wheeze on the relative safety of the shore. Then I head for a phone box in the shadow of a palm tree, and fish around in my damp pocket for change, and call the only number that's ever stuck in my head.

'01234 567899 Naan by Numbers Mohit speaking may I take your order please?'

'Mohit,' I say. 'It's Harry Temple.'

'May I take your order please?'

'Harry *Temple*,' I repeat. 'Onion bhajis, chicken passanda and vegetable biryani every Sunday Harry Temple.'

Mohit's voice changes. 'My apologies. The number was not recognised. Twenty minutes for your food, OK?'

The phone box is eating my change too quickly. I tell Mohit as much.

'I have not had a telephone conversation like this since 1998,' says Mohit.

'I'm in Portugal.'

'I'm sorry but we cannot deliver in Portugal.'

'This isn't about food, Mohit. Do you have my mum's number?'

'Chicken dopiaza and jasmine rice? Of course I have her number. You want her number?'

I memorise the number Mohit gives me and slam the phone down before it slides out of my head. How did people ever do this without mobiles?

Mum sounds worn out when I reach her. In the background I hear one of the dogs barking, shrill and fierce. She detonates when I speak.

'Harry! Why haven't you called? Why haven't you texted?'

'My phone,' I begin.

'You're just like your father, off on your own thing and never a thought for the ones you leave behind!'

'I'm sorry,' I say. 'My phone broke and I'm in Portugal and things out here have been a bit crazy.'

'Are you eating? When are you coming home? Harry, are you looking after yourself? I'm reading about kidnappers in Portugal, are you talking to strangers?'

I squint at myself in the reflective glass hood of the phone box. 'Depends how you define strange.'

'Your father spent his life talking to strangers and look how that worked out,' Mum says fretfully. 'You're turning into him, aren't you?'

Oh the irony.

'I have to go,' I say. 'I'm in a phone box. And out of change. I'll be home when I can. Look after yourself.'

There's two dogs barking in harmony behind Mum now. 'Harry, come back to me safely. Promise me!'

Putting the phone down takes a couple of attempts because I'm struggling to see the cradle. I remember now, with a stab of blinding guilt, how Mum would lurk by the phone for hours until Dad made one of his infrequent 'Whoa, that hurricane was wild, we almost didn't make it' calls from whatever godforsaken bit of the ocean he'd found himself in. I had always wondered how he could leave us both twisting in the wind the way he did.

I'll call more often from now on.

No rucksack equals no fresh clothes. Making a choice between garish and even more garish at the gypsy stand by the roadside, I buy blue board shorts, grey T-shirt, blue flip-flops. I throw in a blue and green baseball cap emblazoned with the legend *PORTIMÃO? PORTIMORE!* and add a pair of sunglasses, bringing Precious's money down to a magnificent four euros and thirty cents. Then I celebrate by dumping all my old clothes on top of a load of ice-cream wrappers with attendant wasps in a roadside bin and heading up the boardwalk dividing the estuary from a neat rank of blue sea-facing hotel accommodation.

Four euros and thirty cents. No passport. No ticket home. What a bloody mess.

A boat is coming towards me across the water from the castle side of the river mouth. I stop and watch its progress. A girl, tall and slim with short black hair blowing in the wind is standing in the boat, braced like a figurehead on the prow of a sailing ship. Her dress billows like a mint-coloured sail around her body. I feel as if someone has struck me hard around the head with one of the mooring posts that stand sentry along the dock.

It's Precious.

Confusion covers me from the tips of my new flip-flops to the peaked brim of my *PORTIMÃO? PORTIMORE!* cap. I swear she wasn't that tall this morning. Maybe it's the shoes. What has she done with the guys who took her? There's no one else in the boat apart from the driver.

At a table a few yards from where I'm standing, a woman sets her phone down and gets to her feet, shading her eyes with a tanned and manicured hand. The wind catches at her blond hair, teasing it into heavily sprayed clumps. She's tall. Almost as tall as Precious, to whom she bears a passing resemblance. But she also appears to be shrinking right before my eyes.

The boat bumps and clinks against the dockside. Men appear from several sides to assist Precious out of the boat. She ignores them all. Straightening her sea-coloured dress and adjusting her sunglasses, she walks towards me. I panic, tug my blue and green brim down and pull my head back into my neck like an ineffectual tortoise. What am I going to say to her? What is she going to say to me?

Before she reaches me, however, she stops beside the blond woman. They exchange a look so loaded I'm surprised their eyeballs don't hit the boardwalk like ball bearings. The woman bursts into tears.

'Baby, I've been so worried! Where have you been? What have you done to your hair? The papers are saying you were kidnapped. Did you escape? I should have known as soon as that boat went up in flames that your father was into something dangerous and illegal, I should never have left you here by yourself—'

Precious holds up a hand like a glamorous traffic enforcement officer. A man with a large camera appears from the hotel, pointing a lens the size of the Post Office Tower at the pair of them. The sound of the shutter resembles gunfire.

'I know it was you,' says Precious.

The woman glances at the photographer. 'Baby, you're tired and emotional,' she says. 'It must have been a terrible couple of days but really, it wasn't supposed to go on for this long. They were supposed to deliver you to me yesterday but then you ran and they couldn't find you and I have been *beside* myself. There's a suite in the hotel for a few days, we can stay here a while. I will explain all of this and we can talk?'

'I'd prefer not to do that,' says Precious. 'Did you even *have* a meeting with Howarth Steele?'

'I had the meeting, of course I did, but then I flew back. You should have been here *yesterday*, that's what they said, none of this should have happened. I know it's absurd but your father gave me no—'

Precious is vibrating like a bowstring at a medieval siege. 'Stop talking,' she says.

'You won't believe what that man is trying to get away with. Hazel Howarth says—'

'I said *stop*.'

The woman tries again. 'Let's have a drink and talk about this like adults.'

'I'd rather have a drink with a velociraptor.' Precious turns her hand, palm up. 'But I'll take the extra grand. You know, the cash you were going to give the Terminator Twins to stop me losing my ears.'

Her mother flushes. 'Where are . . .?'

'In hospital. Nasty car crash.'

Precious's tone of voice dares a question that doesn't come. Instead her mother bows her head and, scrabbling in her purse, pulls out a wad of cash. Precious takes it, counts it and walks on up the boardwalk away from us both, lifting her middle finger in a traditional teenage farewell. I can't take my eyes off her.

Mrs Silva stuffs her purse back into her bag. The photographer is watching Precious and fingering his shutter button.

'Give me your camera,' she snaps at him.

The camera man opens his mouth.

'GIVE me your CAMERA, Mario bloody Testino.'

The memory card is removed and flung into the glittering water. A black-headed gull dips after it, then wheels away in disappointment. Muttering, the photographer sidles away.

Mrs Silva glances at me with eyes that are bright with tears and an overload of mascara. 'Enjoy the show?' she asks bitterly.

I want to go after Precious and tell her how magnificent she just was. On the basis of that performance, I wouldn't be surprised if she had evaporated the Terminator Twins with the point of a finger. But I'm still struggling to get my head around the fact that her mother appears to have had her own daughter kidnapped in order to score points in her divorce.

'Very much, thanks,' I say, getting up and straightening my cap. 'And I must say, the best woman won.'

# PRECIOUS

A thousand euros crinkles in my hand. Together with what's left of the Terminator Twins' stash, it's a nice sum. What do you spend blood money on? More clothes seem a bit dull. A hotel would be nice. There are plenty of flashy ones around here, all massages and towels folded into swans. Maybe rose petals on the bed. Only trouble is, hotels require passports, and mine is somewhere on a seabed, beside my credit cards and Harry's rucksack.

I glance very briefly over my shoulder to check that she isn't following. A few tourists are strolling along the marina some distance behind me, one in a particularly hideous baseball cap. No sign of my mother.

I flag a taxi. About three stop at once. It's taken me sixteen years, but I've finally found some presence.

'Hotel Sebastian,' I tell the first one, getting in.

The cab interior smells of suncream and the cabbie's cigarette of choice. For the first time since it happened, I let my thoughts sidle cautiously up to the figure I saw on the grassy verge beside the golf course. And, more particularly, his full suit of armour, engraved and shining in silver and gold. Dazzling enough to blind a golfer.

The taxi cruises through the grittier end of Praia da Rocha towards a wilder stretch of coast, passing palm trees, purple bougainvillea cascading down white houses, the back ends of apartment blocks. The tyres thump and twist on cobbles and I shut my eyes as we pass through the wide iron gates of the Hotel Sebastian with its neatly tended verges of pink oleander and hibiscus and the plink of golf balls in the distance.

Dad used to tell me how he went out on his father's boat when he was eight years old, hauling heavy drift nets that broke the skin on his hands. When the water was rough, he stared at the big house on top of the cliff and kept its steady lights in his salt-swollen gaze and promised himself that he would own it one day. For all his faults, he never lacked ambition.

The Sebastian. Dad's first hotel. The jewel in his questionable crown.

Paying the cabbie with a fifty, I head for the wide stone steps, through the pillars and into the lobby. It's dark and soothing, the tiles gleaming and the black and white marble floor so cool that I just want to lie on it. The furniture is brightly upholstered, clashing happily with the ornate panelling, and there is chatter and the clinking of glasses in the bright bar beyond the wide wooden staircase with its tiled battle friezes. The opulence of the place has my father stamped all over it.

'A room please, Luisa,' I say, pocketing my phone. 'A suite if you have one.'

Luisa's lacquered nails hang in mid-air over the reception keyboard. 'I'm sorry,' she says, looking blank. 'Do you have a reservation?'

Luisa has known me since I was a little kid. My makeover has clearly had more of a dramatic effect on my appearance than I realise. I take off my sunglasses and fix my eyes on hers.

'It's me,' I say.

Luisa attempts to cover her shock. My father's hotel staff are good at that.

'Miss Silva?' she says. 'You're here? But the newspapers—'

'Don't believe everything you read.'

She recovers. 'It has been two years since we saw you. You have – grown up.'

I tap my aqua nails on the marble reception top. 'Yes,' I say. 'So do you have a suite?'

She checks her screen, glancing curiously at me as she scrolls. I wonder what she's thinking.

'We have a balcony suite available tonight,' she says. 'Very quiet with a beautiful view. Your father is expected later. Would you like me to tell him that you are here?'

My heart thumps at the mention of Dad. I'm not ready for him yet. I take the key – a heavy metal one with a wooden tag.

'No,' I say. 'And if anyone else calls for me, I'm not here.'

'You have bags?'

'No bags.'

I feel Luisa's gaze follow me as I take myself through the bar and the double doors to the pool terrace. My suite is in a modern wing to one side of the pool, with a glass balcony with blue and yellow tiled sides and the kind of light that fills you up like a balloon. I collapse on the bright white linen and stare at the ceiling, which is painted with ships and fish. Kind of weird, painting a ceiling with fish. Then I spend twenty minutes underneath the fiercest jets of water that the state-of-the-art solar-powered system can muster. This way, even I can't tell if I'm crying or simply washing my face.

# HARRY

'Hotel Sebastian.' I heard her loud and clear as she got into her taxi and pulled away.

'Sebastian was a king.' The cabbie looks at me in his rear-view mirror a little too often for my liking. 'Very sad, a lost king of Portugal. Is she your girlfriend?'

'How do you lose a king?'

He lets go of the steering wheel entirely for two very long seconds, gesturing in the air. 'Big battle, terrible disaster.'

I eye the meter. It's ticking down quickly. 'Will four euros thirty get me to the Sebastian?'

It didn't. So now I'm standing on the side of a road with nothing in my pockets at all, a half-hour's walk from my destination. I start moving, the roadside gravel crunching beneath my flip-flops. The sea softly reflects the darkening sky on my left, glimpsed between buildings as I make my way. Nightjars are churring like tiny motorbikes, deep in the trees that line the verge.

I'm following Precious mainly out of curiosity. There's also an element of need because she has cash and I don't and I would like to eat sometime in the next few days. I would obviously like to kiss her as well, although there was something about her on the dockside which is making my palms sweat at the thought of trying.

*Can't you smell the adventure?*

The road is branching. I take a left, working on the assumption that any hotel Precious chooses will be close to the sea, which is fine by me. The air is scented and warm, the sound of the waves close by. The nightjars churr louder.

*Doesn't it thrill you? Make you feel alive?*

'I'm not doing this for you,' I tell Dad. 'If that's what you're getting at.'

My stomach rumbles. The croquettes were a long time ago. I take a swig of water and adjust my hat. But when I reach the gates of the Hotel Sebastian, footsore and a little sweaty, I pause. Setting foot on the cobbled drive with its scented flowers and lights in the low-hanging trees in a market-bought baseball cap feels like a desecration. I lose my nerve about ten feet in, and scuttle sideways on to the close-cropped grass. I then move, ninja-like, from shadow to shadow, waiting for the searchlights, the machine-gun fire. *Shoot all board shorts on sight.*

It's a long driveway. Every now and again I leap into a shrub as a set of gleaming headlights sweeps up or down the neatly arranged cobbles. Cicadas saw away, slicing through the strong smell of jasmine with their wings. The hotel looms like a wedding cake up ahead, set against palm trees and glittering ocean.

The drive widens into an elegant turning circle of patterned grey and white before a flight of marble steps to the hotel lobby. I stop in the last puddle of shadow, and attempt to find my courage. Millionaires wear T-shirts and board shorts, I reason. Look at Mark Zuckerberg.

I take one final sideways shrub-jump as a long black Bentley sweeps around the turning circle and stops. A white Boxster follows hard behind. A couple of flunkies in blue and yellow jackets hurry into view, and I hear the expensive clunk of several hundred grand's worth of car door being opened and voices exchanging greetings. Peeping out from my bush, I observe Ricky Silva himself buttoning his jacket and making his way up the hotel steps. I recognise him right away from the papers. Precious echoes at me through his large brown eyes and the set of his jaw.

Two people get out of the Boxster: a guy I don't recognise, and a guy I do. Nathan Payne passes so close to my chosen shrub that I can smell his shower gel. He is having a conversation with the man in front, too low for Ricky Silva to overhear.

'But they grabbed her, Dad! What was I supposed to do?'
'Wait in the car.'
'I don't want to wait in the car, I want—'
The casual force of the backhanded slap that sends Nathan staggering backwards makes me catch my breath.
'I said,' the older man repeats, 'wait in the bloody car.'

Nathan leans against the car door as his father mounts the steps of the hotel. With his head bowed, he gets back into the Boxster.

Sorry as I now feel for the poor bastard, I switch my attention back to the lobby, where Precious's dad and Payne Senior are at the main desk. They head left. I take several bunny-hops left as well, keeping in the shadows until I am round the side of the hotel. There is a bench nestled beneath a window, and that's where I sit down. The window, helpfully, is open. Voices drift over my head.

'Your boy not joining us?'

'He isn't feeling well. Sends his apologies. You know what kids are like.'

'Not really. My daughter and I aren't close.'

It's easy enough to tell the voices apart. Payne Senior's voice is smooth and wide as the mouth of the River Thames. Ricky Silva's accent has a grain to it like a smoky oak lintel above a pub fireplace. I catch the sound of a clinking glass, the expensive gurgle of something poured over ice.

'Come now, Ricky. That daughter of yours is the apple of your eye.'

'We don't grow many apples in Portugal, Aiden. Whisky?'

'The papers are all over her disappearance. Must be hard. Any news?'

There is the sound of a cut-glass tumbler being placed with some force on a table. 'No.'

'Kids have minds of their own these days,' Aiden Payne says sympathetically. 'Never think to let their parents know what they're going to do next. I'm so sorry about your boat too. But I imagine it was insured?'

Ricky Silva is silent.

'Ah,' says Aiden Payne.

More whisky. More clinking.

'In all the years that we've known each other, you have come through everything, Ricky. This can't be the end.'

'Even I have my limits.'

'Have you thought any more about the site I mentioned last month?'

'I don't want to sell.'

'You know how expensive it will be to develop.'

'I don't want to sell,' Ricky repeats.

'You may have to.'

There is silence for a while.

'Let's take a look at the site together on Tuesday,' Aiden Payne suggests. 'I've only ever seen it on paper.'

'We can look,' Ricky concedes. It sounds like someone's pulling his teeth out.

A cicada screeches so close to my ear that I almost leap from my bench.

'Tennis in the morning?' Aiden Payne says. 'That, at least, you can win.'

Ricky Silva sighs. 'I am winning very little at the moment. Why will tennis be any different?'

'I think I'll join you in that whisky now,' says Aiden Payne.

'I'm no longer thirsty, help yourself. I will see you in the morning, seven o'clock on the court. I hope that you have a comfortable night in my hotel.'

The sound of a door shutting, followed by that of more whisky pouring into a glass and the single bleep of speed dial.

'Any word yet?' Aiden Payne says to whoever's on the other end.

There's a pause. From all the clinking, it sounds like he's drinking the whisky faster than he should.

'Any idea where she went?' he says eventually. 'Stay where you are in case she calls. Let me know. Yes. Yes. Me too.'

I hear another beep signifying that the conversation is over.

'*Women*,' Aiden Payne mutters.

# PRECIOUS

The contents of a mini-bar don't last nearly as long as you think they will. I squint at the empties. Jack Daniel's: grim. Port: pure hangover. The Amarguinha was my favourite. Sweet and almondy. Swalmondy.

I reach for the phone.

'Bottle of Amarguinha to suite 104. Lots of ice.'

I'm feeling slurry, and slurry is good when you speak my father's language. My language. Half my language, half my blood cells. When the Amarguinha arrives, I take it out on to the balcony and plonk it down on the table alongside the bucket of ice and a glass. I offer the glass hospitably to the tiled Sebastian standing beside me with his blue and yellow shield and his dark blue eyes, but he doesn't take me up on the offer. So what if he shows up naked on beaches? Or wears armour on a golf course?

The first glass goes down like molten marzipan. The second coats my teeth in a kind of almond veneer. By the third, it's probably my imagination but Harry Temple appears to be standing below my balcony and shouting something.

'Piss off,' I say, squinting at him through the middle of my glass.

He does. Satisfied, I pour the fourth glass and drink it all in one go.

Someone is banging on my door now. I'm illogically pleased to see that it's Harry, and fling my arms round him before I remember that he dumped me in Albufeira. So then I hit him instead, and it's just like it was in the mist when Sebastian first showed up to screw with my head.

'You're drunk,' says Harry as he fends me off.

I stop hitting him and collapse on the bed. 'You *left*,' I accuse.

He wavers unnervingly above me. 'You left first. Your father's here, by the way. So is Nathan, and Nathan's dad. Is this your dad's hotel?'

'*One* of my dad's hotels,' I correct. I squint at him. 'I don't like your hat.'

He removes the green and blue monstrosity so his hair tumbles around his face and then he sits beside me on the bed. 'I heard Nathan's dad and your dad talking earlier. There was all this stuff about your father's business being in trouble and then Nathan's dad made this strange call—'

'You smell salty,' I say.

Harry sighs, rubs his face. 'I had a wash in the sea.'

'Ooh. Naked?'

'What kind of question is that?'

193

Naked makes me think of the rambler in the mist on the beach. I peer out on to the balcony, but Sebastian is tucked round the side and out of sight. And also grouted on to the balcony wall. The room swims. Suddenly the fish on the ceiling make sense.

Harry pushes a glass of water into my hand. I drink it, make a face.

'Where did you get that?' he asks, eyeing the phone on the bedside table. 'Does it belong to the Terminators? Where *are* the Terminators?'

I take a lock of Harry's hair between my fingers. It's rough and dry and loaded with salt. I realise I'd like to smell it, so I pull it closer. Harry's face follows. His nose is now only a couple of centimetres from mine.

'Sebastian caused the car accident,' I confide. 'He was wearing a suit of armour at the time.'

'Is this the Nathan Payne game, level two?'

I rub Harry's hair between my fingers and breathe in the deep salt smell of him. I place the curl on my top lip and imagine myself with a caramel-coloured salt-smelling moustache. 'The naked rambler was Sebastian too,' I say. It all makes perfect sense inside my head, but I'm not sure I'm conveying it very well. 'King Sebastian.'

Harry puts his hands on mine, trying to remove his hair from my fingers.

'I don't know why he was naked the first time I saw him,' I continue, trying to see the answers through the almond fog. 'I guess he hadn't had time to get dressed. I'd only just summoned him, you see. With my hair.'

'You summoned him with your hair,' Harry repeats.

'He comes when you need him.' I seem to have both hands on Harry's face now. Which is interesting. 'When I threw my hair in the sea, he heard me. Like a sort of . . . hairy text alert. With hair.'

Harry Temple, super close. Blue eyes. Long eyelashes.

'And then he was wearing armour by the roadside.' I give his face an experimental tug and he comes closer. Our noses touch. 'So he dazzled the golfer who hit the ball that smashed the windscreen that lived in the house that Jack built.'

'Precious,' says Harry. 'I don't think—'

Kissing Harry Temple is a bit like kissing the sea. There are waves, rising and falling and swirling about. Salt and moisture. A surging current that catches me and pulls me down to mysterious blue-green depths.

'Oh God,' Harry mumbles against my mouth. 'This is such a bad idea.'

The feel of his shoulder blades under my fingers takes me straight back to the misty beach. I imagine we look pretty sexy, him with his hair and brown back which appears to have shed its T-shirt and me in a robe that's half fallen off. I still have my phone in one hand.

Harry jerks back, breathing hard. 'What are you doing?'

We're out of focus. I ditch the clip, disappointed.

'Were you *filming* that?'

'No need to make it sound pervy,' I object. 'Everyone does it.'

'I don't.'

He gets to his feet and finds his T-shirt, which has migrated across the room.

'That shouldn't have happened,' he says, looking pained.

More rejection. Just what I need.

'It was only a kiss,' I mutter, pulling my robe back round myself. 'You don't have to be all dramatic about it.'

'Right,' he says after a moment. 'Can I take a shower?'

'Do what you like.'

He disappears into the bathroom. Irritably, I stalk back on to the balcony and help myself to more Amarguinha. Briefly I consider checking out Harry in the shower, but decide against it. Because I've just seen something *much* more interesting down by the pool terrace.

# HARRY

I turn the shower to its coldest setting and stand there with my face pointing straight up at the stinging water. I didn't think I was the kind of person who made out with girls too drunk to know their own names. But I clearly hit some kind of reset button the day I looked into Medusa's eyes and put my feet in the waves.

What if this whole descent-into-madness thing extends further than a simple inability to survive away from the sea? Nathan Payne isn't the only one living on the edge, I realise with a dull sense of irony.

I turn the shower up, shave with a complimentary razor and wash myself thoroughly from head to toe with real soap and proper shampoo. A vast amount of dirt swills down the drain by my feet. Who was Aiden Payne calling? What site were he and Ricky Silva talking about? I wish I knew what was going on. As I work the hotel toothbrush around my teeth, I think about the taste of almonds on Precious's tongue, and am forced to turn the shower to cold again.

After about twenty minutes, I re-emerge. Precious isn't in the suite. Spying half a club sandwich lying on a plate on the balcony table, I sidle outside and finish it off, feeling like a ravenous tramp on a bin-dive.

I nearly leap into the hotel garden at the sight of someone standing just to my right. It's a tiled figure set into the dividing wall between this balcony and the next one. The figure is around my height, with a shield and a full set of armour. *EL REI DOM SEBASTIÃO* it says over his head. Sebastian. The cabbie's king. And also apparently a naked rambler who shows up on roadsides wearing armour. The words *O DESEJADO* are written in smaller letters underneath his name. Trailing through my scant knowledge of Spanish and zero knowledge of Portuguese, I try and fail to fit a meaning to the word.

I wonder if Precious has gone to the main building to find her dad. I wonder if she even *heard* me when I mentioned her dad. I hope she'll talk to me when she's sobered up. Maybe she won't even remember what happened. I wish I could forget too.

I reach for the suite phone.

'Twice in one day?' says Mum in some astonishment. 'Have you eaten? Do you need money?'

I need a rail ticket and a passport too, but I don't mention that.

'I'll organise a transfer in the morning,' she says when I agree that money might be an idea. 'Where should I send it to? We went on holiday to Lagos a few years back when Dad was in his paragliding phase, I don't suppose you're anywhere near Lagos?'

'I think it's the next place along the coast,' I say.

'Are you on the coast? You don't like the coast.'

'It's growing on me.' Like fungus.

She promises to get the bank on to the money transfer first thing tomorrow, because despite today being Sunday, she has contacts who can do that kind of thing. One of the dogs has bad breath and needs eight teeth taken out. Another one has dodgy anal glands. Life at the bank ticks on. Usual takeaway earlier, Mohit asked about me. I look out of the window at the dark night, and listen to the gentle sound of splashing around the softly lit pool and the nightjars and cicadas and faintly barking dogs way off in the distance, and breathe in the scent of the night flowers.

'But you're OK and that's the main thing,' Mum concludes. 'When are you coming back?'

'When I can,' I say truthfully.

The suite is lovely and peaceful and the gentle hum of the air-con is making me yawn. As I hang up the phone, I realise how exhausted I am. I've hardly slept in the past forty-eight hours, and the weeks prior to that weren't exactly restful.

I lie cautiously on the edge of the bed closest to the bathroom and furthest from the door. Just a quick nap, I think. Then I'll move to the sofa. It'll be better on the sofa. Safer, for when she returns. If she returns.

What am I going to do when she returns?

# NATHAN

Leaning against the tiles beneath the surface of the pool, I poke moodily at my back tooth with my tongue. It feels loose.

Dad is angry but won't explain why. I don't know if I was supposed to stop the kidnappers or whether – when he said that stuff about 'leave the sharks alone' he meant that the sharks worked for him somehow or . . . I don't *know* what he meant.

*You'll work it out, Nathan. You're my son.*

Except I can't work out a single bloody thing. Dad makes all this shit look easy, and it's not.

I spread my arms out on the smooth marble edges of the pool and study my body. My chest looks good from this angle. Any girl would be lucky to have me.

'Nathan Payne who's not in Spain. Why are you in my father's pool?'

I stare. Precious Silva is balancing on the diving board at the deep end, pointing her toes like a deranged ballerina.

Her hair has somehow improved. She's wearing a toweling robe and in the dim pool lighting I can see a flash of her long brown legs.

'Why aren't you in the back of a car?' I manage to say.

'Accident.'

'And the two guys—'

'Hospital,' she says, squinting at me. 'I think.'

The sharks are in hospital. A faint spark of understanding glows inside me. Is that why Dad was mad? I lost Precious, but then the sharks got her, but then they lost her too? *But now I have her back.* I can still fix this. Prove to Dad that I'm not the waste of space he thinks I am.

'What are you, some kind of secret ninja?' I say in delight.

'Maybe,' she says, doing a few bleary karate moves. The diving board thrums beneath her feet. 'And now I'm thinking about swimming. With you.' She wobbles and rights herself. 'Only *I don't have anything on underneath,*' she says in a theatrical whisper.

She wasn't this interesting in London. I dip into the water, whip my trunks off and wave them in the air like a damp blue flag. It's clearly the funniest thing she's ever seen, and she laughs until she chokes. The flash from her phone makes angels dance across my eyeballs.

'Are you coming in?' I say in my most inviting voice.

She lets the robe drop to her feet and kicks it off to the side. There's now around six feet of nakedness on the board above me, whooping and bouncing. It's unsettling, how easily she does it. Watching her cleave the water reminds me of a heron I saw once, darting deep with its long beak and skinny neck. Something about her makes me put my trunks back on.

When she comes to the surface, she lies on her back and wafts her arms from side to side. 'Seals can sleep under the sea,' she tells the stars in the sky. 'Did you know that?'

'How much have you drunk?' I find myself asking.

'Boring question. I'm going to go again.'

'Keep your voice down,' I say uneasily.

She swims and sloshes towards the steps. 'I'm naked,' she sings, giggling as she goes. 'I'm naked, I'm naked.'

People are starting to peer out of the windows in the bar. At any minute, Ricky Silva or my dad will see. I feel the situation slipping out of my control.

'I don't think you should dive again,' I begin as she skips back towards the diving board. 'We'll get turned out of the pool, and my dad won't—'

She flicks two fingers at me. Bounces a little higher, dives a little deeper. She's under for such a long time that I start to wonder if she's ever coming up. I peer beneath the dark surface of the pool and try to pick out her shape against the ripples. A darkness flows past my feet, and I almost scream. I am at the point of believing that she's drowned when she resurfaces.

'I really think you should get out now,' I plead.

'You're so handsome with your lovely shiny wet chest.'

Weirdly, I feel more naked than I did with my trunks off.

'Your cheekbones make me want to cry,' she continues. 'Kiss me. What's the matter with you? You're a guy, I'm a girl. Isn't this how it's supposed to go?'

'Sir? Madam?' says a voice. 'Would you mind getting out of the pool? Some of our guests have complained at the noise.'

I blink water out of my eyes to see the night manager standing by the side of the pool. He's holding Precious's towelling robe.

Embarrassed, I pull Precious towards the shallow end at arm's length, bundle her out and wrap her in her robe. Gripping her swaying body with one hand, I fumble in the pocket of my own robe. 'You won't tell my father, will you?' I say to the night manager as I press a note into his hands.

Precious pouts as the manager disappears back inside the hotel. 'Well that was boring,' she says, reaching for my hand. 'Let's go to your room.'

The girl's a runaway train. I don't much like being strapped to the rails.

'Don't you have a room?' I try.

'I want to come to YOUR room,' she says, loudly.

'Fine.' I make little shooing motions with my hands, ushering her along. 'Just move, will you? People are *looking*.'

She takes the stairs ahead of me, swinging her skinny hips from side to side and singing at the top of her voice. I find myself missing the girl who looked at me with passive brown eyes and never said a word.

My room is big, white and airy, and there's a tiled dude on a horse out on the balcony. Precious strikes a pose, hands on hips, and looks down her long nose at me.

'Come on then,' she says with a hiccup. 'Show me what the fuss is about.'

'You're here to sleep,' I say, averting my eyes. 'Just sleep, OK?'

I head into the bathroom, shut the door and lean my forehead against the mirror above the basin. I've got her. Dad will be pleased. I mustn't lose her again. The memory of Ricky Silva's broken boat brushes at me like a cobweb.

I leave the bathroom with caution, looking around in case she jumps on me. She's out cold, thank God. I head outside, slide the glass door shut and take out my phone. A trick of perspective makes the tiled guy on my balcony wall looks like he's turning his horse towards me.

'This better be good,' says Dad.

'I've got Precious,' I tell him.

I savour his disbelief.

'I've got her,' I repeat. 'And before you ask, Ricky doesn't know she's here.'

Dad is quiet for ages. 'Good,' he says at last.

I glow.

'Take her somewhere tomorrow. I'm playing tennis with Ricky at seven, you need to have left by then. We're visiting the site on Tuesday, when, all being well, we'll complete the deal. I'll let you know when I'm done.'

'But it's Sunday today,' I say, feeling a sudden kick of dismay. 'What am I going to do with her for two days?'

'Use your imagination. I don't care where you go, just keep her away from the coast. I don't want her anywhere near me, do you understand?'

'Two days is a long time,' I begin.

Dad is getting irritable. 'You have money. You have the car. A lot is riding on this, Nathan. If you get it wrong, then we are very much back to the beginning of your rehabilitation into a useful member of this family.'

'Dad,' I say. 'The guys who took her yesterday, were they working—'

But he hangs up halfway through my question.

I head back inside. Precious is sprawled sideways across the bed with her mouth open, so I set the alarm on my watch and lie down on the sofa. As I close my eyes, I swear the tiled guy starts galloping towards me through the balcony doors, sword outstretched.

# HARRY

When I wake up, the light pouring through the uncurtained window is hard and bright. The other side of the bed remains rumpled from our drunken snog last night, but it's clear no one has slept in it. Where is Precious? I fall back on to the pillow. When am I allowed to stop worrying about her?

Her dad is here, I remind myself. She's probably with him in some kind of Presidential Suite at the top of the hotel with a roof terrace and a masseur and everything.

After another long shower, I make my way across the beautifully mown lawn, around some big orange flowers that look like pterodactyls and past a few lemon trees which I'm stupidly thrilled to see have actual live lemons on them. I stand for a moment to watch the gleaming swallows dipping down for a dainty drink at the pool, then enter the cool of the hotel dining room through the terrace doors. Trying to look as if I belong.

The place is half empty. After giving the room number to the waitress, I take a seat by the window, eyeing the breakfast spread with something approaching awe. There's fruit on there I've never seen before. Meats and cheeses and salads and bright yellow pastries. A rainbow of juices, silver state-of-the-art coffee machines, an elaborate tower of bread as high as my head. I come away with a large doughnut and a slice of watermelon, which I eat with my gaze on the wide, shifting, sparkling ocean beyond the white deck parasols around the pool.

Halfway through a third round of food – sesame-seed bagels, cream cheese and slices of smoked salmon – loud voices make me turn towards the tiled and panelled reception room through the dining-room doors. I rise automatically from my seat, brushing doughnut crumbs from my shirt, as Ricky Silva comes into the dining room, a pair of hairy ham-like legs protruding from a large pair of very white tennis shorts.

He's not very tall, I realise. In fact, he probably comes up to my shoulder: a fact I failed to clock last night as he took the hotel steps two at a time. But the power of the man has nothing to do with his size. He takes a seat by the window and a waitress brings him a huge coffee and a large plate of pastries as soon as his bum hits the chair. I glance behind him, hoping to see Precious following in his wake. Instead, I get an eyeful of Aiden Payne, his streaked grey-blond hair slicked away from his face. Like Ricky, he's in tennis whites.

Ricky Silva indicates the chair opposite with a flick of his heavy, bear-like fingers. Aiden Payne's hands by contrast are slim and long-fingered. He pulls out the chair offered, nods at the waitress who brings coffee.

I sit there, irresolute.

*Talk to the man. Tell him his daughter was here. Ask him if he's seen her.*

For once, my father is talking sense.

'Can I help you?' says Aiden Payne, glancing up at me like he's the one in charge.

'Mr Silva?' I say.

Ricky Silva attacks his pastries with a sort of dog-like ferocity. 'I'm busy,' he says through a mouthful.

'It's about your daughter,' I begin.

He's on his feet so fast that I step back. A hairy paw takes the collar of my shirt and begins to twist. The fur on his hands is soft, so it feels like being slowly strangled by a cat. Aiden Payne pours himself a cup of coffee.

'What do you want?' says Ricky Silva.

'I don't want . . . anything,' I wheeze. Apart from being allowed to breathe.

'Do you have my daughter? Do you know where she is?'

'No,' I squeak. I want to explain but I can't get the words out.

'Leave the kid alone, Ricky,' says Payne, munching on a croissant. 'You just have to look at him to see he couldn't kidnap a kitten. Read about Ricky's daughter have you, kid? Thought you'd try it on?'

The world is dancing, receding into spots. With a snort, Silva drops me. Rubbing my throat, I back away from the table. I've lost my appetite.

If her own father hasn't seen her, and the Terminators are out of the picture, then where the hell is she? I sidle fretfully out of the dining room and into the tiled hallway with its massive Cinderella staircase.

'Has Precious Silva checked out?' I ask at the reception desk.

The lady stops tapping at her keyboard and looks me straight in the eye. 'Miss Silva is not staying here,' she says.

I squint at her name badge. 'Sorry to disagree with you, Luisa, but I know she's staying here. I've seen her.'

I feel a hairy hand on my shoulder.

'What's your name, son?' says Ricky Silva very close to my ear.

Shit. He's come to finish the job.

'Harry Temple,' I say, swallowing. 'Sir.'

'Tell me what you know about my daughter, Harry Temple.'

Perhaps he's not going to strangle me this time.

'Well,' I begin cautiously as he pushes me towards the marble steps and down towards to the big cobbled turning circle outside, 'she was here last night.'

His face sags. 'Here?'

'We've been travelling together on and off for the past couple of days,' I tell him. 'But yesterday she disappeared, and then I found her here and she was drunk and weird. Something crazy happened with her mother and a couple of kidnappers, but otherwise she was in good shape. I was in her room.'

His already near-black eyes darken to midnight.

'Nothing happened,' I add quickly. 'Well, there was a bit of snogging but that's as far as it went. We only met two days ago.'

Ricky Silva, hotel-owning criminal mogul. *Protective* hotel-owning criminal mogul. Ricky Silva loves his daughter. I'm telling Ricky Silva I spent the night in his daughter's room after only having met her two days ago. All these thoughts and more tumble through my head as his hairy hand bites into my shoulder and I think about broken collarbones.

'We'll discuss the room thing another time,' he growls. 'What did you say about her mother?'

'I think her mother had Precious kidnapped,' I say helplessly. 'But she got away yesterday and now I can't find her.'

'Why would my wife kidnap our daughter?'

'Something to do with your divorce.' This is getting a bit personal, like I'm waving his grubby boxers under his nose. 'I don't know the details, I just know what I heard.'

'And where is Precious now?'

'That's what I'm trying to tell you,' I say, swallowing. 'I don't—'

The Boxster is no longer parked on the cobbled sweep, where it was last night. Once again, I have the answer to an unasked question.

Nathan Payne.

'Actually, I think I *do* know where she is,' I say as clarity dawns. 'Or who she's with anyway. And can I just add, when I say we were snogging—'

Aiden Payne appears, coffee cup in hand. 'Want me to fetch hotel security, Ricky?'

Ricky Silva shoves me down the steps so I stumble and almost land flat on my face on the cobbles at the bottom. He puts his hand into his pocket and pulls something out. For a long and awful moment, I think he's going to shoot me. Instead, a roll of something hits me hard in the eye.

'You shouldn't pay these people.' Leaning against the door, Aiden Payne takes a sip of coffee. 'They only come back for more.'

'This one won't,' Ricky says. 'Will you, son?'

With one hand over my watering eye, I pick up the fat roll of coloured paper notes. I've heard of throwing money at people, but I never thought anyone would throw it at me. Aiden Payne disappears back into the wooden darkness of the lobby, but Ricky Silva's eyes are still full of questions. I take a risk.

'You shouldn't trust him,' I say, nodding at Aiden Payne's back.

I think I'm telling Ricky something he already knows.

'Find her,' he says quietly.

And then he's gone.

# PRECIOUS

'Shit,' says Nathan in horror.

I mop my mouth as he squeals the car into the shabby little petrol station and slams on the brakes. 'I'm sorry,' I begin, sitting lower in the Boxster's bucket seat.

'It's all down the side!'

'At least I got it outside the car.'

I definitely feel better, but those almonds have a lot to answer for. It's almost cool, puking down a Porsche. I would post something about it, only I can't find the Terminator phone.

'Go into the petrol station and get antiseptic wipes! And air freshener. God!'

It's been an interesting morning already, and it's hardly begun. In addition to waking up in Nathan Payne's bed with the headache from hell and zero recollection of how I got there, I have been offered a room-service breakfast at dawn that I was very much not ready for, and treated to the sight of Nathan in the shower whilst wearing Nathan's polo shirt and a pair of his cargo shorts. I still have Mum's money, which was in the pocket of the bathrobe I apparently slept in, so I should be able to buy more clothes and yet another pair of shoes when we get to wherever it is we're going. The shoe thing is getting a little out of control this week.

I pad barefoot to the till to buy the wipes and air freshener and a packet of mints. There isn't much traffic yet. Set against the deep blue sky up ahead, the mountains are looking considerably higher than they did yesterday.

Nathan is hosing the side of the Boxster with the garage jet spray. He snatches the wipes from my hand and attempts to clean up the bit around the window.

'Did you already tell me where we're going?' I ask, chewing mints to take my mind off my unsettled stomach. 'I've forgotten.'

'Monchique,' he says, stopping to wipe his forehead.

I squint up at the mountains. 'Why are we going there?'

'You said you wanted to last night.'

I stare at him in surprise. As a kid I used to gaze at the mountains of Monchique from the deck of the boat while Mum took pictures of herself in her latest range of bikinis and Dad took telephone calls and smoked cigars and occasionally steered us away from over-ambitious jet-skiers. The mountains had seemed far away, but on clear days also close enough to touch. I don't remember ever wanting to go there, though. I was more interested in sailing where the sea grew wilder. Maybe one day reaching the end of the world.

'OK,' I say doubtfully.

Nathan's got a bit wet with the hosing, and his linen shirt is turning see-through. A little bit of chest hair is developing in the tiny vee on his collarbone. The sudden stab of lust dissolves quite a lot of my confusion. Another perfect post that will have to stay in my imagination. I must have left the phone back at the hotel, along with most of my memory. I bite my lip in vexation.

'I'm sorry to ask you this,' I say, 'but did we . . .? Last night?'

Nathan hoses the passenger door harder. 'No.'

'Did we, um, kiss?' I seem to remember a kiss.

'No.'

All the insecurities I've been trying so hard to overcome crash back over my aching head in a terrible wave. First Harry, leaving like he did. Now Nathan. I slump back into the antiseptic-smelling Boxster. There's only so much reinvention a girl can do. Underneath I'm still me.

'I suppose you didn't fancy me,' I say glumly.

Nathan puts the jet hose carefully back on its little metal cradle, then rubs his hands through his hair. It stands up all over his head in dark tufts.

'You were drunk,' he says.

I slide my sunglasses up my nose, the better to hide behind. I'm getting another wave of Amarguinha repeating on me, like an almond-scented horseman of the apocalypse.

'Either you fancied me or you didn't,' I mutter.

He finishes buffing the car door and blasts the air freshener a bit too close to my nose. 'You weren't the same

Precious who skulks around the edge of parties in London, that's for sure.'

'That's good, though, right?' I say. 'London Precious was boring with bad hair. I don't want to be her any more.'

He gets back into the car, turns on the purring engine and we swing back on to the road. 'Be whoever you want to be, Precious Metal,' he says, keeping his eyes straight ahead. 'If you can.'

I'd like to close my eyes, but that just makes me feel ill again. I wish I could remember more. I lost track quite early on. I do, however, remember all too clearly that it was my own mother who brought me to this point.

'What drives you, do you think?' I ask as we twist around the roads, passing the occasional glimpse of blue sea between the hills.

'What?'

'We're all driven by something.' I put up my hand, turning my palm this way and that. The wind buffets my fingers. 'With my dad, it's ambition. With my mother, it's money. You're driving this car, but what's driving you?'

'This car's automatic. It pretty much drives itself.'

'I think I'm driven by rage,' I say.

He glances at me. 'You don't seem the angry type.'

'You don't know me,' I point out. 'Apart from calling me a deckchair once, I don't think you ever said one word to me before yesterday afternoon. So how do you know I'm not the angry type?'

The automatic gearbox changes again. The road flies away beneath our wheels.

'What are your parents like?' I say presently.

He takes a sharp corner. The Boxster holds the road like Spider-Man on the Empire State Building. 'They're parents,' he says.

'My mother is the demon witch from hell,' I inform him. 'She had me kidnapped, can you believe it?'

'Your mother hired the sharks?' Nathan says in surprise.

'To prove my dad was an unfit parent or something,' I say. It feels just as unbelievable now as it did yesterday. How can a mother do that to her own child? 'All she did was prove herself even more of an unfit parent than him.'

Does this perspective shift change things where Dad's concerned? I decide to consider the question when my head isn't hurting quite so much.

In the absence of my phone, I fiddle around with the contents of the Boxster's glove compartment. There's a sketch pad in there, filled with scribbled faces: children playing, an old man sleeping, skateboarders in full flight, one or two dogs. I recognise Nathan's style from all the work that used to hang in the corridors at school.

I realise with a sudden shock that my results come through next week. Which means A-level results are through already. I wonder if Nathan knows his. The ones he took, at least. I can hear it now, the gossip that followed us out of school and into the first couple of weeks of the holidays. *Nathan Payne, artist. Nathan Payne, Sixth Form Art Prize. Nathan Payne, definitely heading to Art School. Nathan Payne no-show. Nathan Payne absent.*

'Why didn't you show up for your last Art exam?' I ask outright, showing once again my natural talent for diplomacy.

A spray of gravel spatters the windscreen as a large truck rattles past, tipping on its wheels towards a dizzying drop through the trees.

'I was busy,' he says.

'Busy?' I echo disbelievingly. 'It was an A-level.'

'Anyone can do Art. You don't need an A-level to prove it.'

'You need one to go to Art School, though.'

'Maybe I don't want to go to Art School.'

I laugh, which hurts my head. 'But you're famous for wanting to go to Art School! It's all anyone talks about when they talk about you.'

'Who talks about it?'

'Every girl in school. Half the boys too.'

'Well, I'm famous for the wrong reasons then.'

I put the sketchbook back in the glove compartment and rest my head against the window, letting the cool glass press against my pounding temple. The mountains are getting greener as I watch, with a hint of eucalyptus that wafts uninvited into the car. My ears are starting to pop. In my mind I catch the flash of sunlight on armour. I *want* to believe it was him. Does that make me insane?

'Do you believe in the supernatural?' I ask next.

'Do you ever stop asking questions?'

Maybe I shouldn't have said what I said about Art School.

'Ignore me if you want,' I say, apologetically.

He sighs. 'Do you mean, like, ghosts?'

217

'Sebastian's not a ghost, exactly,' I say, feeling my way around my hangover. 'He's more of a legend.'

'Sebastian's the saint who's always stuck with arrows in art galleries.'

'Not that one. The Portuguese king. He went into battle with twenty thousand men in Africa and they all got killed. His body was never found so there are all these conspiracy theories about him, about how he'll return one day. Like King Arthur, or Elvis.'

In this wind, Nathan's hair looks like a cool, chocolate Mr Whippy. 'Did your dad name the hotel after him?'

I lift a shoulder. 'Dad named his whole business after him.'

'I thought your dad's business was *Desejado* something.'

'Sebastian is *O Desejado*. It means the Desired One. Dad's obsessed with all the Portuguese legends, but especially Sebastian. When he chose Sebastian for the hotel, no one was surprised except Mum, who wanted him to name it after her.' I frown. 'I don't remember telling you the Sebastian was my dad's hotel.'

'You told me a lot of things last night.' The car purrs a bit louder, like someone's tickling its belly. 'When you weren't getting naked on the hotel diving board.'

I snort in shock. 'I didn't.'

'Oh, you did.'

That means Nathan has seen my . . . He's . . . And he still didn't kiss me?

'Nathan,' I say quietly. 'Are you gay?'

He shoots me the kind of look that would once have destroyed me, but which now just makes me want to take a close-up of his face. I think perhaps I'm still drunk.

'No,' he says.

What's the next level up on mortally embarrassed? *Im*mortally embarrassed?

'I think I'd like to get out of the car,' I whisper.

'It's only five kilometres to this place.' The sun is reflecting on Nathan's sunglasses, turning his eyes into twin pools of fire. 'You can get out there.'

'You don't have to babysit me.' I don't want to cry, that will completely wreck the illusion that I'm sophisticated and cool and worth all this time and effort.

'I'm not babysitting you. I'm trying to work out what I think of you.'

I blink hard. 'It seems pretty clear to me.'

Nathan slows the car down and pulls into the side of the road. Shifting round in his seat, he takes off his sunglasses and studies me. He has such green eyes, like a cat or maybe a snake.

'You were a bit scary last night,' he says. 'I'm not used to girls taking charge.'

I feel a stir of indignation, followed by surprise. I took charge?

'Why shouldn't girls take charge?' I say.

What follows has a touch of VR about it. I see him coming towards me. I see a 3D world on either side of him, with some flapping floral-printed laundry, a green mountainside and a white church with a bell tucked into its little hat. Then I feel his lips and, apart from worrying that I might still taste of sick, I think wow, technology *has* moved on.

It's a weird thing, kissing, when you think about it.

I wrap my arms around the back of his head and join in with as much enthusiasm as my dehydrated brain allows. This is my fantasy! Right here! I'm in an awesome car with Nathan Payne and we are SNOGGING. Lotta wouldn't believe her eyes. The only thing that gives me slight pause is the unavoidable fact that Nathan was not responsible for the kiss I remember from last night. Without wishing to get too graphic, there's something about his method which is different. This is a little worrying. What else have I forgotten about yesterday?

'So,' he says, releasing me. 'Are we still going to this Monchique place?'

'Will you draw me when we get there?' I ask, trying to catch my breath.

'Maybe.'

I wonder if I should take his hand, but I don't want to push my luck. An image of Harry's hand holding mine in the Albufeira café sneaks into my head and I feel irrationally guilty for thinking about Nathan's hand in the first place.

We drive on, passing a number of pottery outlets and souvenir shops, and stop at a gypsy stall for some underwear, a T-shirt dress and a pair of pumps for less than thirty euros (what?) which I wear right off.

Onwards and upwards. The sides of the road are lifting away and above us now, stepped and green like wide, winding staircases in a crazed giant's castle. There are tiny bridges over scary ravines, and the air is cooler, with as much shadow as sunshine. I start wishing I'd bought a jumper from the gypsies as well. I twist round and peer into the narrow back seat, hoping Nathan's thought to bring one.

Something is lying in the footwell. But it's very much not a jumper.

'Nathan,' I say slowly. 'Why have you got Harry's guitar?'

# HARRY

I keep walking until I reach the main road where the cabbie dropped me last night. The cash in my pocket has been counted and verified, and I can now confirm that I have two and a half thousand euros in my possession. Ricky Silva expects me to find his daughter. Me. I can't decide if I feel proud or freaked out by the responsibility.

If I hadn't lost my passport, with this amount of cash I could head back to Faro and fly home. Except my paymaster is a mogul with friends who probably own firearms. Besides, Precious is someone that I have kissed, and I can't abandon someone that I have kissed and would in all honesty like to kiss again. And also, if I abandon her, Nathan Payne wins, and that won't do at all.

I flag down a taxi.

'Where you wanna go?' says the cabbie, a lady with candyfloss hair and a wart on her chin.

'Lagos,' I say, thinking of the money Mum's painstakingly transferred for me. There will be a hundred phone calls to consulates and embassies to confirm my passport-free identity in case I am a terrorist or a bank robber, and I'll be super-aware of Mr Silva's cash burning a hole in my pocket the whole time, but I have to do it so Mum can stop worrying. 'Take the road closest to the coast. Can I wind the window down?'

*The high-pitched sound of an engine whirs towards us over the hissing of the sea.*

*'It's a seagull,' Mum says as I squint at a dot in the sapphire sky.*

*'There's no such actual thing as a seagull,' I tell her. 'There's herring gulls and terns and stormy petrels and other birds I haven't learned yet. But it's not a bird anyway because birds don't look like that and they don't have engines either.'*

*'I'm sure you're right, David Attenborough,' says Mum.*

*She says she's tired of staring up at the sky and she wants a coffee. I pick myself up from the beach and dust the sand from my knees. We cross the road and a square patterned with grey and white stones, and head down a long street lined with cafés towards a statue made of grey stone with a pink coloured face and what looks like a cowpat on its head. A space helmet sits by its feet.*

*'Oh dear,' says Mum, squinting at the statue as we sit down at a table with a red awning over our heads. 'Who is that supposed to be?'*

*I have a chocolate milkshake. Mum has a tall coffee with a long silver spoon and a doughnut with very yellow custard inside.*

*Every time we hear a buzzing sound in the sky, we look up in case it's Dad.*

*'He won't crash, will he?' I ask.*

*Mum squeezes my hand across the black plastic table. Her expression makes me nervous. Anxiety fills my mouth, taking the taste of chocolate milk away.*

*'Of course not,' she says. 'I promise.'*

*I have a sense that you can't promise things like that. I push my milkshake away. I don't want it any more.*

A guy is playing the guitar outside the bank in Lagos, his fingers flashing away to the accompanying clink of coins falling into his guitar case, and I sit at a café for a while and listen enviously as I try to formulate a plan. Guys in movies come up with plans in less time than I take to sneeze. This plan isn't coming that fast.

I have Mum's two hundred euros in one pocket and Ricky Silva's roll of cash in the other. I decide to buy a pay-as-you-go phone and some credit to start with. Private detectives on TV are always buying phones. I feel furtive as I hand over the cash. The guy in the shop doesn't even watch me as I leave.

Outside the phone shop, there's a familiar statue standing on a plinth at the heart of a ripple of concentric cobbles, groups of people sitting around the space helmet by its feet feeding pigeons and eating ice-creams. The plinth says *EL REI D. SEBASTIÃO 1973*. This Sebastian looks like a girl, with a feminine face and very strange hair. He's nothing like the guy on the tiles at the hotel.

224

I try to see past his foolish, pink marble face. He looks lost, gazing towards the sea over the heads of the chattering families at his feet. In my mind, Dad bumbles over my head on his paraglider. We went out for pizza when he landed, and he bought me an inflatable crocodile. I rode on its green plastic head on the balcony of our holiday apartment and screamed every time Mum suggested I took it to the pool.

An idea puts its head cautiously over the parapet. I head back to the taxi rank on the waterfront.

'Sure I speak English,' the cabbie says when I check. 'Where do you want to go?'

I fumble in my pocket, doing my best not to pull out all the euros at once and scatter the cash like confetti along the street. 'How many other taxi drivers can you speak to on your radio?'

He considers. 'One hundred, maybe?'

'Can you ask them if they've seen a white Porsche Boxster in the area today? Spanish number plate, 1975 ADP. The driver is around my age. Brown hair, pleased with himself. He's with a girl who looks like a black-haired, bug-eyed giraffe.'

The cabbie takes the cash and I wait as he puts out a call on his handset. There is a lot of crackling, and a few jokes if the laughter is anything to go by. Maybe it's the giraffe thing.

'Two persons have seen a car and passengers like that,' the cabbie informs me after a while.

I feel a little astonished at my success. 'Where?'

'Driving to the Serra de Monchique.' At my blank face, the cabbie thumbs roughly beyond the town.

I have a bad feeling. 'This Serra place,' I say. 'Is it on the coast?'

The driver rubs his beard. 'No, no. Forty minutes away from the sea, maybe forty-five. You want to go there?'

# NATHAN

Precious said the sharks were hired by her mother. Nothing to do with Dad at all. The deeper I go into all of this, the less I understand.

We're really high up now, mountain tops peeping over the red roofs covered in pink flowers. Why the hell did I pick this place? The road is getting narrower all the time. As I squeeze around rough corners with millimetres to spare, I feel like a rat in a maze. I've often wondered what they do with the rats that fail. I imagine they get euthanised.

I can still smell vomit.

'How much space do I have on your side?' I check with Precious.

'*Turn around where possible,*' says the satnav.

Ladies pegging out their washing stare at the car as if it's a spaceship. The air smells of lemons and sunny cobblestones. I want to shout with relief as the road widens a little beside a rough, upward-leading path. We're the only ones here this early in the day. My heart rate slows and settles back to something normal as I park in front of a shed and get out of the car. The guitar stays tucked into the footwell. No one's going to steal something so bent, brown and – frankly – crap.

'You'll never see him again, you know,' Precious says, sliding out of her seat.

'It seemed a shame just leaving it in the café,' I repeat.

'Bring the sketch pad so you can draw me,' Precious suggests.

I let her scramble up the path ahead of me. Her bum looks decent in that T-shirt dress. I suppose I could do some drawing while we're here. Dad's not watching.

Even as I'm thinking this, my phone goes off. Sometimes it's like he's inside my brain, with me all the time, whether I want him there or not.

'Where are you, Nathan?'

My throat feels dry. 'Somewhere called Monchique. It's in the mountains, away from the coast like you said.' Away from pretty much everywhere, really.

'Stay there and don't screw up.'

I hate that phrase. 'The sharks were hired by Precious's mother,' I tell him. 'Did you know?'

'Just stay there,' Dad repeats, and hangs up.

I shove the phone into my back pocket and tackle the rising path in a wash of sudden energy. I think sometimes I'm driven by rage too.

It's a five-minute walk up through the trees. The building at the top doesn't look like a ruin at first, but the state of it becomes clearer the closer we get. The sound of guitar music drifts among the trees, as if Hairy Harry's guitar is serenading us from the car. It's a little creepy.

'What is this place?' Precious says, looking up at the doorway.

I check my phone. 'The Monastery of Our Lady of something. *Desterro*?'

'That means exile.' She moves into the shady atrium, trailing her fingers around the huge stone blocks. The inner door into the church bit is welded shut with a large piece of rust-red metal. 'Banishment.'

I almost jump out of my skin at the sound of cackling. Chickens, somewhere. There's a weathered stone shield set above the church door, depicting a lion wearing a crown. He's on his back feet, front paws raised in challenge, toothless but fearsome too.

*'O leão de Pero da Silva.'*

I spin round. The guy's hands are full of eggs, their flesh-coloured shells wedged between his dirty fingers. Behind him, a scruffy assortment of chickens cluck their rage. Precious shields her eyes against the sun. Portuguese coils out of her like rusty wire. The chicken farmer brightens and answers her, his words as tangled as hers.

'How's this for crazy?' Precious says. 'The lion over the door is the symbol of the Silva family. He says we can go in if we want. There are tiles. You'll like them, you're an artist.'

We follow the farmer through the ruin, picking our way over mops and buckets and a load of mysterious old-guy stuff. The monastery courtyard is a flagged, mossy space, almost entirely taken over by an enormous tree growing right in the middle. The chickens scratch and run around our feet. Sunlight slants in as best it can through the close-leaved branches over our heads. The tiles in one of the side ruins are translucent blue and white and very old, shaded by a fig tree nearly as big as the one in the main courtyard. There is falling masonry everywhere I look, and holes in the roof and walls. The air tastes neglected, damp and sad.

'Why did I say I wanted to come here, exactly?' Her eyes are looking clearer now, less hungover. 'I mean, it's sort of cool, but . . .'

'I bet this place hasn't changed for hundreds of years,' I say, keen to change the subject. 'What's through there?'

She moves through a sunlit door that makes me think about portals to other places. The farmer shoos me over with his dirty hands, and I follow her into a large, bright space where the patterned brick ceiling above has almost all collapsed and the windows are boarded up. I picture old priests in ruffs and nuns praying daily for deliverance, and I know how they feel. How am I going to keep Precious here for two whole days? It isn't exactly Disneyland.

'You said you would draw me,' she says, leaning back through the portal. 'Come on.'

She gives the farmer a fifty-euro note that makes him cluck as much as his chickens and we return to full daylight. There's a sunny patch of soft grass outside, beneath a large green tree, where she sits down. She isn't a natural model. She can't relax into position, moving her legs from side to side and tilting her head and making awkward faces. I'm taken powerfully back to life class, most particularly to a girl I had sex with in the art cupboard.

'Just look at the view,' I suggest.

My stuff is digging into my hip, so I take everything out of my pocket and set it on the ground as she settles down and stares with concentration at the scenery. The pad feels heavy in my hand and my fingers are weak. I haven't drawn anything since I did Ricky Silva as a shark, and you can tell.

'Can I talk?' she asks, gazing at the green ocean of hills and trees and roofs below us.

'Can I stop you?'

'I didn't use to talk this much.' Her jawline makes a hard line of shadow against her neck, which is long like a swan's. 'I had a lot of conversations inside my head, though, with myself. It must be that, coming out now.'

'Must be.'

'Do you have any brothers or sisters?'

'Not that I know about.'

'Why were you busy the day of your Art exam?'

I can still taste the blood at the back of my mouth. I wonder sometimes if it'll ever go away. I can hear the doctors too, discussing the chaos and violence of the party with Dad, how unfortunate it was that it grew so out of control. *No, he doesn't want to press charges. Do you, Nathan?*

'I just was,' I say. 'Stay still.'

It takes three attempts to get her proportions right. Modigliani and Giacometti would have loved her with her endless legs and curving neck. Now she's relaxing, she's not bad at keeping the pose. Leaning closer to the sketch pad, I shade the dimples in her collarbone. My fingers are starting to feel easier. I haven't lost it.

I'm so absorbed that I don't notice the point where she falls asleep. Sleep is good. Sleep kills time. I sketch some variations on a theme, putting a lion's head on her shoulders in one version and turning her into a grasshopper in another. The articulation of her elbows and knees and ankles and wrists is a bit like that of the wooden model figures we used to bend into compromising positions.

The sound of the guitar has returned, wafting through the air along with the birdsong and the clucking of the chickens. It's hard to shake the idea that Harry's guitar is roaming around the woods below us, hunting us down. Apart from the disembodied music, it's incredibly quiet. Something with large dark wings is circling, high in the deep blue sky like a surveillance drone.

My breathing suddenly feels shallow. I set the pad down and stand up and head towards the trees as if I can leave behind the unpleasant sense of being watched, along with Precious and the sketch pad. I'm trying to locate the music, I tell myself. I'm not running away.

Down the path, a figure flits between the trunks with a guitar around its neck. The sight freaks me out so much that I almost pee myself.

'Harry?' Hearing my own voice makes me feel slightly more secure. 'Is that you?'

Of course it's not Harry. That would be impossible. I left him yesterday on a roadside near Portimão. What possible reason—

I shriek like one of the chickens when a crazy man looms out from behind a tree. He has a hat tied with scarves, a dirty brown chest, no shoes and a guitar, and the smell coming off him is something special.

It's not Harry.

'If you're a street performer, mate,' I say, with my hand pressed to my hammering chest, 'you might want to find somewhere with more passing trade.'

He flits away into the trees like a bad dream, trailing dust and stink and a waterfall of poorly tuned notes. My legs feel weak as I try to even out my breathing. I now want to get out of here very badly indeed. Even more badly than I did with the circling bird drone and the pencil like a lead weight in my hand. Except, of course, I can't, because Precious is still up by the monastery and I'm supposed to be with her, watching her, looking after her.

It's almost midday, and my shrunken shadow squats hard and black on the path at my feet. The end of the path isn't far. I can see a little shop with postcards in the window, on the corner of two converging streets below where I have parked the car. I reason myself back to something approaching calm. Precious is asleep. I haven't screwed up. I'll simply buy a couple of bottles of water and, when

233

I am feeling less paranoid, I will return to the top of the hill.

Emerging from the stuffy little shop with two bottles of water five minutes later, I stop dead.

Somehow, Hairy Harry Temple is standing on the cobbles in front of me.

# HARRY

I want to say that I don't know who is more surprised, me or him. But seeing how I have been tracking him since eight o'clock this morning, it's probably fair to say that Nathan is considerably more surprised than I am. He drops the bottles of water he's holding, and they roll towards me, and then past me, and then they pick up speed and bounce clear out of sight on their own gravitational mystery tour. I clutch my own bottle tightly, feeling the dips and dimples in its plastic surface.

'Where's Precious?' I ask, as steadily as I can.

We gaze at each other across the hot cobbles. I squeeze my bottle harder. I have left my cabbie in the square at the bottom of the hill. He didn't want to dent the sides of his taxi, and also I think he fancied a coffee.

'Earth to Nathan Payne,' I say.

Nathan's eyes are like ping-pong balls. The kink in his nose is more obvious from this angle, and I wonder if perhaps he broke it.

'You can have your guitar,' he says randomly.

'I don't want my guitar,' I say.

I find that I do, in fact, want my guitar. It's nice to know that it's still in the back of the white Boxster parked so carefully up the street there, in what little shade there is.

'Where's Precious?' I repeat.

He's wary as a well-dressed cat now. 'What makes you think she's here?'

I didn't actually *see* Precious get into the car with him, but the way his eyes are spinning about in their sockets confirms that she's here. I feel a flush of triumph. Another tick on the private-eye CV.

'She's not interested in you,' Nathan adds, which rather adds proof to my theory. 'Piss off.'

In many ways there's nothing I'd rather do than piss off, away from this landlocked place where my heart is racing like I'm on caffeine pills. But two thousand euros and plain, blind obstinacy won't let me. I try to see behind him into the shop, but it's dark and he's in the way.

'Precious?' I shout. 'Precious, are you in there?'

I try to shoulder past Nathan into the shop but he shoves me sideways, and I have to shoot out my free hand to catch the wall and stop myself from falling. He squares up, panting a little, holding his arms martial-arts style like a poor man's Jason Statham.

'What do you want?' he says. 'Why are you here?'

'I know something's going on.' I flick my eyes about for Precious. 'Did your dad tell you to keep Precious out of the way while he did a deal with Ricky Silva?'

*What do you think they're going to do to her?*

*Use her as leverage, you pillock. It's what I'd do.*

'Is your father using her as leverage?' I say. 'Promising to bring Precious back once Ricky signs the deal?'

Nathan shakes his head.

'What if he doesn't sign? What does your dad want you to do with her then?'

He shakes his head again and his eyes are wild.

'If he told you to get rid of her, would you?' I'm feeling more and more like a cop from a TV show.

Sweat is pouring down Nathan's face and pooling in the hollow at the base of his throat. 'No one tells me what to do. She's here because she wants to be.'

I hold more firmly on to my bottle. 'Let's ask her.'

His fist slams at me in a rush of air. I duck. Again with the fist. Again I duck. This time, however, the side of my head connects with the wall beside the shop doorway. The world shrinks to a pinpoint, then balloons back into focus with a lovely accompanying throb.

'What the hell are you doing?' I say, staggering upright.

He wipes his forehead with the back of his hand, then puts up his arms again. 'Why are you following me?'

A couple of people have stuck their heads out of their windows to watch the fun. I get the sense that not a lot happens in this mountain town. I don't want to get slammed into the door frame again. It's time to approach this from a different angle.

'I was at the hotel last night,' I begin. 'I saw your dad hit you.'

Nathan goes very pale.

'No one deserves that.'

I open my hands out, away from my body, the way my grief counsellor did, to show that it's OK to say anything and everything and no one will judge you for feeling the way you feel.

I discover that it also opens your stomach up to a lovely punch. Gasping on impact as much in shock as pain, I lower a shoulder and barge into Nathan before he can do it again. I like to think that we collide with the grace and masculinity of fighting stags, but two cats in a bag is probably more accurate. There's a lot of grappling, made doubly hard by the bottle. Nathan grabs my hair and yanks it. I rip the button off his polo shirt. If a Hollywood director choreographed this, the audience would leave the auditorium in disgust.

Next, my feet go from underneath me. Suddenly all I can see is sky and some very hard cobbles. With a thud, Nathan lands on top of me. Like the water bottles, we start rolling, picking up speed until we collide with the side of a building about a hundred yards down the hill in a bruised and gasping pile of limbs.

At which point, we both hear the distinctive grumble of the Boxster.

# PRECIOUS

I am alone in a vast and silent place, on top of a green world. The monastery is nothing but rotten walls and broken tiles. There's no sign of the farmer. Even the chickens are quiet.

When I woke up ten minutes ago, heavy-headed with heat and the passing shadow of almonds, I fell headlong into paranoia. Nathan has vanished in a puff of dust and chicken shit, leaving only his sketch pad, phone and car keys to prove that he was here at all. Or perhaps it's me that's vanished, slid sideways into the realm of the forgotten. I feel transparent. Not here at all.

*Exile*, I think with a kind of cinematic dread. *Banishment*.

'Where did you go? Nathan, where are you?'

This frightened squeak is apparently my voice. The circling bird in the great dome of blue sky will mistake me for a vole and snatch me up in his yellow claws and peck at my eyes with his scimitar beak. Why does everyone leave?

The stones on the path slip and slide beneath my feet as I make my way down the path, clutching Nathan's stuff so tightly that I can feel the car keys leaving a red welt in the palm of my hand. What if I get to the bottom and the car has gone? What then?

I stop halfway down the path, lean against a tree and squeeze my eyes tightly shut. Girls on the run don't freak about stuff like this. Girls on the run take control of their own destinies. Girls on the run are explorers, adventurers. Bartolomeu Dias wasn't scared of the silence of the Indian Ocean. Ferdinand Magellan didn't turn back halfway round the world. The air blows around me and the leaves whisper overhead and the tree trunk is rough and comforting beneath my hand. Within a few breaths, I hear the snap of sails in my head and I'm back in my crow's nest with the crows, sailing above a waving grass ocean.

I feel bright and clear when I open my eyes. Perhaps I've finally slipped into a part of myself that's always been there. Whatever the reason, I discover something important.

I know where I want to go.

Towards the bottom of the path, a guy is sitting up a tree with his hat on his nose, playing the guitar. He tips his brim up as I pass beneath him and peers at me with eyes as bright as the monastery chickens'.

'*Onde vai?*'

'*Oeste,*' I inform him.

He nods agreeably and strums a chord. '*Boa viagem, a senhora navegadora.*'

I'm a navigator, navigating my way to myself. That's good. I like that.

240

The car is still where Nathan parked it, facing down the hill. The leather seats look hot enough to griddle eggs. If I wait, then he will eventually show up.

But then I see something.

About a hundred metres from the car bumper, down a steep section of the road, Nathan is pummelling Harry Temple with a raised fist. Harry's hair is fanned out on the cobbles around his head, his skinny arms up in defence. They are both screeching like badly oiled brakes and rolling downhill.

I stare for about half a second, processing the extreme weirdness of this. Why is Harry here? Why is Nathan pounding him into the cobbles? I have no answers to those particular questions, but one thing is abundantly clear as the guitar man's words echo in my head and I weigh the Boxster keys in my hand.

I don't have to wait for anyone.

The driver's seat is on the shadier side of the car, and my thighs only give a very faint sizzle as I settle into the leather and stroke the steering wheel. I've never driven before, but how hard can it be? Nathan said this car practically drives itself.

I have barely touched the keys to the starter panel when the engine growls at me and the twin exhausts at the back start to throb. There's a bit of bunny-hopping as I work out how to release the handbrake. The car rolls itself forward, purring. Now it's just a case of keeping my foot on the accelerator. Or, it transpires, *off* the accelerator and on the other pedal, which turns out to be the brake.

Nathan and Harry crash into a wall, which stops the whole downward motion thing. Lying flat on the cobbles, they look up, fists frozen.

'Oh my God!' Nathan screeches.

It isn't quite true that the Boxster drives itself. Anything heavier than two fingers on the steering wheel makes it swing alarmingly towards the wall, and I have to remind myself that this isn't an arcade game. The car gathers speed, and I stomp on the brake, panicking slightly at the incline, and judder over the shiny cobbles and slide a bit. When I swing away from Harry and Nathan and make it round the corner with only the slightest of *dinks* against the white wheel arch, I give a whoop of triumph.

Harry and Nathan have stopped fighting and are on their feet, I see in the rear-view mirror. They both start running after me, taking a comically uneven line down the road. I watch them in the mirror for slightly too long, taking one hand off the steering wheel to offer a cheery wave. There's another *dink* and a screeching noise as I plough too near one of the whitewashed houses that line the road.

Nathan's screaming fades pleasantly behind me as I bump on down the hill. The road's a bit wider here, so easier to navigate. The next corner comes up a lot faster than expected, though, and I swing the back of the car a bit too close to the roundabout.

Harry is still running after me, waving a water bottle in the air.

'Precious!' he shouts. 'Where are you going?'

'Where all good navigators go,' I shout back, flinging both arms into the air. There's another *clonk* and the Boxster's hubcap chips away a bit of pavement. 'WEST!'

# HARRY

It's hard to hear myself think through Nathan's howling. He is rocking where he sits, his arms wrapped around his shins and his head pressed tightly against his knees and his oh-so-perfect hair no longer oh-so-perfect but badly dishevelled with gravel in it. I look at the bottle in my hand for a couple of seconds, trying to draw strength from its contents.

A couple of ladies come out of a house a little way across, clucking like agitated hens. Tearing my eyes from the last speck of white Porsche Boxster that I can see as it veers wildly through the toy town spread at our feet, I wave them off with the international sign for 'Thanks but everything's OK' and then sit down on the cobbles beside him.

'Listen,' I begin.

He rears up. 'This is your fault!'

'For what, showing up?'

'Oh God,' he groans. 'Dad's going to break every bone in my body.'

Despite the blazing sun and the scalding heat surging up from the cobbles beneath us, I feel a nasty chill. From what I've seen of Aiden Payne, that doesn't sound too much of an exaggeration.

He wipes his nose. 'What am I going to do?'

The look in his eyes reminds me of the look Precious gave me outside the shoe shop in Quarteira a hundred lifetimes ago.

'We could try to follow her,' I suggest.

I hope my cabbie hasn't finished his coffee yet. I meant to give him a retainer from the wodge of cash in my back pocket, but the thought slid out of my brain the moment the guy in the café said that a white Porsche with Spanish plates had taken the road up the hill. I suspect he's buggered off. No one warns you how much planning ahead is required in this business.

'Let's see if we can find a cab.'

I find myself holding out my hand. He looks at it wordlessly and gets himself to his feet unaided. I wipe my palm on my shorts self-consciously.

It's a steep and silent walk back down to the square. One or two people are sitting in the cafés near a rusty waterwheel that isn't working. There are no cabs in sight. No cabbies either, unsurprisingly. All the cars parked at angles along the cobbled pavement are empty with no way of telling if the owners are nearby. The only manned vehicle I can see is an ancient blue scooter thing with a covered seat and boxes of something green in the corrugated bit on the back.

Nathan has sat on the low wall edging a line of sprinkling fountains with his head drooping like a flower in need of water. It's very tempting to give him a brisk shove backwards and provide. I eye the guy unloading green veg from the scooter van and finger the cash in my pocket.

*I don't think they have Uber in the Algarve.*

'I have a plan,' I say. 'But you're not going to like it.'

Nathan looks up dully. 'I'm dead anyway. Just do it.'

At first, the veg guy thinks I'm trying to buy his lettuce. It takes some bad miming and a large chunk of Ricky Silva's money to convince him that it's not his veg I'm after but something larger, with three wheels, basic handlebar controls, a torn vinyl seat and an extensive collection of dents and rust patches. When he twigs, he shakes his head and takes around two-thirds of Ricky's money and almost throws the keys at me. This is pretty momentous, when you think about it. I have bought my first vehicle. I think it's a keeper.

'Hop in then,' I say, sliding into the sardine can and settling my water bottle carefully at my feet.

'You're shitting me,' Nathan says.

I am pleased when the tiny engine starts up like an asthmatic bumblebee.

'Told you you wouldn't like it,' I say over the buzzing. 'Are you coming or not?'

Nathan looks up and down the square.

'There are no cabs,' I say. 'I am your only ticket out of here.'

It's a squeeze as we set off. The handlebars are helpfully set in the middle of the cab, so my elbow is in Nathan's ear as we putter away at a neck-breaking speed of 10 kph. His arse takes up more than half the tattered seat.

'I can't believe this,' he says at intervals.

'I'm having so much fun,' I say. I'm already developing a crick in my spine from twisting my body around him to reach the handlebars. 'It's great sharing it with you.'

'You're a loser.'

'You didn't have to come.'

The gears work just like a scooter, with a twisting action on the handlebars. I drove a hired scooter in Paris, so I kind of know what I'm doing. Well, technically Sasha did the driving and I hung on at the back, closing my eyes as we went round the Arc de Triomphe, but I'm clear on the theory. The water bottle rolls around by my feet.

'The Boxster has over three hundred brake horsepower and goes from nought to sixty in under five seconds,' Nathan gripes as we wheeze up the hill and out of town.

'And I'm sure Precious is enjoying smashing it around.'

'God, I could *walk* faster than this thing.'

'Why don't you drive, Lewis Hamilton?' I suggest.

I pull over, to the loud relief of the line of cars that has accumulated behind us, and get out. Then I get back in again, realising that you don't have to change seats in a scooter van with centred handlebars.

Nathan has picked up my water bottle and is tipping it towards his mouth.

'Wait,' I begin.

But I'm too late. His eyes bulge as much as his mouth. He sprays the contents around in a fine mist and the bottle falls out of his hands and I dive for it before the entirety of the contents pours into the footwell.

'Jesus!' he croaks. 'Why the hell have you got seawater in a bottle?'

I screw the lid on with trembling fingers as he dry-retches in my ear. There isn't much left, but it will have to do. What other options are there, this high in the hills?

'Are you driving or not?' I snap.

I get it, *says Dad as I tighten the lid and wipe my sandy fingers on my shorts.*

'It's dumb,' I say. *I squint at the cabbie, waiting for me on the road above the beach. If he's curious, he's hiding it well.*

You'll come back though?

*I slip the bottle into my pocket. You can't take water through airport security.*

'Yes,' I say. 'I'll come back.'

We still have a lot to talk about, you and me.

'I know.'

My stomach is still turning over like a broken engine as we approach a junction on our right.

'Which way?' Nathan asks.

Why does everyone think I have the answers? At nought to sixty in under five seconds, Precious could be anywhere, assuming she hasn't wrapped herself around a tree.

A flash of silver in a ray of sunlight catches at the corner of my eye. I twist in my seat in one of those spur-of-the-minute decisions that, half a second later, make you wonder if you're sane.

The car is grey this time, not black. It passes our scooter at a comfortable purr, hugging the road towards Monchique. The driver doesn't spare us a glance, tucked as he is behind mirrored sunglasses.

'Which way?' Nathan repeats, more loudly.

Returning my thoughts to the floppy-haired idiot beside me, I probably reply more sharply than necessary. 'Let's ask the state-of-the-art satnav.'

The bald dashboard with its single analogue dial looks reproachfully at us.

'Well, which way is west? You said she was going west.'

This is a bad time to ask me questions. 'I don't *know*, OK?'

'This was your idea!' Nathan shouts.

'Use your own brain for once!' I shout back.

We sit on the hard shoulder opposite the junction for about five seconds of hard and mutual loathing. If Nathan Payne hadn't shown up in Albufeira, none of this would have happened. I tell him as much.

'What's with the seawater?' he fires back. 'Are you a mermaid?'

'What's with doing what Daddy says? Are you a doormat?'

'My father's a bastard.'

'So was mine!'

Dad wasn't really a bastard. He just expected too much, asked me to do things that I couldn't do. By comparison to Nathan's prize specimen, he was a bloody saint.

'Hits you too, does he?' Nathan hurls at me. 'I don't blame him.'

My anger falls away.

'He's dead,' I say. I lean my head back on the beaten metal panel behind our heads. 'He drowned. And I have to be near the sea, near him, or I feel like I'm going to die too. If that means I have to put the sea in a bottle, then I'll put the sea in a bottle, if it's all the same to you.'

It sounds even stupider than I thought it would, out loud.

'Is that why you almost puked in the Porsche yesterday?' Nathan says after an awkward silence. 'No seawater?'

'Yes.' Nothing like sharing your weaknesses with the enemy.

'That's pretty messed up.'

I grit my teeth. 'Don't you think I know that?'

There's a streak of burned rubber on the road by the junction. Hot, black. Evidence of a corner taken at speed and with an uncertain level of control.

'Precious might have done a wheelie in that direction,' I say, relieved at the opportunity to change the subject. I think again about the mirrored sunglasses, and feel uneasy. 'Let's assume right is west.'

Nathan starts up the scooter van again. We turn right.

# NATHAN

'Get your elbow out of my ear.'

'Move your bony arse,' I return. 'Do you fancy me or something?'

The van has more personality than my travelling companion. The air conditioning comprises two windows on flaps. There's no suspension, a couple of dubious switches on the dash, and an analogue speedometer. The whole thing is like one of those fierce, bandy-legged old ladies you see at bus stops. I clamp my hands tightly on the handlebars and change gear as the smell of herbs wafts around us through the rust-eaten corrugated bodywork like someone's burning an expensive candle in the back. Coriander maybe, or basil, green and fresh and wet.

'Green Doris,' I say aloud as we pass a climbing tower of blue flowers like a silent fireworks display on the side of the road. The views outside the flappy windows are full of colour – yellow houses and purple flowers and green trees with blinding red bark.

'What is it with the over-privileged and their cryptic conversation?'

'It's what you should call the tin can,' I say. 'Green Doris.'

'But it's blue,' says Harry.

'It smells green. And it's old. And it's kind of funny that it's blue. So Green Dor . . . forget it.'

I suddenly realise that I left my phone in Monchique. How is Dad going to contact me now? Why do I get it wrong all the time?

'What now?' says Harry when I groan.

'I don't have my phone.' Please God, don't let me cry in front of him again.

'I've got one if you need it.'

He produces a small Lego brick from his pocket. Even in the horror of the moment, I burst out laughing.

'What the hell is that?'

'A communication device.' He puts it away again, a little irritably. 'I hear they're all the rage.'

'I'll let you know if I need to call anyone in 1998.'

'You do that. Get your elbow out of my fricking EAR.'

It takes a couple of miles for the panic to go. When I can think straight again, new thoughts begin to fly at me. Dad doesn't know where I am or who I'm with. I could disappear. Head north and never come back. Draw things as I go, sketch tourist portraits in holiday towns. Grow my hair back, get a tattoo. Lose Nathan Payne all together.

Harry is rolling his bottle between his palms. I take one

hand off Green Doris's handlebars for long enough to wipe a hot trickle of sweat from between my eyebrows and decide to tackle the thing we have in common.

'Do you like her? Precious?'

He eyes me. 'Do you?'

'I don't do girlfriends,' I say. 'I do girls, but not girlfriends.'

'Nice,' says Harry. I think he's being sarcastic. 'But not what I asked.'

'Not what I asked either.' This feels like a boxing match.

'She's all right,' Harry says presently. 'If you like giraffes.'

I think about kissing Precious. She was unexpectedly enthusiastic. I should have kissed her in the pool, made the most of the opportunity. And I should definitely have kissed her awake in Monchique. Girls like that kind of shit. Maybe I'll try again when we find her. If we find her.

'Why are you following her if you don't like her?' I ask next.

'I didn't say that I didn't like her.'

'I could get her,' I say. 'If I wanted.'

Harry rolls his bottle again. 'She's not a raffle prize, you twat.'

Next up, a Boxster wing mirror lying on a verge. Silently, I pick it up and place it in the back of the van.

'At least we're on the right track.'

It's the first thing Harry has said in fifteen kilometres. He keeps looking over his shoulder at the empty road, which is making me nervous. All sense of good cheer has gone as I slam Green Doris back into gear. 'I'm still a dead man,' I mutter.

'Don't you ever fight back?'

I finger the bridge of my nose. 'No point.'

'Do you want me to drive?'

'I'm good.' I'm feeling possessive of Green Doris's handlebars. 'Thanks, though.'

Something like a ceasefire has descended. Harry senses it.

'What happened to your nose?' he says.

I haven't told anyone what happened to my nose. Maybe because saying it out loud would make it more real. Harry saw that crap at the hotel, so I guess I wouldn't be telling him anything he doesn't already know. It's tempting, the chance to offload on someone I'll never see again.

'Why do you want to know?' I say.

'You know my problem. It seems fair that I should know yours.'

A problem shared is a problem out in the wider world, where it can grow teeth and turn into a weapon to be used against you. Although the hairy mermaid may have a point. Two problems, two weapons. Isn't that the whole theory behind the nuclear deterrent?

'Plus,' Harry adds, 'Green Doris has no radio. And I'm bored shitless.'

# PRECIOUS

I'm annoyed about the wing mirror. I really thought I had the steering thing under control. There's hardly any traffic on the road, so I accelerate because I can. I'm ripping up the road, tearing it to shreds, and the trees are whipping by. I feel the salt spray of the waves in my face and the force of the wind in my sails. The sense of power is unbelievable. No wonder Magellan made it the whole way round the world.

Seeing a brown sign up ahead for a viewpoint, I swing the steering wheel round and cruise up the gravelled slope. The road twists up through the trees until there's no road left, so I park the car and test the locks, and I find the Terminator phone tucked into the driver's door. That's strange. How did it get there? Did Nathan pick it up from the hotel after all?

After staring at the phone for a while, I think about checking Instagram. Right now it feels kind of irrelevant. I can't imagine the explorers bothering, even if they'd had the technology.

@vascodagama
Pumped to reach India! #pleasetheking #cash
#jewels #exploringrocks

@pedrocabral100
Beautiful Brazil #pleasetheking #gold #parrots

I take the Terminator phone with me up what remains of
the gravelled slope and squat at the top, weighing it in my
hand. It's overflowing with texts.

Please talk to me baby

I know you're mad with me

Why aren't you answering?

I'm sorry

I'm so so sorry xxxx

I don't know what I was thinking

Are you dead?

Baby I'm going insane, PLEASE CALL

'I'm not dead,' I say coolly when she snatches up my call on
the first ring.

She's breathing the way she does when she's frightened in a movie or we've had a near miss at school drop-off with someone's bumper.

'Where have you been? They wouldn't have hurt you, Aiden promised me they would only hold you for a little while, just so we could get the press on my side, only you disappeared and they didn't call me and I had no idea where you were—'

When Mum cries, it's usually around the mouth and not around the eyes or the forehead, depending on when she last had the Botox. Aiden . . . The streaky guy?

'This was *Bacon's* idea?' I say.

Mum is still weeping. 'He was so nice to me in London and I was so lonely after that man did what he did in Spain—'

I try to keep up. 'I thought you met Bacon at the club last week?'

'Oh no, we met in London, why do you keep calling him Bacon? He was the one who suggested I joined you in the Algarve, and it seemed like such a good idea, a chance to talk to your father about the divorce and have a little break, and then that idiotic kidnap was all very spur of the moment because Aiden knew these men he uses sometimes – he's in oil, did I say? – and then you sent me that awful text about your ears and I almost *died*.'

There's a lot here that I don't know and need to think about.

'Oil?' I say. 'As in, NO TO THE OILGARVE?'

257

'Why, who says that? Oh, baby, I saw you coming towards me over the water like some kind of goddess, and you were so amazing and beautiful and powerful and I felt like the world's *worst* mother.'

'Maybe not the worst,' I say, mollified by the awe in Mum's voice and her use of words like 'powerful'. 'But definitely not very good.'

'I've been so lonely,' she says again.

'You've had me.'

'But you're not a man, are you?' Mum says earnestly.

'What's that supposed to mean?' If she starts talking about Needs, I'm going to throw up.

'You'll understand better when you're my age. Trust me when I say that men cause you to lose your mind.'

'Mum,' I say. 'In order to lose your mind to a guy, you have to give your mind to the guy first. I'm only just discovering my mind. I'm not planning to give it to anyone.'

'Oh, Precious,' says Mum with a sigh. 'You have so much to learn.'

'You're the one getting the divorce and kidnapping your own daughter,' I point out caustically. 'I think you're the one who needs to do the learning, don't you?'

Was Mum always like this? Or am I only just noticing?

Back at the Boxster, Nathan's phone is screeching like an offended owl on the front seat. It stops just as I reach it. He's missed three calls from his dad.

I hope it's nothing important.

# HARRY

It's a good thing Precious is so crap at driving. Pretty much everywhere we've stopped, people have pointed and told us which way the Boxster went. Somewhere around Marmelete, Nathan couldn't stand asking any more, so left the questions to me. He hasn't explained his nose yet. If he ever does, I think it's going to be bad.

The sensation of being followed itches between my shoulder blades. The driver of the grey car *couldn't* be the one who chased us down the beach at Quarteira. He and his fat mate crashed out of the game, literally. Precious confronted her mum about it. It *must* be over. What's the point of continuing when everyone's been found out? But all the logic in the world fails to make the feeling go away.

We stop in Aljezur because Nathan needs a piss. When I suggest that I could drive and he could piss out of the open side of Green Doris because we ought to keep driving, he threatens to top up my water bottle.

'Unlike you, Mermaid, I'm not a frickin' animal,' he says, and I have to let him park up beside the municipal market building and nip into the café tacked on the front.

The car park is large, and there is no shade. Nowhere to hide either, and in plain sight of the main road that squeezes through this scattered little town. All Sunglasses has to do is stop at the first place in Monchique and ask about the Porsche. In a matter of minutes, he'll be backtracking to that junction, spotting the tyre marks on the road and making an educated guess, and all of this at twice the speed of Green Doris. He could be as little as ten minutes behind us, maybe less.

*How's your hornet, Harry boy? Tasty?*

'Shut up,' I say, loudly. 'I'm trying to think.'

I keep my hands on the handlebars for insurance, counting the seconds until Nathan returns. How long can one piss take? The longer he's out of sight, the more convinced I feel that the hunt is still on. It'll be a tragic sight, me attempting a get-away wheelie at the sight of the powerful grey car, but it's the best I've got.

Four minutes. Five.

I slide out of Green Doris and into the café, where Nathan – *bloody* Nathan – appears to be chatting up the girl behind the bar, holding a bottle of water and one packet of crisps.

'He's with me,' I tell the girl. I grab his sleeve. 'Come on, sugar tits. Remember how angry Daddy is going to be when he learns that you've lost Precious.' I shove him in the small of the back to keep him moving towards the door with its chequered metal grille. 'The longer we hang around, the less chance we have of finding her. And on top of everything else, I think we're being—'

A dark grey car is gliding into a space outside. The driver's mirrored sunglasses cover the plaster on his forehead nicely as he turns off the engine and opens the door. I don't seem able to move my feet as he studies the key fob in his hand and plips the locks.

Finally, I move, grabbing a handful of Nathan's shirt and hauling him backwards. 'Questions later,' I say through his spluttering as I hustle him through a back door in the café and into the market building itself.

I'm not into markets. Too smelly and full of dead things that I'd prefer to see alive. This one is neat and well kept, and full of light with a planked ceiling and square terracotta floor tiles. A few late shoppers loiter beside trays of sad-eyed seafood, cartons of fruit and vegetables, jars of honey, boxes of pebble-like clams shining in their beds of ice. A powerful smell of fish hangs over everything like a heavy mackerel-infused curtain.

Nathan's pupils dart around like tadpoles. 'Harry,' he says, but I'm already off, dodging trays of tomatoes, aiming for the large double doors at the back. I've never seen a running hare, but I have no doubt that it would bear no resemblance to me at all. We need to get round to the front again and miraculously find Green Doris has a booster button, a hyperdrive, *anything* to get us away from Sunglasses before he sees us.

After a split second, Nathan runs after me.

'Harry, I know him!' he shouts. 'I KNOW him!"

I'm so pumped that it takes a while for his words to spin and settle into sense. When they do, I whirl about, reach for the floppy collar of his polo shirt, and slam him up against a pungent tower of blue fish crates.

'*What?*'

Nathan struggles. 'He does security for Dad. He's – there's usually two of them, Tico and Matteo—'

Two lines of thought collide in my head, ringing and roaring side by side. Everything is clear, and nothing makes sense. Nathan wriggles in my grip, gasping and cursing. I am apparently stronger than I look.

'Does your dad know Precious's mother?'

'I don't know – get *off* me . . .'

'Are you on Sunglasses' side, or mine?' We can clear that up, at least.

The door at the café end of the market swings open. Sunglasses whips off his shades to adjust to the dim light, and as he glances around the big space I shove Nathan deep into the shadow of the crates.

'Now would be a really good time to decide,' I say.

# NATHAN

Tico scared me from the moment I first saw him, the day Dad took me to the refinery. Through the stink and the clatter of the place, he stood out, watchful and still as a scorpion. Matteo not so much, although he wore a decent watch. If I had to run away from one of them, I'd pick Matteo. Seems like I've been Plan B all along. It's surprising, how much that hurts.

Tico is padding like a cat towards us, his aviators dangling from one hand, taking his time. I pull Harry's hands from my neck, gasping for air.

'He's seen us,' I croak.

Harry's eyes burn me like gas flames. 'Are you with him?' he says again. 'Or me?'

It's over, I think. Dad's pet shark can take Harry, and find Precious, and the responsibility won't be mine any more. Tico won't hurt me. He'll just deliver me to Dad, and Dad will hurt me instead.

'You,' I say.

Harry nods.

'This doesn't mean I like you,' I add, rubbing my neck.

'Likewise,' Harry says. 'Run.'

We break away from the crates. But even as we start running for the main doors, Tico is blocking our path. He seems puzzled, probably wondering whether we've tucked Precious inside a box of oranges. I skid, and spin about, and run the other way. Tico's eyes flicker. He wasn't expecting that.

The tiny break in concentration gives Harry a chance to join me. A bank of marble fish counters now stands solidly between us and Tico. We move one way, he moves the other. We feint and shuffle, and so does he, and all the while he holds our gaze above the gold, copper, bronze and silver flanks of fish whose colours shift and shine and change with every tiny movement.

'This could take a while,' says Harry under his breath.

The market workers have noticed that something is up. Eyes are on us and the volume is rising, echoing off the high ceiling. As we edge closer to the central point of the counters, where one enormous trophy fish stares at us with dead eyes, Tico stretches out his arms like a goalkeeper covering all possible penalty directions.

'Two ways out,' I say suddenly. 'The main doors and the café door. He doesn't know which way we'll go. If we split up and make a run for it, at least one of us—'

'Not the problem,' Harry hisses back. 'Even if we make it to Green Doris, how is she meant to outrun a Lexus?'

And I remember that we don't have a Porsche any more. We have a three-wheeled tin can.

Tico's acceleration comes from nowhere. One minute he's standing opposite us; the next, he's backed up and is leaping – almost flying – over the counter. The fish sellers duck. Harry yells in shock, flinging his arms up.

I also yell, but my arms go somewhere else. *My* arms go for the massive fish, the sad sea monster on the counter, who has been watching this whole charade with its milky, plate-sized eyes. I wrap my arms almost lovingly around its huge, slippery head, and I sink my fingers into its gills, and I heave it upwards with all my strength.

The long silver body arcs and whips and clatters into Tico's groin. He grunts in pain and surprise, and loses his momentum mid-air, his feet shooting out as he tries to right himself. He catches the side of a tray with his heel, sending a glittering spray of tiger-striped fish flashing through the air. Cursing, he hits the counter with his backside and skids off, across the floor tiles, spinning like a puck on an ice rink.

My weapon of choice is unexpectedly heavy. I'm still whirling like an Olympic hammer-thrower, trying to keep my grip on the gills and stay upright at the same time. In an act of sheer self-preservation, my fingers let go of the fish entirely. The whole room seems to hold its breath as the turbot/halibut/whale soars through the air, on its final flight – and smacks into the back of Tico's head as he spins. Soundlessly, he drops face first to the ground and lies entirely still.

The volume in the market rises to an impossible level as sellers and buyers crowd around the body sprawled on the floor. No one is paying us any attention – apart from the fish seller, whose voice is louder than the rest put together as he yells and points at his fish and yells again.

I grab Harry and I pull him behind me like a kite in a tough headwind, whooping like a WWE wrestler. 'Did you see that?' I'm on the biggest high of my life. 'Did you *see* that?'

'I need to pay the fish guy,' Harry says.

'Did you SEE that?' I roar again, but Harry is stuffing bank notes into the fish seller's cold red fingers and patting his back and apologising. It's not really the response I'm after.

Good ideas come in pairs. As we run back through the café, I grab a used glass from a table and break it on the metal door grille.

'Classy,' pants Harry as we race for Green Doris. 'Why not smash the café windows too?'

'Four tyres,' I inform him. I lob him half the broken glass, which he catches with a wince and a curse. 'Two each. You take that side, and I'll take this.' I carve a gash in one of the Lexus tyres and whoop again. 'Did you *see* me throw that bastard fish?'

# HARRY

Green Doris bumps gingerly down a cobbled track towards a vast west-facing beach, hemmed in by cliffs that make the ones on the south coast look like skateboard ramps. The surfers – midget dots on matchstick boards far out on the long, cresting waves – give you the only real sense of scale. You'd struggle to fill the beach, but there's a scatter of brightly coloured umbrellas across the sandy expanse. A tiny harbour filled with weary-looking boats juts into the water in the northern corner of the bay, its skinny arm doing what it can to ward off the hammer blow of the sea.

What's left of the Porsche is parked in front of the one seafront restaurant in this place. Nathan turns the colour of concrete at the full extent of Precious's handiwork. The scrapes down both sides of the car have gone through to the silvery metal underneath. There are dents in the bonnet and the bumper, and kinks in the wheel arches. The missing wing mirror we know about. The spider crack in the windscreen, not so much. She's parked nose down and left the handbrake off, so that the car bonnet is crushed up against the little wall separating the tiny parking area from a five-foot drop to the sand. My guitar is still sitting alone in the back.

'I'm so dead,' groans Nathan. All the fish elation has gone.

It's around four o'clock. Walking on the soft sand is tough, but it gets easier the closer to the water's edge we get. The power of this churning western sea is chilling, even as the sun beats down on my head. There is nothing between us and the coast of America here. You can feel it, all those billions of cubic metres of water, pulsing and pushing and eating at the land, gorging on the rocks and mashing up the sea bed. The noise is immense. Overhead, the gulls don't stand a chance of making themselves heard over the boom of the sea.

After half an hour, I sit down on the sand and contemplate the stretch of beach we have yet to cover. Precious could be anywhere. Beside me, Nathan scrapes at the sand with his toe. He took off his deck shoes forty minutes ago, and his shirt twenty minutes after that. I get the impression that he's shedding more than his clothes.

'Look,' he says. 'Green Doris embracing her future.'

I squint at his sand sketch of the van. He's made her wheels all thin and speedy, as if she's tanking along at seventy.

'You should have sat that exam,' I say.

Nathan wipes his forehead with the back of his hand. 'If you remember, I had a bandage across my face.'

We went through it on the road from Aljezur, and it was bad. Really bad. But, being blunt, it's not the full and complete excuse Nathan Payne wants it to be.

'The bandage wasn't on your fingers,' I say, trying to be tactful.

'Might as well have been. Everyone expects me to be . . .' He waves at his face.

'An idiot?'

'Pretty.'

'You could still have taken it.'

'Dad says art is for girls.'

'Your dad also thinks your face is a punchbag.'

He shrugs. 'You know what it's like, trying to live up to what they expect.'

Trying, and failing about as hard as you can. That's the worst thing.

'I guess so,' I say.

The waves crest and crash and boom, spitting surfers like grape pips on to the beach. Several girls come out of the water, hair wet and gleaming, boards under their arms, whispering as they look at Nathan. He leans back, smirks, opens his chest like he's on *World's Strongest Man*. I stop feeling sorry for him.

'I'm going to tell Precious what you're doing,' I say. 'Despite the fact that you took out a Terminator with a fish.'

'Do that and I'll tell her you're on Ricky's payroll.'

I open my mouth.

'I worked it out, Mermaid, don't bother denying it. Where else would someone like you get enough money to buy Green Doris right off?' He winks at one of the passing girls. 'Precious doesn't like her dad much. How is she going to react when I tell her he paid you to hunt her down?'

I feel almost admiring. 'Oh, you're good.'

He smirks. 'You know it.'

# PRECIOUS

The rise and fall of a sea like this beneath the shallow hulls of the caravels must have been terrifying, but the explorers still went out there, sailing west. Most of them didn't even know what they were looking for. Me? I'm screaming. Shrieking my head off. The board buzzes like a living thing under my knees and the wave foams around me and the salt is singing in my mouth and stinging in my eyes. Any remnants of my hangover have been scoured from my head and my brain rinsed clean. I'm no more in control of the board than I was of the Boxster and it's *wild*.

The beach is flying towards me with its charcoal cliff arms outstretched to welcome me back to solid ground and I don't want the ride to end. But like all good things, it does. I crash and tumble head over heels on to the beach with the tether yanking at my ankles and the sand scraping at my arms.

'Next time, I'll do it right,' I tell the blue sky above me.

'Next time maybe you'll want a wetsuit.'

271

There's a hairy silhouette above me with his hands on his skinny hips.

'Hello, Barry,' I say.

I gaze up at him and he gazes back down at me. Lurking at the back of my brain, I have an odd memory of holding his hair. I can feel it now, dry and salty between my fingers. Why would I hold his hair?

He wipes his face with both hands in a downwards motion. 'My dad would have liked you, Precious Silva.'

I have a feeling my bra has gone a bit see-through. 'Because I go surfing in my pants?'

'Because you're grasping the nettle. And also surfing in your pants, yes.' He pauses. 'Why *are* you surfing in your pants?'

'I didn't want to hire a wetsuit. The surfboard was expensive enough.'

'What happened to Fifty-Euro Girl?'

'What happened to you in Albufeira?' I counter.

'I've seen you since Albufeira. Don't you remember?'

'There's plenty of things I don't remember,' I admit. 'I got drunk at Dad's hotel last night and everything's a blur. How did you find me?'

Harry seems to be recalibrating. 'A white Porsche isn't hard to track,' he says. 'By the way, you can't drive for shit.'

'I was annoyed about the wing mirror,' I confess.

'So was the wing mirror. We found it in the road. Nathan put it in the back of Green Doris.'

I want to ask who Green Doris is, but a second silhouette has joined Harry. Broader, but a bit shorter. Whippy hair. Nice chest.

'Oh, good,' says Harry.

'Hello, Nathan Payne,' I say in delight.

Having Nathan and Harry here at the beach means they must have followed me all the way from Monchique. At parties, when I head for the stairs, I head for the stairs alone. I'm turning into a person interesting enough to follow, in a literal sense instead of just an online one.

Nathan offers me a hand so I can get up, but I quite like lying where I am with the wet sand against my soggy pants and the little washing waves tickling my toes so I don't take it.

'Why are you both here?' I ask, propping myself up on my elbows. 'Why were you wrestling in Monchique?'

When Harry rubs his chin, he leaves a streak of sand on his cheek. 'You had my guitar,' he says.

'Nathan had your guitar,' I correct. 'You left it in the café when you bolted. I don't know what's going on with either of you.'

'I'm actually quite worried about where to begin,' Harry says.

'Come surfing with me,' I suggest. 'The sea will clear your head.'

His skinny body tenses up like a wire. 'I went into the sea in Portimão. I went bloody *through* the sea at Quarteira.'

'He's got a thing about the sea,' says Nathan.

'I know he has a thing about the sea,' I say. 'His father drowned. He told me all about it.'

'He has to carry seawater in a bottle,' Nathan adds. 'Otherwise he pukes.'

'Whoa,' I say in interest. That's a new development.

'I am here, you know,' says Harry.

I'm getting cold so I pick up my board. 'It's nice chatting and all, but I'm going in again. Are you coming, Barry?'

'The Porsche is more likely to regrow its wing mirror,' Harry says.

'I'll come,' says Nathan. 'Do I have to surf in my underwear too?'

'Underwear optional,' I say, before realising how inappropriate that sounds.

'Wait here and I'll hire the stuff,' Nathan's saying, backing towards the surf shack at the foot of the cobbled slipway that leads on to the beach. 'Harry can keep you company. Remember what we were talking about just now, Harry? You could tell her about that, maybe.'

There's a weird vibe here. Are they in some kind of competition with each other? Over me? If they are, then Nathan is winning, obviously, with the kiss in the Boxster, but Harry . . . Harry appears to be in the race too. Following me around is one thing, but this feels – wrong.

'Harry,' I say uncertainly. 'Am I a bet?'

He's pacing a safe distance from the water, glancing every now and then at Nathan over by the surf shack. 'What?'

'A bet,' I repeat. I think about kissing Nathan in the car and feel anxious. 'Like, when two guys chase a girl, but it's more about the win than the girl?'

Harry looks horrified. 'Of course not!'

I'm not sure I believe him.

# NATHAN

According to the great artists, there are three types of women: maidens, mothers and crones. Precious is in the maiden category, which makes me a knight on a foaming white steed. There's something about her recklessness that makes me want to do my best. As we wait together, feeling the dip and pull of the water, I squint at the beach, where I note with satisfaction the small hairy figure of Harry Temple making his way to the restaurant by the slipway. One–nil.

I wish I could tell her about my stunt with the fish. But that would lead to complicated questions that I don't want to answer.

'It's not difficult,' Precious shouts at me across the spray. 'You just hold the board and jump on. I haven't stood up yet but I've been quite close.'

'I have done this before.' I feel a little irritated that she thinks I need guidance. 'In Cornwall. Quite a few times.'

'Can you stand up?'

'Of course I can,' I retort, because what else do you say?

The foam crests quicker than I expect, and I miss the first ride. Precious cruises in, screaming, on her hands and knees, and waves at me when she hits the sand. I wave back, pretending that I'm waiting for the next one. A cluster of surfers bobbing along out here appear to have done the same as me. Squinting over my shoulder, I notice a large hump of water travelling at speed towards me.

Confidently I start paddling. The water rises. I paddle harder, and jump. And slip. Now I'm cartwheeling through the blue, with the surfboard battering at my legs and the tether pulling like a mad dog on my ankle. Shit, I'm upside down. I'm fricking UPSIDE DOWN. The water is pummeling at my head. I cartwheel some more, choking in terror and desperation, flailing my arms above my head.

The beach strikes me like a wall, scraping the skin off my face. I feel the blood well up and the caustic sensation of salt on raw flesh as I roll and tumble, the tether still heaving at my leg, until I am literally face-down in a puddle, where I lie, my nose and throat burning with water, gasping like a dying sardine.

Precious takes my hand to pull me up. I snatch it back, choking and heaving, furious and humiliated that she should see me like this. My cheek is hurting like hell. So much for being a knight. If I'd done that Art exam like Harry said, I'd have got the top mark in the school. But instead I'm here, a bleeding failure in a puddle. At the moment, she probably thinks I fail at everything I do.

'Aren't you going to laugh?' I say, feeling sour. 'Girls always laugh when guys mess up.'

'You jumped too soon,' she says. 'Does it hurt?'

'Of course it bloody hurts.'

She touches my face with her long bony fingers, moving very lightly over the graze. She then leans in close to me and puckers her mouth and blows on the raw place. Her breath is cool.

'What are you doing?' I say, jerking back.

'I always blow on grazes. The cool feeling helps. Don't you think?'

'I don't know,' I say, confounded. 'No one ever did it to me before.'

'Not even your mother?'

'No.'

'Your dad then.'

I want to laugh. 'Oh, he blows. But not like that.'

Her question catches me by surprise as I'm trying to brush the sand off my wetsuit.

'Am I a bet, Nathan? Between you and Harry?'

My face throbs harder than ever. 'No!'

She shakes her head. 'I'll be really mad if you're lying.'

'I'm not lying,' I say. 'I . . . I swear.'

'You're not OK though,' she says.

'I'm fine,' I snap. 'It's only a scratch.'

'I'm not talking about your face.'

She blows on my cheek again, a bit harder. I try to keep my feet on the sand but I feel untethered. Like I might float away.

# HARRY

Precious does the talking as we eat, her expression changing like the clouds that break and scud overhead. Nathan on the other hand is almost silent, his fingers touching the graze on his cheek every few seconds. The wipeout has deflated him. I don't feel surprised when he pushes away from the restaurant table the minute the soup bowls are taken away.

We watch him head back down to the beach. When he reaches the sea, he stands up to his ankles in the frilly white bubbles and stares morosely at the horizon.

'What are you doing here, Harry? Really?'

Precious looks at me very intently as she asks this. I remember the taste of her mouth, all heat and almonds, and the feel of her hands on my back.

'I told you,' I say, clearing my throat. 'You had my guitar.'

Nathan has started splashing away to the right now, heading for the rocks uncovered by the retreating tide, towards the noses of the fishing boats tucked into the tiny harbour.

'You ran off without it in Albufeira easily enough,' she says. Her brow creases. 'That was a shitty thing to do, leaving like that.'

There's no point in evading Precious's questions. I know from experience that she'll just keep asking them.

'I didn't run away. That's just what Nathan told you. I was in the café toilet. When I came out, you'd gone. And then you were snatched. I got a lift from Nathan along the coast' – I neglect to mention how he dumped me on the side of the road – 'and . . . I followed you to the Sebastian.'

'The Sebastian?'

'Yes,' I say. I feel terrible.

A reddish colour starts creeping up Precious's neck. It blooms at the base of her throat and spreads upwards until her whole face is a gentle reddish-pink. She's remembering.

'There's a statue of Sebastian in Lagos,' I say randomly. 'I went to Lagos yesterday and saw him and he was a bit crap.'

She catches up a piece of my hair and rolls it like a cigar between her finger and her thumb. She hasn't looked into my eyes yet.

'Do you know that statue?' I say a bit desperately. 'I thought he looked like a pre-pubescent Justin Bieber in armour. You said something about armour yesterday but to be honest, I didn't really catch it because it was quite hard to concentrate at that point.'

'Harry,' she begins.

'It's OK,' I interrupt. 'Honestly. You were drunk and I was – well, not drunk – and stuff happens sometimes. On holiday.'

That makes it sound like we had sex.

'We didn't have sex,' I add.

Precious keeps staring at the bit of hair she's got in her fingers. I think about how she pulled me towards her last night and how pushing her off was the hardest thing in the world.

'Harry,' she says again, very quietly indeed.

I steel myself.

'Who is Green Doris?'

I blink. 'She's my van. I bought her in Monchique. And even though she's rusty blue, Nathan called her Green Doris so we kept calling her that.'

She gazes over the open balcony of the restaurant to where Green Doris is parked, listing ever so slightly to one side.

'Nathan should paint her,' she says. 'He'd do an amazing job. He really regrets not doing his A-level. Painting Green Doris might help him get over it.'

She looks at me now, and I feel like Augustus Gloop falling into the hot chocolate river.

'Would you do it again?' she says.

She's not talking about Green Doris this time. I hesitate. Is it a question or a request? If it's a question, then the answer is undoubtedly yes, although preferably with her sober. If it's a request, then once again a table is in the way.

She drops her gaze, and I realise that it was both a question AND a request and I have taken far too long to answer or respond to either. What's known in the business as a Window of Opportunity just shut in my lightly sweating face.

'Let's go and find Nathan,' she says, pushing away from the table.

'Great,' I say, raining heavy curses on my pathetic head. 'Let's.'

# NATHAN

God knows what they put in this stuff, but it wouldn't pass any kind of health or safety rules back in England. Green, yellow, red, blue, white, black. The sun is sinking into the sea, casting a low light on everything, and it's getting difficult to tell which colour I'm using.

There's something Egyptian about the way the eyes slant upwards and outwards across the bands of colour that I've painted on to Green Doris's flanks. The fishermen in the harbour told me they painted eyes on their boats for good luck, before selling me their leftover paint with a shrug. They got a lot more than the going rate. I outline the second eye for the last time in a sweeping line of black. I'm going to need all the luck I can get tomorrow.

'See?' says Precious when I put the paintbrush down and join her and Harry on to the cooling sand, where they've built a small fire.

'If I bought up more of these tin can scooters, I could do a whole fleet,' I say, enjoying her admiration. The paint fumes uncork my ambition. 'There are probably loads of them being used like donkeys for fruit and vegetables around here. I could buy them for peanuts and paint them and sell them to surfers and holidaymakers. What's the plural of Doris? Dorii?'

Harry's twanging on his guitar, making a bloody awful noise. 'Green Doris is mine, in case you'd forgotten,' he says.

'I'll buy her off you,' I say grandly.

'What if I don't want to sell?'

'I paint a masterpiece on your crappy van and that's all you can say?'

We drink some warm beers that Harry bought from the restaurant hours ago. One or two lights twinkle on the road way above us. One or two twinkle out at sea as well. Oil rigs maybe. Dad says there's loads of oil along this coast. Or perhaps it's smugglers, or a haunted ship like in *Pirates of the Caribbean*.

'Does anyone know a creepy story?' I ask hopefully.

Precious launches into a gruesome one about a prince who fell in love with the wrong girl. 'The king didn't approve and so she was murdered,' she tells us as the flames flicker and the wood crackles. 'When the prince became king, he executed his lover's murderers by ripping out their hearts. And then he dug up her body and he put a crown on her corpse and a ring on her finger and made all his nobles kiss her hand with her putrid flesh hanging off the finger bone.'

We sit there in silence, picturing it.

'That's one of Dad's.' Precious prods the fire. 'All my stories are from my dad.'

The moon has risen clear above our heads now, bobbing above the cliffs and casting a milky light on the water in front of us as we sit with our backs to the land. Harry absently starts twanging again.

'I want to ask a serious question,' Precious says.

'Yes, Harry is still a virgin,' I say, and Harry scuffs sand at me.

Precious tuts but laughs at the same time. 'What's your worst fear?' she says.

'You know that already,' says Harry.

'Mine's being alone.' She rests her chin on her kneecaps. 'But I'm starting to conquer that. You could conquer your fear of the sea too, Harry, if you tried.'

They exchange a look that makes me feel like I shouldn't be there.

'I'm scared of flamingos,' I say.

'There are flamingos in the Algarve.' Harry lies back in the sand with one hand behind his head. 'If they are really your worst fear, you wouldn't be here.'

'You're scared of the sea, but you carry the sea around with you,' I point out. 'That's like a vampire carrying around a bulb of garlic for luck.'

'It's not the sea's fault that your father died, Harry,' Precious says.

'Except it is,' Harry says. 'Because he drowned in it.'

'He chose to go out there.'

'He didn't choose to get sunk.'

They're excluding me again.

'I'm scared of flamingos because they have pink zombie eyes and skull-crushing beaks,' I say. 'And their legs bend backwards.'

'They don't.' Harry shifts a little closer to the fire. 'They bend forwards but the knee joints are inside their bodies. The bits you see are their ankles.'

'I'll probably cover bird anatomy at Art School,' I say without thinking.

There is a long silence, punctuated by the whispering sea. When Precious puts her hand on my arm, I jump.

'It's not too late to retake,' she says.

'Dad won't let me,' I say in despair. 'And even if he did, it would cost over six thousand pounds. I have four hundred euros in my wallet and two grand in my personal account, and he will take all of it to pay for the damage to his car. He'll stop my allowance altogether, in fact. Probably for ever.'

'You could find a way round it.'

'Like Hairy Harry can get round that?' I gesture dramatically at the ocean. 'I should be facing the cliff right now, not the sea. It's a better representation of my options.'

Precious seems to be staring in the direction of Green Doris, although it's hard to tell in the dark.

'I have a thousand euros,' she says. 'How much have you got, Harry?'

Harry shifts position. 'About five hundred. Although I owe you twenty-five of that.'

Precious claps her hands. 'If we put everything together, we could buy another Green Doris. Nathan could paint it and sell it for a profit and then we could buy another, and another, and before you know it he would have the six thousand he needs for the retake.'

I digest this.

'Are you saying you'd invest?' I say uncertainly. 'In me?'

'It's a business opportunity. Dad always taught me to look for business opportunities. You don't succeed by sitting around, apparently.'

'You'd do that?'

'She said she would, didn't she?' grunts Harry.

'How much was Green Doris?' Precious asks.

'About fifteen hundred,' I say, trying to still the rising excitement in my gut.

'Sixteen,' Harry corrects.

Precious's eyes gleam in the firelight. 'I bet you could sell her again for closer to two thousand now you've painted her,' she says. 'Add the profit to my thousand, Nathan's four hundred and your five hundred, and you—'

She pauses as if she just ran into a wall.

'Harry Temple,' she says. 'Since when do you have five hundred euros?'

# PRECIOUS

'Four hundred and seventy-five,' says Harry after a long pause.

'How did you buy Green Doris?' It suddenly strikes me how little I know here. 'You have no money. You couldn't even buy fishcakes in Albufeira.'

The fire crackles between us.

'Tell me,' I say.

Harry rubs his eyes. I start feeling worried. Has he robbed someone?

'Tell me,' I say more loudly.

'This is going to sound bad,' he begins.

'Really bad,' Nathan agrees, lounging back in the sand.

I snatch up a stick from the campfire and point it at Harry. 'Tell. Me,' I say.

Harry clears his throat. 'Fine. But you're not going to like it. It's . . . You . . .'

'Your dad paid him to look for you,' Nathan says.

I'm so shocked that I drop the flaming stick. Paranoia rushes through me in a wild ocean wave. Harry on the beach, Harry holding my hand in the café, Harry kissing me. I've been feeling his kiss ever since he reminded me about it in the beach restaurant.

'He *paid* you?'

It's like Harry said on the beach. *You've never done real before.* None of this has been real.

'When did he pay you?' I discover that I've stood up. 'In the airport? At the train station?'

Harry's on his feet too. 'This morning at the hotel. Only this morning, I swear.'

'I don't believe you.' I shove him in the middle of the chest so he staggers over the glowing embers. 'Why were you at the hotel if he hadn't already paid you to be there?'

'Because I was worried about you.'

'Worried?' I say incredulously. 'You don't even know me.'

'But I do,' he says.

I shake my head. I wish I hadn't dropped the stick.

'I felt awful when the Terminators got you in Albufeira. I made Nathan drive around after the Terminators took you. I wanted to find you. And then I did and I kissed you and you disappeared again. And then I met your dad in the hotel this morning and he paid me to find you. That's it, that's the whole story, I swear.'

'You kissed her?' says Nathan, looking up from poking at the campfire. 'You didn't tell me you kissed her.'

Harry glares. 'Why would I tell you I kissed her?'

'I kissed her too.'

'When did *you* kiss her?'

289

'In Monchique before you came blundering in.'

'I kissed her at the hotel.'

'And it was so good that she forgot all about it,' Nathan says. 'And disappeared right after.'

'Well, *you* only kissed her so Daddy doesn't take away your allowance,' Harry says. 'Tell her about the deal. Go on.'

They look like they're going to start fighting again like they did in Monchique. I wish I could enjoy the unlikely nature of this conversation.

'You're a liar,' I tell Harry, breathless with confusion. 'What deal?'

Nathan spreads his hands. 'My father is doing a deal with your father for some land on the south coast. He wanted me to keep you company while the deal was going through, that's all—'

'Keep her away, you mean,' Harry interrupts. 'Frighten her father into thinking he'd only get her back if the deal was signed. Nathan's worst fear isn't flamingos, Precious. It's his dad.'

Nathan gapes. 'And Harry's worst fear is the feel of my fist in his mouth!'

I am hot and cold, all at once. This is all much worse than a bet. Harry is here because Dad paid him. Nathan is here because his dad is doing a deal with mine. Everyone is here on false pretences.

'Don't come near me,' I say, my voice rising. 'Either of you. I do karate and I will HURT you.'

Nathan looks worried. Harry makes an explosive noise and rubs his hair with both his hands so that it stands up around his head in a raffia tangle.

I back away from them both. 'I'm going to sleep in the Boxster and neither of you is coming in there with me.'

Muttering, Harry snatches up his guitar and strides off down the beach in the direction of the harbour. He's invisible by the time I take the cobbled slipway in three furious bounds.

'So where am I going to sleep?' Nathan asks, following me. 'I thought we would both go in the Box—'

I'm in the car and pressing buttons until the roof slides up from beneath its special lid to seal me in. I lock the doors and bang buttons and yank levers and savagely twist wheels until the soft leather seat starts reclining. Nathan raps forlornly at the passenger window. I turn my face away, grab the linen jacket hanging over the back of the seat and drape myself in it. Then I ignore him until he goes away.

My brain hurts from all the pieces in this puzzle. Mum and Bacon. Harry and Dad. Harry's kiss, Nathan's kiss. Land and deals, airports and Terminators, car crashes and ghosts and armour and oil. All I did was go on holiday with people I thought were my friends.

I stare at the roof of the car, listening to the swell of the sea. It sounds like it's lapping up the slipway, perhaps even brushing at the wheels of the Porsche. I wish it would just carry me away, far out into the western seas. All the way to the end of the world.

# HARRY

I've chased Precious Silva halfway across the country with nothing but a bottle of seawater and a self-regarding idiot to keep me company, and this is what I get. So what if her father paid me to look for her? Doesn't that mean he cares? *I* care.

I try to get more comfortable on the damp planks. It's not easy when your muscles are cramped with anger. There's some tarpaulin that I have draped between the sides of the boat so that I have a small covered space in which to toss and turn and talk to myself. Which I do. Loudly.

'You wouldn't have paid a bean for anyone to come and find *me*.'

*Says who?*

'Oh, come ON. We both know I was a massive disappointment to you in life. Let's not pretend I'm not a massive disappointment to you in death too.'

I press my hands to my eyes.

*I'm sorry.*

My father has never apologised before. Tears roll hot and fierce down my cheeks.

'I'm the one who should be sorry,' I groan. 'I'm the . . . I'm the one . . .'

It's as if the waves are inside the boat with me, drenching me, drowning me. I wrap my arms around my head and squeeze my eyes as tight as they will go. I have a whole ocean inside me, and it's all coming out of my eyes and my nose and my skin.

*The argument has worn transparent at the edges. My passport is in order, my kit is packed, everything is in place except my final decision. Which I made several months ago, and which Dad is still refusing to hear.*

*'It'll be the most magical experience of your life, Harry boy.'*

*The croissants are still warm. I carefully unravel mine, praying that my father will stop being so obtuse and accept that I will never board his yacht, never in a million aeons. This last-minute assault on my resolve is not going to work.*

*Dad attacks his pastries with his usual vigour, so that there are crumbs spread in all corners of the kitchen. 'Most sailors in past centuries couldn't swim. They got by.'*

*'Until they drowned,' I say.*

*Dad waves a croissant. More crumbs fly about. 'We all live in life jackets. There's a man-overboard procedure that we can do blindfolded. The crew is a great bunch of guys, you'll like them. It'll only take around fifteen or sixteen days from Bermuda to the*

*Azores, then eight days home. Twenty-four days of magic, son. Twenty-four days of watching seagulls.'*

*Twenty-four days of pitiless sea, waves like mountains, stomach fizzing with terror.*

*'There's no such thing as a seagull,' I say automatically.*

*'There'll be purposes too,' says Mum.*

*'She said that on porpoise,' says Dad, following up his joke with such a massive gust of laughter that he practically blows the teapot off the table.*

*'I don't want to go,' I say doggedly.*

*'The navy took apprentices at twelve. You're fourteen. You're strong, you're tall. Imagine how it will feel, sailing into Portsmouth harbour with your old dad when it's all done. Imagine that!'*

*I'm imagining it all too well.*

*'I don't want to GO,' I repeat.*

*Dad tries one last time after lunch as Mum assembles everything by the front door, and checks his passport, and kisses him each time she walks past, and locks herself in the toilet for a silent cry that only I am aware of.*

*'Last chance, Harry,' he says, laying his great hand on my shoulder.*

*I shut my ears to the hope in his voice and aim for the stairs, shaking my head as I go.*

I sleep somehow. From exhaustion, perhaps. I'm in a pool, wide and blue. I'm resting my head on my inflatable crocodile, my arms around its neck and my face pressed against the hot, tacky plastic. The water dips and rolls under me, supporting me. There are sound effects and everything.

I sit up abruptly, the guitar in my arms, and get a mouthful of tarpaulin. There's a shout, and the heavy sound of boots. I fling my arms over my head to shield myself from whatever is ripping back the tarp, and squint into the pale morning light. An oil-covered man in a battered red cap and several days' beard growth is staring at me.

'*Puta que pariu!*'

It's fair to say that he sounds startled. The boat dips, and I clutch for the side. The stink of salt and fish assails me. There's sea all around. Sea everywhere. Sea, sea, more sea.

A younger man appears from behind the little cabin at the front of the boat. His Guns 'n' Roses T-shirt has seen better days, but his teeth are whiter than you see on TV.

'Why are you in this boat?'

I'm struggling with such a primal level of fear that I just keep saying, '*Shit!*' I'm floating on a LOT of sea. There's nothing between me and the monsters but a line of creaking planks. Guns 'n' Roses clicks his tongue and says something to Red Cap, who laughs.

'You want to work?' says Guns 'n' Roses, gazing down at me.

I want to throw up. Of all the places to sleep in, I chose a boat?

'I have money,' I manage. 'Can you take me back?'

'We are maybe five kilometres out, we will go back in some hours. You can work?'

My hands reach, trembling, for my back pocket. I don't know how much I pull out, but I wave it at Guns 'n' Roses who takes it, studies it and pockets it.

'Work, don't work,' he says. 'Where do you want to go?'

'Back,' I repeat helplessly.

Guns 'n' Roses scratches his head. 'The tide at Arrifana is out now, we don't go back to the harbour for some hours until we have the fish. The current take us to the south.'

South sounds like something that's not made of water.

'South is fine,' I say, trying to keep my voice steady. I'll work out how to find Precious from there. I'm on the bastard SEA.

Guns 'n' Roses rattles something at Red Cap, who grins and fires something back.

'My father say we can go to the Cabo São Vicente if the current is OK,' says Guns 'n' Roses. 'It is the end of the world. You want to go to the end of the world?'

'Already there, mate,' I say, clinging dumbly to the boat. 'Already there.'

# NATHAN

My feet are sticking out of Green Doris with the wind on my toes. My cheek is still hurting and I have a headache because the smell of paint isn't evaporating, even in the brisk – and it's pretty bloody brisk – wind whistling across the sea and up my trouser legs. It's a design flaw that will need rethinking if Precious meant what she said last night about a Green Doris fleet.

I'd pinch myself if I thought it would help. She offered me a thousand euros so I can retake an exam I shouldn't have missed in the first place. No demands, no questions. She's angry right now, but she seems madder at Harry, so that's OK.

A thousand euros, just like that.

There's obviously a catch because nothing in life is free, not even love. I press my hand to the unwounded side of my face, curl my legs up to my stomach, turn on my side and stare at Green Doris's corrugated wall. I fall asleep, trying to work out what the catch might be.

# PRECIOUS

As daylight brightens through the Boxster window, I run my tongue around my furry teeth. A number of things have become clear overnight. Things that require direct action. Dental hygiene will have to wait.

The petrol gauge is still quite high. I flex my fingers and run my fingertips over the ridged leather of the steering wheel. Then I start up the engine and attempt to get out of my parking space without scraping anything. I fail pretty dramatically.

Leaving Green Doris in my rear-view mirror, I climb the cobbled hill in fits and starts, and hope I don't meet any early-morning surf buses hurtling down to greet the day. These corners are sharp. How did I get down here yesterday without removing the second wing-mirror as well?

There are surf buses parked along the road at the top, blatantly defying the 'NO PARKING OVERNIGHT' signs stapled to the wooden fence posts separating the cars from the cliffs. A couple of guys are brewing a cup of something on a tiny gas stove outside their camper, sitting on mismatched chairs and already wearing their wetsuits. They gaze at me as I rush by, and shout something that gets lost on the wind.

Nathan said his father and mine were doing a deal for some land on the south coast. That's a lot of coast. Where do I begin? I veer into the verge in the shadow of a great whirring wind turbine, fumble for the glove box and pull out the Terminator phone to Google Dad's development plans. Nathan's phone rolls out as well. I'd forgotten I still had that.

**Desejado Developments Ricky Silva**
**Desejado Developments Payne Silva**
**Desejado Developments property deal**

I get hundreds of hits ranging through Dad's misadventures. A new golfing hotel with a blight of moles, a chunk of land polluted by run-off from a cement factory. My stomach turns when I find an article all about the *Amalia*, on which Dad apparently owes millions. I can picture wads of fifty-euro notes without too much trouble, but millions is something else. I don't learn anything specific about Dad and Mr Payne, but I do get a strong sense that Dad is in trouble. *Bankrupt that man is not!* As with most things, my mother might just be wrong.

I drive on, thinking about what I've read. I pass more wind turbines, and blackened chunks of forest damaged by recent fires. There are road cones (I hit a couple), and diggers, and men in fluorescent jackets working in the shimmering heat. A new motorway for the deserted west coast. More opportunities for people like my dad to build hotels and create jobs.

I realise that I don't want him to fail.

I check Nathan's phone next, to see if I can gather anything useful from his father's voice messages. 'Why the hell aren't you answering your phone?' is Mr Payne's main drift, which tells me nothing useful. He sounds stressed and angry, and faintly familiar.

A brown sign on the right catches my eye. *Cabo São Vicente.* The Cape of St Vincent.

*'And the body of the holy Saint Vincent sailed alone from the coast of Africa, his sightless eyes looking up to heaven as the waves tossed him and the monsters clashed their jaws and the whirlpools sucked at the boat and tried to drag him to hell.'*

*Dad lowers his voice.*

*'And down from the sky flew the ravens. Four ravens, with wings black and shining in the sun. Two settled at Saint Vincent's head and two at his feet, and they brought him through the waves and the serpents and the whirlpools to the Cape. What could we do except give his name to the place where he came to safety?' He says this like he was personally responsible for the decision.*

*'He wasn't safe though,' I point out, imagining the ravens rowing the boat with their great black wings. 'He was dead.'*

*'Yes,' Dad replies, undeterred. 'But he was in Portugal.'*

Dad would never sail us as far as Cape St Vincent. Too many strange and unpredictable currents, where the sea from the south meets the sea from the west and the two invariably argue. So I've never been.

I turn the wheel.

The stories drift through my head as I drive. Inês de Castro and her skeletal fingers. Mad Queen Maria screaming around her palace, King Sebastian and his lost army, the cooked cockerel of Barcelos crowing at the feast. And the explorers aboard their tiny boats, leaving a small country at the end of the world, to find there's no end to the world at all.

The road gets narrower, then turns to dust and rocks. The Boxster bumps and grinds over the rougher potholes, occasionally sliding off the road altogether. The sea is near. The whole horizon glows with it. When the road opens up again into a long, straight stretch of perfectly empty tarmac, I put my foot down and fly – faster, faster, faster – until the horizon resolves into a perfect line of blue. The little finger of a lighthouse, striped red and white, sticks jauntily into the air, and I floor it some more, until I'm parking at an uneven angle beside a large SUV with French number plates. The car almost rolls into the barriers until I remember the handbrake.

Most of the people wandering through the dusty car park are studying the view of the sea and the waves and the lighthouse through the viewfinder on their phones. With the lighthouse on my left, I walk to the very edge of the rocks, as far as I can go, and I sit cross-legged on a yellow-lichened rock spattered with punky pink flowers and I look at the ocean and I smell the salt in the air. I think about Mum, too lonely to notice so many things, and Dad, struggling under a burden of debt and divorce, and Nathan's hopelessness. I think about sea and dragons too. I let myself remember the feel of Harry's skinny arms around me in the mist and his skin on my skin at the hotel and the salt taste of his lips on mine.

Then I take out the Terminator phone.

'Mum,' I say when she answers, as breathless and anxious as yesterday. 'What's Bacon's full name?'

# HARRY

Fish, loud and flapping and shining. The sun turns their scales to gold. The smell of the boat's diesel engine mingles with brine and sweat and the air holds the sounds of crashing water and the screams of the gulls and the creaking planks of the boat. The fish themselves don't smell as they did in Aljezur. They smell of the cold unknown, which smells of nothing at all.

We have been at sea for several hours. Guns 'n' Roses has told me his name is José and he studies English in Lagos at weekends. I have told him my name and that I'm going to study Environmental Sciences at Birmingham in September if I make it back to England alive. The word for petrified in Portuguese is *petrificado*.

'Throw them in the sea,' shouts José, scooping the air at me now. His soggy T-shirt clings to his skinny chest. 'They are too small, throw them in the sea before they die.'

I put my hands mindlessly in the slithering, gleaming mass and fling handfuls of fish over the side. Gulls swoop, water droplets on their wings, rushing to catch at the tails and fins as the surviving fish break for safety. Some succeed. Some don't. A little way ahead, by the distant headland José says is the Cape of St Vincent, the water breaks in three cascading curves of dove grey. Dolphins.

*Look, son. See what I wanted to show you.*

# NATHAN

I'm enjoying the admiring looks so much that I almost forget the gut-melting horror of waking up two hours ago and finding Precious and the Boxster gone.

Almost.

I'm driving south. Precious will also be driving south, to the coast, because that's exactly where my father doesn't want her to go. Dad will know for sure what a cock-up I have made of everything because Tico will have told him. What's worse, incompetence or treachery? I wipe at the layer of sweat on my top lip and squeeze hard on Green Doris's handlebars. He hasn't even seen the state of his car yet.

Every driver smiles at Green Doris as I drive past. Every single one. It gives me courage, and I push the dark thoughts of Dad to the back of my mind. Now all I have to do is keep them there.

*Green Doris artwork by Nathan Payne. All designs considered. Call now for a customised quote.*

# PRECIOUS

I'm not all that surprised when I see a sign for DESEJADO DEVELOPMENTS COMING SOON! beside a sign for a beach called Praia Dom Sebastião. What does surprise me, however, is that I'm barely five kilometres from where I started, at the Cape with its lollipop lighthouse and punky pink cliff flowers.

The wooden posts are splintered and raw and smell of resin more than they smell of salt. There is nothing here but rocks and sand, and COMING SOON! strikes me as optimistic. This far west, the landscape is a lot wilder than where Dad's other hotels are. The few buildings that exist are low, crouched into the ground, and there are no trees at all. The sea has bitten a row of sandy golden arcs out of the south-facing black-grey cliffs that plunge away to my right. How do black rocks produce golden sand?

The wind of yesterday has dropped and the clear, mint-leaf sea is calm. A catamaran is moored on the opposite headland, and a small fishing boat is cruising towards the shore with the usual escort of seagulls. More Desejado Developments signs stand at angles around a small, scrubby car park containing just one other car. A car I recognise.

My palms start sweating. I haven't seen Dad in three months. Three months is a long time not to see someone you've just remembered that you love.

The car park is right by the uneven cliff edge, so I'm extra careful to put the handbrake on when I get out of the Porsche. As soon as I'm upright, smoothing down my T-shirt dress with nervous hands, I spot a path marked by a series of waist-high metal poles leading down the cliff.

The path is narrow. Not really a path at all. And the handholds are set a long way apart. Slipping and sliding as I descend, stretching my arms from pole to pole, it's a long five minutes before I see the reason why Dad might have bought the site. A squat little Bond-villain fortress built of grey stone clings on halfway down the cliff face. Parts of the building overhang the sea, with one or two surfers bobbing disconsolately on the lazy waves below. It's a glorious leap of imagination to see the crumbling fortress as it might once have been, but the position is unbelievable.

An empty golden beach sweeps away below the fort. No one but a crazy person would attempt to get a beach umbrella down this path. I can only assume the surfers bobbed along from the next beach by mistake.

Two men are standing further down, holding one metal pole each.

'It's the best offer the board can make,' Bacon Payne is saying. 'I'm sorry it's not higher, but extracting the oil is going to be difficult.'

Dad's voice is distant, like he's not really concentrating. 'It is a good offer, in the circumstances.'

They walk on, along a stretch not much wider than a window ledge. The path dips and turns like a roller coaster, and Bacon staggers and grabs the metal posts once or twice. When I am satisfied that they are out of sight, I follow, doing my best not to send any pebbles skittering ahead of me.

'We can draw up the papers when we get back to the hotel.' Bacon's voice drifts towards me over the rock, more out of breath than before. 'I've arranged for my lawyer to meet us there.'

'This is good of you, Aiden. Helping me in this way.'

'Not at all, not at all. Business is business.'

They make the final scramble to the fortress itself. The moment they disappear through a sea-facing archway, I scamper after them like a lizard. Moving a little too eagerly on the last stretch of path, I almost lose my footing just as Dad pops up through a second sea-facing doorway in the fortress wall.

I do my best to hold his startled gaze and to tell him that I'm OK and that I have his back if he needs it. And that I'm sorry I didn't wait for his men at the airport and how very much I would like to spend the rest of the summer with him after all.

Dad breaks into a smile. Now that he has seen me and I have seen him, I hurtle up the path without caring too much about the dizzying drop to my right and stoop to bury my face in his warm shirt and smell that combination of cigars and lavender soap that I haven't smelled in a long time.

Stepping out of the doorway behind Dad, Bacon freezes, one leg in the air, streaky hair blowing back from his beaky face. His eyes, seen close up, are pink-rimmed. Perhaps Nathan's fear of flamingos isn't so strange after all.

'Aiden,' says Dad. 'Have you met my daughter?'

'I haven't had the pleasure,' Bacon says, sounding worried.

'Yes you have,' I say, lifting my face from Dad's shoulder. 'Mum introduced us. Don't you remember?'

'I . . . no?'

'Of course you do.' I reach out and give Bacon a friendly jab in the belly. 'We met at the Swintons' villa. You weren't very happy about it. I thought that was because you wanted Mum to yourself, but it was because you knew I'd recognise you if we met again.'

Bacon's face is turning as pink as his eyes.

'Has Nathan ever said you look like a flamingo?' I ask curiously. 'Out of interest?'

'What?'

'Sorry, off-topic,' I say. 'Let's go back to the Terminator Twins. The men you use sometimes, for your dirty work.'

'I don't know what men you're—'

I hold up my hand. It's a surprisingly effective way of stopping adults from talking bollocks. 'You sent them to grab me at the airport.'

'What?' Bacon says again, a little more quietly.

'Mum conveniently forgot to sort out my paperwork before she left.' That part still hurts. 'So you both knew I wouldn't be able to catch my plane. Then Mum flew back in for the happy reunion. You let her take responsibility for the whole thing, telling her to spin the photos to her advantage and get the press on her side for a decent divorce payout. You even paid for the room we were supposed to stay in at the Jacaranda Hotel until the deal was done.'

'Terrible hotel,' says Dad with interest. 'Not one of mine.'

I glance at the cliffs, the scrub, the beach, the sea. 'There must be a lot of oil here for you to go to all this trouble,' I say. 'I mean, a *lot*. You're trying to say YES TO THE OILGARVE, aren't you, Bacon?'

Bacon looks perplexed, possibly by the Bacon thing. 'Really, Ricky, your daughter doesn't understand any of this.'

'She appears to understand more than me,' says Dad.

I tut at Bacon for interrupting. 'Anyway,' I say. 'I escaped and you had to send Nathan after me. I escaped from him too, by the way. Oh, and I nicked your car.'

Bacon's eyes dart up to the top of the cliff, where the Boxster's nose can just be seen. It's even closer to the edge than I realised when I parked it.

'Don't worry,' I add. 'I put the handbrake on.'

'That's a very valuable vehicle,' Bacon says in horror. 'If you've damaged it, I'll know where to send the bill.'

'Yes,' I say, pulling a face. 'About that.'

He pales. 'What have you done?'

'You should probably see for yourself,' I suggest. 'It's not great, to be honest.'

My father takes my hand in his big hairy paw. We follow Bacon back up the cliff. Every now and again, Bacon glances back at me with loathing. I don't think he likes women much.

'You and I need to talk about this, Ricky,' he pants, flicking his flamingo gaze to Dad as we climb. 'Man to man. You still need to pay for your boat. You are in debt up to your eyes. I'm doing you a favour by offering to buy this plot from you. We both know it. Any damage your daughter has caused to my car can probably be offset by a fair price for the lan—'

Bacon stops as the sound of breaking glass floats over the cliff edge.

# NATHAN

I don't know whether to feel relief or despair when I spot the Boxster parked at a strange angle on the cliff edge. It looks even worse than it did at the beach. Ricky's big black Bentley is here too. So, presumably, are Ricky and my dad. My stomach turns to liquid.

I change gears and swing off the road, feeling every bump in the gravel as I do. For all her charms, Green Doris isn't that hot on suspension. I get out and try to calm myself down. The hard grey-yellow rocks beneath my feet seem solid enough, so why do I feel like I could tip over the cliff?

'I'm here to talk to Precious,' I say out loud, to bolster my courage. 'I'm here to ask her to invest in me. This has nothing to do with my father. I don't need my father.'

Hearing it out loud makes it sound ridiculous. I can't do this. I can't be an artist. I wouldn't survive. How many times has Dad told me that? I know it, I've always known it. My stupid little cloud of hope is evaporating into the big blue sky with every step I take towards the Boxster.

I'm in awe at how thoroughly Precious has wrecked it. The bodywork is ripped to pieces. The bumper is dented. The chip in the windscreen has spread. The wheels are white with dust and all four hub caps are ruined. Wow. Just . . . wow.

Do freak-outs have levels? Exactly how bad can it get?

I mean, really?

I pull back my foot and kick the passenger door with a clang. The rush is like nothing on earth. I kick the door again. The metal buckles. With each kick I find a fresh source of energy and kick harder. My foot complains at the pain but I don't care. I bend at the waist and batter the driver's window with my heel. The glass wobbles and twists in the frame.

'Don't . . . screw . . . up . . .' I pant. 'Don't . . . mess . . . up. Always said you were useless. Now who's . . . useless?'

The driver's window caves. Glass spills through the leather interior even as it cuts the skin on my ankle. I feel a glimmer of sympathy for the car, the beautiful car, whose only mistake was to belong to my father. But then the moment is gone. I kick out both headlights, stumble on to the bonnet and start driving my bloodied feet at the windscreen.

When the bonnet buckles under my weight, I lose my balance, tipping sideways off the car and grabbing hold of the remaining wing mirror. My palms are cut too, I see. The realisation of how close I am to the edge of the cliff slaps me in the face and the madness ends as abruptly as it began. I am weak, loose-limbed, untethered like I was when Precious blew on my cheek.

Dad's head suddenly emerges over the edge of the cliff. Precious appears behind him, followed by her father. I'd be creeped out if I had enough energy left. Instead, I simply wait for them to come closer. I even wave, a little breathlessly, and push my sweaty hair back from my face with a bloodied palm. I'm growing it back, starting from today.

Precious claps her hands to her face. Dad's beaky mouth works soundlessly.

'Don't come any closer,' I advise. 'The handbrake is off.'

Reaching through the busted driver's window, I put my hand on the brake, press my thumb on the button and gently – ever so gently – lower the lever all the way down.

'At least, it is now,' I say.

Pebbles crunch as the wheels roll forward. Dad shrieks, and lunges, and falls to his knees as the car cruises off the edge, where it briefly tries to ride the first few metres of the cliff face with all four wheels before abandoning the attempt and flipping over, and over, and over, until it smashes into the rocks below with a boom and a crunch. There's no explosion, which is disappointing.

Oh. Wait.

There it is.

The smell of burning petrol and billowing smoke is eye-watering. We all gaze over the cliff at the wreckage, apart from Dad, who doesn't seem able to move from his dog-like position on the pebbles. Behind us on the road, cars slow and drivers crane their necks, trying to see what has happened.

Ricky helps Dad to his feet but Dad wrenches free from his hairy grasp. He is clearly fighting an enormous battle with his emotions. He showed more love for that car than he's ever shown me, or Mum. I decide to make his day a bit worse.

'I blew up your boat, Mr Silva,' I say.

I see why Roman Catholics get such a kick out of confession. Precious's brown eyes get even buggier. Dad puts a dusty, long-fingered hand to his face. Ricky Silva's eyebrows twitch, but that's about it. He's a tough man to surprise, I think.

'I didn't know it was a bomb.' It's such a relief to say it out loud. 'Dad just told me to put a packet on your boat in Vilamoura. I thought it was . . .' I wave my hand, because what I thought isn't important. 'Anyway, I was just doing what I was told. I do that a lot.'

Dad groans.

'I arranged the moles on your golf course too,' I add, because now is as good a time as any. 'And put in the call to a guy Dad knows at the cement factory that polluted your land. I didn't want to do it but I should probably take responsibility.' I look hopefully at Ricky Silva. 'Unless maybe you want my dad to take that?'

# HARRY

The water is clearer than I thought it would be, this far out. Peaceful too. I hang my face over the side and gaze at the blue ridges way down on the sand below. The dolphins that have been following us since we rounded the Cape have disappeared. I lift my head and look at the horizon, hoping to see them breach the surface again, but the water is like a mirror and nothing moves but the gulls that bob on the surface and watch us with their keen yellow eyes.

It's like coming out of a trance when José lays a hand on my shoulder.

'We will land at Baleeira, the port in Sagres. My father will call the harbour so they know we are coming.'

'The French word for whale is *baleine*,' I say.

'In Portuguese, *baleeira* is the boat that catches the whale.'

I would have seen a whale if I had gone with Dad. The Azores is famous for them. But then, I would be dead, and there would be no one to tell.

'I'd like to see a whale,' I say.

José smiles and points. Squinting along the line of his finger, I see something black and white curving out of the water. Before I blink, it's gone.

'Orca,' he says agreeably, like we just saw a blackbird in a hedge.

I stare at the spot where the orca sank away, and am rewarded almost at once by two more. They are absolutely massive but somehow not scary at all, although they clearly have something to do with the disappearance of the dolphins. I am silent, lost in wonderment.

*I can still show you these things. I can show you so much.*

José's father brings the fishing boat closer to the shore. There are beaches all along this side of the coast, curving and golden and almost entirely empty. The cliffs are a multitude of colours layered together, cake-style. I've never seen beaches from this angle before, or appreciated the way the sea changes from deep blue to pale aqua as it approaches the shore. There are lots of things I've never seen before, including a white car tipping off a clifftop. Right there, above a glimmering beach with no one on it.

It seems to move in slow motion. Two wheels, then four. The long nose tipping south, the sloping headlights. I know that car.

I jump to my feet. 'Take me to that beach.'

José looks startled. 'But Baleeira—'

The car bounces down the cliff face, flips over a few times and hits the sand with a silent puff. There's a boom,

317

like a toy cannon firing way in the distance, and a leap of flame. Four little figures stand at the top of the cliff, their silhouettes like tiny smudges of darkness against the yellow-grey rock. Four people. Precious, Nathan, her dad, his dad: maybe.

But only maybe.

I start racing up and down the boat like a rat in a trap, roaring and swerving among the crates of fish set into their great boxes of ice. José and his father watch in bemusement. I don't know what to do, I don't know where to go. The boat is too *small*.

My voice doesn't sound like my voice but it must be because I can see José and his dad and neither of them is speaking. 'You have to take me to that beach as quickly as you can. I'll pay you more, I'll pay you everything I have.'

José translates. His dad puts the fishing boat into some kind of higher gear and I'm thrown backwards, landing butt-down in a box of fish. By the time I struggle upright again, the four smudgy figures have started climbing down the path to the smoking wreckage. Impossible to tell if they are men or women. Impossible to tell if Precious is with them, or lying in the burned shell at the foot of the cliff.

'Faster,' I roar. 'FASTER.'

'We cannot land on this beach,' protests José. 'There is no harbour like at Baleeira. We can take you in maybe some metres from the shore, but then—'

I know what's coming.

'Then,' José finishes, as I know he will, 'you must swim.'

# PRECIOUS

The tide is coming in, creeping towards us beneath the overhang of the little fortress on our left. The power of a high tide can clear away most things but not, I suspect, an entire car.

'We will arrange for a salvage boat,' Dad is telling Bacon, who has come down here with us and is now sitting on a rock with both hands on his head. 'Access is difficult but not impossible.'

Nathan's made it down here despite his injured feet and hands, and is staring out at a fishing boat on the horizon. I'm glad he hasn't tried to talk to me since revealing his part in blowing up the *Amalia*. It's another thing Dad has taken surprisingly well. Better than me, that's for sure.

'There is no more that we can do down here,' Dad says.

He takes the first stretch of path at a brisk jog, swinging from metal pole to metal pole like some kind of beach-dwelling monkey. Aiden Payne gets to his feet and follows.

Nathan doesn't want to meet my eye. I wouldn't want to meet my eye either. I turn my back on him and scramble up the little path behind Bacon. As I reach for the metal handholds, I wish I could pull them out, one by one like pins from a pincushion, before Nathan can use them. I'd like the tide to take him and his pretty face and wash them all far away from me.

There's a shield over the main archway to the fortress that I didn't notice earlier. A royal shield. I duck through the archway to join Dad and Bacon in the courtyard. Nathan edges silently into the fortress behind me. Still unprepared to look at him, I move across the great central space to where the fortress wall is so low that I could stand on the remaining stones and fling myself into the sea like a Mexican cliff-diver. I imagine the walls restored, the roofs replaced, the royal shield repainted. I picture a great sea-facing deck all around the fortress, shoring it up so that it will never fall into the sea. Staying here would feel like riding on the prow of a great stone boat.

'Do you know about our lost king, Sebastian?'

I don't know why Bacon shakes his head. Dad isn't looking at him.

'He came to this place. He brought his musicians and they played for him in the sea caves below us. Imagine the music, Aiden. Can you imagine it? He made them play until the tide was lapping at their feet, rising to the roof of the cave, almost drowning them all because he did not want the music to stop.'

320

Dad runs his hand along the rough stone walls. There are gaps where the wind and the rain and the sea have taken bites out of the structure, and the salt breeze blows around us.

'Sebastian thought that he could take on the might of an empire,' he says. 'But he did not plan ahead. He and his army were slaughtered in North Africa, and all of Portugal was lost to Spain. This country hopes that he will return to save them one day, but the truth is that he couldn't even save himself. I'm glad that he is gone.'

He is building up to something.

'Why name your hotel after a failure?' Bacon asks cautiously.

'To remind me not to make the same mistakes,' Dad says, surprised by the question.

Bacon rubs his forehead. 'What do you want, Ricky?'

'What I've always wanted.' Dad indicates the view with his hand. 'This.'

'But you need to sell,' Bacon begins.

'Ah yes,' says Dad. 'To pay my debts. A few million from you, a change of hands on this place and my business can begin to recover. But things are different now, aren't they, Aiden? Now that I know what you have done to me.'

The way my father's voice changes from genial to icy-cold over the course of one simple sentence is enough to make Bacon eye the fortress archway, clearly calculating the quickest way out.

'Nathan,' he says, addressing his son for the first time since the car thing. 'We're leaving.'

The speed at which Dad moves is breathtaking. One moment he's gazing up at the deep-blue sky. The next, he has chugged into Bacon with the full force of a train, blasting him across the courtyard. Somehow Nathan's father stays upright, but his feet slide through the pebbles and grass and his hands flail and he squeals like a pig in a slaughterhouse.

I barely have time to leap out of the way before Dad is curling Bacon into a brutal back bend against the broken wall. One or two stones crumble away and sail out of view with a faint plop into the sea below. Bacon squeals again, and grapples with the hairy hands that my father has around his neck.

'No one is leaving,' says Dad.

It's creepy, how calm he sounds. He squeezes harder, pushes Bacon back further. Bacon is gasping, gargling. I stand where I am, unable even to think. On the other side of the courtyard, Nathan also appears to be frozen.

'My marriage.' Squeezing, squeezing all the time. 'My business. My boat. My daughter. And now this place. You try to take all of these things, and you think you are leaving? You are not leaving.'

Nathan has made it across the courtyard and is now attempting to get his hands on my father's shoulders to pull him back. But Dad is as unyielding as the limestone surrounding us. Bacon gasps and groans and shrieks as more stones give way behind him.

Dad's face is set.

Bacon stops gasping.

322

The seriousness of the situation hits me like a bag of cement. No one has ever said outright that my dad's a criminal, but the papers are always hinting. How else does a barefoot kid from a Portuguese fishing village become a millionaire? Rags don't turn themselves to riches without blood and threats and maybe even deaths along the way. Planned, unplanned: deaths all the same. Everything to this point has been a child's game of chase, of fetch, of hide and seek and telling tales. I see that now. For the first time, here in this beautiful and dangerous place, I understand who my father is.

I fling myself on his cigar-scented back. I wrap my arms around his neck and my legs around his waist and I pummel him as Nathan yells and heaves away at his arms. The silent Bacon stops kicking.

'Dad,' I roar. 'Stop. Stop. Stop. DAD!'

The wall is too weak to hold against the weight the four of us are now inflicting on it. It breaks apart with a crack, and we are falling.

All of us are falling.

# NATHAN

This is the bit that ought to be in slow motion. The bit where your arms and legs whirl gently like those little helicopter seeds that fall from the trees in the autumn, and you spin and turn in the air until you cut into the grey-green foam five metres below. But there's nothing slow about this. It's swift and brutal and shocking. Stones from the fortress wall fall alongside us. Precious screams the whole way down, I remember that much. Dad squawks and heaves for breath. Ricky Silva is the only one of us who is silent.

The water is keen to meet us. It seems to brace, like putty that you can snap one minute and bend the next. In only the briefest of seconds as we fall, I glimpse it. It looks as hard as glass.

I don't remember the moment that I shatter the surface. There are bubbles, lots of them. Pain blooms through me. Blue thickens to black. Faces appear in the dark, of people I don't know but who seem to know me. They reach for me with thin arms that blow around me like seaweed. There are boats down here too, inverted somehow, their shadowy black hulls and tattered masts hanging above me like strange, gawky bats. The water fills their sails like wind and they sail away from me on the great invisible sea of air that I know is above us all, but just out of reach.

Dimly I see my father. His eyes are wide and his hair floats about his head. He is reaching for me. I hesitate, not wanting to lift my arms towards him, and the moment is gone. Onwards I go. Down, down, down.

# HARRY

Paddling isn't the easiest thing in the world, but the guitar is useful. I drive it into the water, pushing grimly onwards, the battered red-and-white lifebuoy around my belly both holding me up and holding me back as José and his dad bob at a safe distance from the shore. I wish I could swim like James Bond, cut through this heaving water like a shark, arms slicing clean and smooth through the waves as I power towards the churning cascades at the bottom of these terrifying cliffs, but I can't.

I wish I hadn't thought of sharks. I hope there aren't any fricking sharks.

'I'm coming!' I wheeze, choking as the waves slap at my face and burn up my nose. Not the most heroic figure these seas have seen I think.

Four people hit the water like bombs a couple of minutes ago. I felt the surface judder even as I flailed towards them. I recognised Precious's head, the sheer bulk of Ricky as they plummeted into the blue, only a few metres away from the rocks. The only head I can now see belongs to Nathan's dad, although I keep losing sight of him as the sea slaps away at the base of the cliff with its little fortress stuck halfway down like an old barnacle.

My feet kick. I can't lie on my belly because the lifebuoy won't let me.

'Precious!' I roar, digging the guitar into the waves and heaving with all my strength.

The sea seemed calm when I was on the boat. Seeing it batter at the cliff in front of me now, I'm aware of the sheer quantity of water in the Atlantic Ocean, and how puny this cliff must seem. It wouldn't have blinked at the flea with sails that happened to be carrying my dad. I dig the guitar in again, swerving around a large wave that has an absent-minded look about it. A dog whose waving tail smashes crockery. An elephant whose feet crush birds' eggs.

The sea isn't malicious, I realise. It's just big.

'*Precious!*'

A head. Two heads. Three now. I paddle harder, tracking erratically towards Precious. Her arm is cold as I grasp her wrist. She seems to stare right through me, blinking through her thick wet fringe, and I'm taken back to the beach and the hot dogs and that awful Bacofoil dress.

'Hold on,' I say. This lifebuoy had better be up to taking our combined weight. 'We've got to get to shore.'

Her eyes focus at last, and lock on to mine. She wraps her arms weakly around the buoy. 'You're in the sea, Barry Temple,' she mumbles.

'I'm in the sea for you,' I say, because it's true.

Her face crumples. 'Have you seen my dad?'

I gesture with some difficulty at the second head bobbing nearby. Precious can hardly turn, but when she does, she glimpses Ricky. He is calling to her across the water, but whatever he's saying is lost in the thump and hiss of the waves.

She turns back to me, lays the side of her face on the hard red-white surface of the buoy and shuts her eyes. I'd kiss her if I could but one hand is still plying the guitar and the other is clinging grimly to the lifebuoy in case I slip through the middle, and I can't get the angle right.

I never get the angle right.

'Where's Nathan?' she asks, so faintly that I have to slide a little bit down inside my lifebuoy to hear her, which is unbelievably terrifying.

Other than Precious and her dad, I can only see Aiden Payne out here, swimming in circles by the base of the cliff. He is trying to bellow, but something about his voice isn't working properly.

'Nathan!' he scratches out. 'Nathan! Nathan!'

I attempt to turn round in the lifebuoy, looking for Nathan's fat head. By the time I make a full three-sixty to no effect whatsoever, Precious has gone.

I panic instantly. She's slid off and drowned like Leo DiCaprio off that bloody door. Then I glimpse her lifting herself out of the water – God only knows how – and duck-diving under the surface. Her long legs kick into view for a bit, and then she disappears.

Off she goes, this miracle girl. Hunting for Nathan Payne.

# PRECIOUS

Harry came for me out of nowhere. He swam through his worst thing for me. *I'm in the sea for you.* When he looked at me through those long strands of wet hair, I felt something as deep as the water underneath and all around us.

And now I'm abandoning him, and diving down through these surging waves for someone who tried to kill my father. It makes no sense, but I'm starting to discover that life doesn't. We blame ourselves for so much that we don't have a hope of changing. We give ourselves such importance, and we're nothing at all.

The current is relentless. The suck and saw of the sea, the push and pull of the cliffs, the constant grinding boom reminds me exactly how small and unimportant I am, and I understand Harry's fear. Except fear is the wrong word. Awe is the word I want.

I swim underwater for several metres. When I surface, my head hits a stretch of overhead rock that shouldn't be there. I panic, and I scream, but that just wastes oxygen and so I stop. There are a few inches of air between my nose and this strange ceiling in the sea. I can see ahead, because the rock ceiling slopes up and away. There is plenty of air, but no sky.

'Nathan!'

It's a *cave*. A luminescence fills the rocky space with rippling aqua light, filtering through holes in the walls below the surface of the water. The whole place echoes as I splash around in circles, ducking deep and rising again over and over with nothing to show for my efforts. Movement and sound, light and dark fill me up even as hope and optimism tick away. I can't find him. I'm tiring. I'm struggling to stay afloat.

'*Nathannnnnnn . . .*'

The echo is like the mournful sound of a bow drawn across a string. The cave walls brighten the ghostly music, bending and twisting it so that it ripples like the light. And someone is there, on the small beach hard up against the wet rock face, as still as a hunting cat.

Sebastian sees me, I think, at the same moment that I see him. He smiles, but then he's gone and I am dropping down to the great blue depths, where the whales hold court among all the navigators that didn't make it as far as they would have liked.

'We try,' he whispers in my ear as I sink. 'It's all we can do.'

# HARRY

Precious hasn't come up yet. My eyes burn with the salt but I don't dare to blink. Under my feet, I feel the sudden blessed shock of land. Still paddling with the guitar, I propel myself further inland. As the water gets shallower, I try and fail to stand up. The lifebuoy is heavy, and my legs are about as effective as tentacles. The smoking remains of the Boxster gaze reproachfully at me as I flounder around in the shallows, completely unable to make it fully ashore.

'Nathan!' Aiden Payne rasps away in the distance, still spinning and ducking and splashing by the cliff. 'Nathan! Nathan!'

# PRECIOUS

Something is ahead of me, floating face-down in the darkness like an astronaut in space. Nathan's eyes are closed. I grab his arm, and pull, and kick, and my chest threatens to explode with the pressure. My ears hurt. A lot.

How far up? How far? Further than the Indies, further than Madeira, Brazil, Goa, further than Japan, further than all of them put together. But also no distance at all. Just a brightening of the light.

# HARRY

Ricky Silva ploughs through the water towards me. He seizes the lifebuoy and tows me ashore like a tug boat with a dinghy.

'Where is Precious?' he says when I am coughing on my hands and knees in the surf. 'She was with you. Where is she now?'

I'm incredibly thirsty. Licking my lips doesn't help. The lifebuoy is still foolishly around my waist. 'She went to find Nathan Payne,' I croak.

'Nathan Payne?'

The Nathan Payne game. We are unquestionably at level three.

Ricky gives a bellow of relief and thunders back into the water as Precious pops into view. Her hair is slick to her head. She has Nathan by the chin, in that move a swimming instructor once tried (and naturally enough, failed) to teach me. Aiden Payne flails towards them – 'Nathan! Nathan!' – but she steers around him, aiming steadily for the shore.

Through the shattering burst of relief, I think of sea lions, not giraffes at all.

I wriggle out of the lifebuoy with the last of my strength. I don't want to meet her stuck in this doughnut, that much I know. She is wading up the beach now, pulling the dead weight of Nathan Payne behind her. Water cascades from her long slim body. Her T-shirt dress is a second skin. Now is not the time to notice these things. I get unsteadily to my feet and lay hold of Nathan's shoulders and we pull him up the beach together and dump him in the smoking shadow of the Boxster.

'He isn't breathing.' Precious sounds completely exhausted.

Aiden Payne is sloshing ashore now, with Ricky close behind. They appear to be supporting each other. I get astride Nathan's body and begin mindlessly pumping at his chest. I don't have much strength left, but I give it all I've got. One two three four, how many times? I think of Dad. It's inevitable.

'He's still not breathing,' Precious says.

I steel myself to pinch Nathan Payne's nose and do the kiss thing but Precious is already there, bending over his inert body and putting her lips on his mouth. I want to push her off and make her kiss me instead. What kind of monster does that make me?

'Breathe, breathe, breathe,' I repeat mechanically as Precious kisses Nathan Payne right in front of my eyes. 'Breathe, you bastard, BREATHE.'

# NATHAN

Cold fire tears through my chest. Someone's mouth is pressing firmly on mine, someone's hands are on my skin. My body jerks and rolls and I cough my lungs up at a pair of sandy feet beside my head. So much water, everywhere water, gushing out of me, searing my throat. I cough, and retch, and cough some more. The pain is unbelievable. I almost want to go back into the sea.

'Nathan!' someone croaks.

Even through the dimness and confusion, I jerk away from the thin-fingered hands coming towards me. Nothing good ever comes from those hands. I turn my back instead and curl myself into a ball. Still I cough. I can't imagine ever lifting my limbs off this hard, gritty beach.

'Bloody hell, Nathan Payne,' says Harry Temple, sprawled on the sand beside me.

I blink blearily at him and cough some more.

'Give him room,' says Precious.

It was Precious's mouth on mine moments ago. A tiny thrill fizzes through the exhaustion. 'Kiss me again,' I try to say, but the words are lost in another gush of sea water.

Ricky Silva's big hands are on me now, stroking my hair off my face. The last time I saw *those* hands they were throttling my father, and I was trying to prise them off, because that's what you do for your family, even when that family is more broken than the Boxster nose-down on the sand behind you. My dad sits at a safe distance, staring at the sand by his feet. My chest hurts, mainly because of the seawater, I think. Nothing is black and white, is it?

'You are too young for this,' Ricky Silva says quietly. 'All of you.'

# PRECIOUS

'I saw him again,' I tell Harry. I point at the cliff that juts away from us into the sea. 'There was a cave . . .'

The memory almost eludes me, a tiny fish darting from my grasp in a silver streak. Not because it didn't happen, but because it's hard to pin down. Anyone sane would agree that it was fear, or exhaustion, or my oxygen-starved brain replaying Dad's words inside the fortress: '*He came here once . . .*' Seeing a dead king on a beach inside a sea cave, surrounded by musicians who play as you sink . . . Yeah. Weird.

From his position sprawled on the sand, Harry opens his burning blue eyes and squints up at me. I'm reminded of yesterday at Arrifana, when I was on the sand and Harry was where I am now.

'Maybe you see him like I hear Dad,' he says. 'He's there, as real as anything. But at the same time, he's long gone.'

Yes. Yes, that's it. He's there, but not there. In the mist, on the roadside, in the cave. He's in my mind, but no less real

337

for it. Harry understands. Maybe only Harry will ever understand.

'Come into the sea with me,' I say.

'OK,' he says, surprisingly.

I'm too shy to hold out my hand to help him up. He does it by himself, dusting down the backs of his legs. The guitar lies a short distance from our feet, wetter and more busted than ever. Harry stares at the lifebuoy beside the guitar for a moment, as if trying to recollect why it's there.

'I need to take that to Baleeira,' he says.

'Later,' I suggest.

Nathan is on a stretcher at the foot of the cliff path alongside his dad and mine. Paramedics in red polo tops move around him with oxygen tubes, trying to work out how to winch him up the cliff. A number of them are eyeing the Boxster, wondering exactly what happened in this place.

'Nathan blew up Dad's boat,' I say.

'What a tosser.'

'I'll ask Dad to go easy on him.'

'That would be good,' says Harry.

The water is warm and gentle at first, tickling around our ankles. It grows cooler and stronger, the deeper we go. Our hands brush together as we move side by side.

'This is safe, right?' Harry checks every now and then.

'We won't go far,' I promise him.

'I was meant to go with Dad,' Harry says suddenly. 'On the trip when he died. But I didn't. I don't know how to get past that. I don't think I can.'

We're up to our thighs now. It seems so natural to catch up his fingers in mine that I barely realise I have done it. I turn to face the shore, moving backwards through the pull of the tide, drawing him with me as the water comes up to our waists.

'What would have happened if you had?'

He lifts our hands up to his face, studying them almost as if he's checking that our fingers are properly aligned. 'I would have died too. And Mum would have lost us both.'

'You couldn't have prevented it.' I wave at the sea with our joined hands. 'This is the Atlantic Ocean.'

He nods. 'It's hard, though,' he says. 'Surviving.'

Letting go of my fingers, he moves his hands up my arms instead. My skin pimples under the gentle grazing motion. He stops around shoulder level and frowns.

'Barry,' I say, unable to wait any longer. 'Are you going to kiss me again or not?'

He looks straight at me, startled. 'What?'

I think about the blurry kiss at the hotel. His back, and his hair, and the taste of his mouth. The blush begins its customary journey up my neck towards my cheeks. 'Properly, now I'm concentrating?' I say.

'Concentrating,' he repeats. 'As in, not blind drunk?'

'Mm,' I say. 'I think maybe it was quite good, from the bits I remember.'

'It was.' Harry glances back at the shore. 'But I wondered if maybe Nathan.'

'That's not a sentence.' My arms make their way over his shoulders and my fingers move through the wet tangle of his hair.

'If maybe you and Nathan, you know,' Harry says with difficulty. 'Like each other. Not me. I'm not very . . . likeable.'

'You're asking me that now?'

A smile breaks across his serious face as the cool silk sea moves around us. His hands resume their progress up my shoulders, coming to rest under my ears. I feel his thumbs under my jaw.

'Oh, I'll kiss you,' he says eventually. He moves his head ever so slightly to one side. 'But only if you promise to remember it this time.'

'I promise.' My stomach is about to combust.

He moves a bit closer. 'I might want to talk about it afterwards, you see. And not watch you look completely blank when I mention it.'

'Will there be questions?' I whisper.

His arms come round me and his mouth meets mine. Our bodies match up like wet jigsaw pieces.

'Lots,' he says. I feel his half-smile against my teeth. 'Most likely from you.'

# BACKGROUND

"I could have been a lot of things, if I weren't who I am.'

*Amália Rodrigues*

When you think that 260 million people around the world speak Portuguese, and then you think of Portugal today with its population of around 10 million, it's a pretty graphic demonstration of history in action.

Portugal in the sixteenth century was vastly rich and influential. Using its Atlantic-facing position and seafaring know-how, the Portuguese traded and conquered like good 'uns. Bartolomeu Dias was the first to sail round the Cape of Good Hope, allowing Vasco da Gama to discover the sea route to India. Pedro Álvares Cabral found Brazil when he sailed too far west down the coast of Africa; Ferdinand Magellan's ships made it around the globe before anyone else. Portuguese kids grow up knowing the names of these explorers the way we grow up knowing Henry VIII's six wives.

Mediterranean countries couldn't keep up. Even the greatest trading city of them all, Venice, struggled to compete.

For decades, Portugal had a virtual monopoly on imports from around the world, and the money poured in. Next door, Spain watched in envy.

Sebastian was where it all fell apart.

Sebastian of Portugal was born in 1554, two weeks after his father died. The few portraits that exist show a sensitive young man with a strawberry-blond crewcut and a natty line in ruffs and armour. The crown landed in his small chubby hands when he was just three years old, after which his mother returned with unseemly haste to her native Spain and left the little King to be brought up by priests. Unsurprisingly, he became fanatical about his Catholic faith. There is evidence that he developed a fear and hatred of women; he may also have been gay.

Disaster wasn't long in coming. Remaining steadfastly unmarried, Sebastian focused his mad-eyed energies on a hopeless crusade against the Muslims in North Africa. He was just twenty-four when he and his poorly planned army were crushed in the battle of Alcácer-Quibir in Morocco in 1578. With no feasible heir, Portugal fell like a fat plum into Spain's lap.

Sebastian had held the future of a wealthy, important country in his hands, and had royally ballsed it up. It's no wonder Portugal created the legend of *sebastianismo* around their lost king returning one misty morning to reverse all that had gone so badly wrong. If you want to understand Portuguese culture and the mournful tradition of *saudades* (which roughly translates as 'a longing for the way things used to be'), look back on this orphaned, confused, fanatical strawberry-blond king and you're halfway there.

Most of the legends in this book are genuine, although I made up the ones about the pre-battle feast and the musicians in the sea cave. *Desculpe.*

# ACKNOWLEDGEMENTS

I think maybe this is the book I've always wanted to write. I lived in Portugal for a couple of years in my early twenties, and it made an indelible impression on me. Is it weird to thank a country? Thanks as ever to my stalwart editor Naomi Greenwood and my indefatigable agent Stephanie Thwaites for letting me run amok with an idea which, let's say, unfolded as it went along. Polly Lyall-Grant for holding the helm; Michelle Brackenborough for a cover I want to jump into; and everyone in production, marketing, sales and rights for being brilliant. You all work extremely hard to get my books out there, and I'm so grateful. Thanks to Bill and Isa for hosting our, ahem, research trip at the lovely Casa das Oliveiras near Silves in the Algarve; and last of all, thanks to my husband Will for letting me drive a manual car on the wrong side of the road for the best part of a week without killing us both.

# LUCY COURTENAY

has officially been writing children's
fiction since 1999, and unofficially for
a lot longer than that. Her desk drawers
are full of half-finished stories waiting
for the right moment to emerge and
dance around her study in a shower of
exuberant paperclips. Her latest books
indulge her love of teenage romance.

@LucyCourtenay1

lucycourtenay.com

Can love
be just like
the movies?

'... a perfect read for romantics and movie lovers.
Pretty in Pink for the modern teenager'
*South Wales Evening Post*

'Funny, realistic and an utterly gorgeous teenage love story'
*No Safer Place*